Some have red eyes that glow in the dark.

Some look like the dinosaur ancestors of birds.

Some lumber along like huge bears—with humanoid faces.

Some cry like babies; others whistle or growl.

Some attack with claws; others hide in fear.

They are unearthly creatures of species no naturalist has classified, but they visit the Earth too often to be mere hallucinations. They all have one thing in common; they are

ANIMALS WE NEVER CATCH.

Read what Clark and Coleman have compiled about these strange beasts who have been reported by thousands of people as far back as the twelfth century and are still being seen. They are creatures of the borderland—that area between fantasy and reality, that grey area which may hold the secret to man's role in the universe.

Also By
Jerome Clark & Loren Coleman

The Unidentified

Published by
Warner Books

CREATURES
OF THE
OUTER EDGE

by Jerome Clark and Loren Coleman

WARNER BOOKS

A Warner Communications Company

WARNER BOOKS EDITION

Copyright © 1978 by Jerome Clark and Loren Coleman
All rights reserved

ISBN 0-446-89150-9

Cover art by Chick Bragg

Warner Books, Inc., 75 Rockefeller Plaza, New York, N.Y. 10019

W A Warner Communications Company

Printed in the United States of America

Not associated with Warner Press, Inc. of Anderson, Indiana

First Printing: June, 1978

10   9   8   7   6   5   4   3   2   1

To John Keel, pioneer.

There is not wanting a feast of broad, joyous humor, in this stranger phantasmagoria, where pit and stage, and man and animal, and earth and air, are jumbled in confusion worse confounded.

—Thomas Carlyle

CONTENTS

1995 + 2

BEAR
Box 22
THomAsville GA
31799

CREATURES
OF THE
OUTER EDGE

INTRODUCTION

This is a catalogue of absurd marvels. It is a compilation of impossible events, hundreds of them, stories so ridiculously unlikely that they sound like demented jokes.

The only trouble is, they all happened. Or anyway, they are supposed to have happened, and by the time you have finished reading the last page, you probably will agree that some incredibly strange occurrences which appear to make no sense whatever are going on all around us.

This book is an effort to record a great many data which otherwise would go unnoticed by any but that small and devoted band, among whom the authors proudly number themselves, who call themselves Forteans, after Charles Fort (1874-1932). Fort was the first person to record in any systematic way all manner of decidedly unusual events which practically nobody besides direct witnesses had any idea were occurring. Fort discovered that not only were they occurring, but they were doing so with astonishing frequency.

One of the many subjects which fascinated him was the phenomenon of mystery animals—weird creatures which seem not to belong in this world at all. Sightings of such beasts have increased dramatically since Fort's time. *Creatures of the Outer Edge* is an effort to update the master's work by describing what people are reporting today. Beyond noting some of the general patterns in the sightings, we have kept speculation to a minimum until the last chapter, preferring for the most part to let the cases speak for themselves. And these cases have much to say that is surprising, often shocking. You will very likely discover mystery animals are not what you think they are. As we track these bizarre creatures, we will discover that their trail leads to some unexpected places. We will find that the farther we pursue them, the more impenetrably mysterious they become.

We would like to thank the following people for their generous assistance:

Curtis and Mary Fuller of *Fate*; Terry Catchpole of *Oui*; R.J.M. Rickard of *Fortean Times*; Charles Bowen of *Flying Saucer Review*; Peter Rogerson of *MUFOB*; Paul Willis of *The INFO Journal*; Rod B. Dyke of *UFO Newsclipping Service*; Mark A. Hall, Ron Dobbins, Tim Church, John A. Keel, Don Worley, Lucius Farish, Brad Steiger, Tom Adams, Jim McClarin, John Green, the late George Haas, Dr. James Ulness, Dr. Warren Smerud, Richard Crowe, Dr. Berthold Eric Schwarz, and Robert Jones; plus hundreds of other Forteans, witnesses, newspaper reporters, game wardens and librarians across the nation who have put up with almost twenty years of our questions and queries; plus, of course, Penny, Toni, and Libbet, as well as our mutually supportive families!

Jerome Clark
Loren Coleman, M.S.W.

Illinois
Massachusetts

CHAPTER ONE

Mystery Animals

Some awfully strange things are wandering through our world—things which are supposed to exist only in dreams and nightmares, things which all the laws of reason assure us are flatly impossible. Things which, for a great variety of reasons, are distinctly unwelcome but which nonetheless resolutely refuse to go away.

Two of them appeared in the 1920s, if we are to credit the testimonies of psychical researchers of the period, who claimed to have encountered them during a series of seances. The medium was a man known to us only through the pseudonym "Franek Kluski," a Polish engineer, poet, and writer whom parapsychologists regard as one of the most remarkable psychics of all time. "Kluski" is supposed to have had a spirit guide who called himself Hirkill.

"Accompanying [Hirkill] always was a rapacious beast, the size of a very big dog, of a tawny color,

15

with slender neck, mouth full of large teeth, eyes which glowed in the darkness like a cat's, and which reminded the company of a maneless lion," an article in *Psychic Science* (April 1926) tells us. "It was occasionally wild in its behavior, especially if persons were afraid of it, and neither the human nor the animal apparition was much welcomed by the sitters. . . . The lion, as we may call him, liked to lick the sitters with a moist and prickly tongue, and gave forth the odor of a great feline, and even after the seance, the sitters, especially the medium, were impregnated with this acrid scent as if they had made a long stay in a menagerie among wild beasts."

We have the further testimony of Dr. Gustave Geley, who described another kind of beast which manifested itself during some of "Kluski's" seances:

This being which we have termed Pithecanthropus has shown itself several times at our seances. One of us, at the seance on November 20, 1920, felt its large, shaggy head press hard on his right shoulder and against his cheek. The head was covered with thick, coarse hair. A smell came from it like that of a deer or a wet dog. When one of the sitters put out his hand, the Pithecanthropus seized it and licked it slowly three times. Its tongue was large and soft. At other times, we all felt our legs touched by what seemed to be frolicsome dogs.

And Col. Norbert Ochorowicz wrote:

This ape was of such great strength that it could easily move a heavy bookcase filled with books through the room, carry a sofa over the heads of the sitters, or lift the heaviest persons in their chairs into the air to the height of a tall person. Though the ape's behavior sometimes caused fear, and indicated a low level of intelligence, it was never malignant. Indeed, it often expressed goodwill, gentleness and readiness to obey. . . . After a long stay, a strong animal smell was noticed.

Over forty years later an even more unlikely series of events was taking place in Salem, Ohio, a small community near Youngstown. The episode began one morning in the spring of 1968 when Mrs. Alice Allison happened to glance out a window and observed something hovering over her buckeye tree, which stood about thirty feet high. "It looked like an airplane without wings," she told investigator Mark Swift. "It sounded like a helicopter but it had no propellers." It was black and unlighted, but the top half of the front part was a clear dome, inside which she could see an occupant.

"He was a man and wore a khaki-colored shirt," she said. "He had olive-colored skin, which was slightly tanned, and his eyes were slanted." She thought he might be worried that the craft was about to crash, since it was making sputtering sounds and rocking back and forth in the air.

Mrs. Allison's seven-year-old son Bruce also observed the object, though not the occupant, because he was viewing the phenomenon from the rear.

After about twenty minutes the object finally flew off slowly in a southwesterly direction.

Around that same time the family often saw a large catlike creature, about three feet high and three and a half feet long. Sometimes it would sit out in the driveway, where once, after a rain, the Allisons found three-inch footprints. On another occasion they discovered claw marks half an inch deep and six inches long in a tree near the house.

Both they and the neighbors heard the creature. "My daughter woke up one night and it was growling and panting so loud it seemed as if it were at the foot of the bed," Mrs. Allison said. Catlike prints, far too large to have been made by a domestic cat, appeared on top of a neighbor's car. A check with the nearest zoo in Cleveland, seventy miles away, failed to uncover any reports of escaped animals. The animals known scientifically as *Felis concolor* and popularly as the panther, the cougar, or the mountain lion has been extinct in Ohio for well over a century.

But that was not all. Ever since the appearances of the mystery cat, the Allisons have been sure that *another* strange creature resides in the nearby woods. "I don't know what it was," Mrs. Allison remarked, "but it was big enough to be a man, a big man. It would stand out in the woods and watch the house. All you could see was a black outline, but it definitely wasn't a bear."

Once, as they entered the driveway, they saw the thing dashing into the woods. Bruce recalled, "It's not like a person running through the woods —you trip over stumps, branches, and rocks. It ran so fast it didn't even look like it touched the ground. During the summer you could go out into the woods and see where it had been lying. Right before it started to get cold, you could see this big spot. One night we heard our tomcat fighting with something and after that we never saw it again, but we can still feel its presence. It's out there!"

The Allisons' married daughter, though she had never actually seen the creature, had heard its growling from time to time. Once, in 1971, however, her husband had been driving to work and was just pulling out of Salem Heights when suddenly something like a "very large man" leaped in front of the car and put its hand up against the vehicle as if to avoid being hit. The car thumped hard against the figure, but when the driver jumped out of the car, there was nothing there—only a big dent in the fender and some black hairs sticking to it.

It should be noted here that for a number of years Ohio has reluctantly hosted sightings of creatures or large "monster men" usually described as somewhat apelike and covered with long black hair.

Since the original UFO incident the Allisons have been plagued with odd poltergeistlike phenomena. In addition, they have had further UFO sightings, though none so dramatic as the first.

We cite the alleged experiences of "Kluski" and the Allisons because between them they cover all the perimeters of the "Goblin Universe" (to borrow Dr. John Napier's delightful phrase)—at least those parts of it which define the territory we shall be exploring in the pages ahead.

That territory, the "outer edge" of our title, stretches along the fringes of reality. It is a place where all manner of bizarre events occur. On the surface these events do not seem to be related at all, which is why legions of dedicated people have separately busied themselves trying to prove the existences of 1.) spaceships from other worlds; 2.) psychic phenomena, poltergeists and apparitions; 3.) flesh-and-blood animals not yet known to science, such as the Bigfoot and the eastern panther. In most cases those people who have specialized in one area are only marginally aware of the work of the other specialists, and virtually all of them would deny vehemently that they are really dealing with one single larger phenomenon, only viewing it from different perspectives.

By now there is a large body of literature on the supposedly separate questions of UFOs, psi and unknown animals. Having read a considerable proportion of this literature—and then having conducted our own personal investigations of the phenomena in question—we have learned to be careful about taking the various "authorities," pronouncements at face value. We have discovered that one proposition is "proven" usually at the expense of another. Examining the Allisons' story, a ufologist would ignore the psi and mystery animal (MA) elements. A Bigfoot researcher, assuming he could bring himself to consider the possibility that hairy critters might exist outside the Pacific Northwest region (a notion most Sasquatch hunters firmly reject), would certainly suppress all references to such inconvenient manifestations as UFOs and poltergeists. And of course a parapsychologist would carefully weed out UFO and MA references.

The major point we shall be trying to make here is that all borderline phenomena are related in some mysterious fashion. In our earlier book, *The Unidentified* (Warner Books, 1975), we argued that UFO reports, fairy tales and religious visions arise from the same source. Whatever that source may be, its signals must be filtered through human consciousness and perception, which shape the manifestations to conform to certain archetypal forms that are both strange and yet oddly familiar to us. Strange because they appear supernatural or extraterrestrial, but familiar because, in a sense, *we have created them*. We have clothed them in the garb of cultural imagination; thus primitive societies which believe nature sprites control the processes of growth and fertility see fairies. People of the late 19th century who awaited the invention of powered flight saw airships with ostensibly human occupants. And our own Space Age culture, filled with visions of interstellar travel and interplanetary visitors, sees flying saucers and little men from other worlds.

That is not to say that these strange phenomena do not exist. These things are not hallucinations, at least as that term is usually understood, nor are all reports of them mere cases of mistaken identity.

In fact, the skeptics' position is demonstrably absurd.

It is not as if, as the present book will show, we are dealing with isolated incidents. Rather we are confronting a vast, and daily growing, tidal wave of reports of peculiar phenomena which threaten to drown us in a sea of madness. Yet most of these reports come not, as various authority figures would have us believe, from liars and lunatics, but from reputable citizens whose testimony on any other matter would not be open to question.

If these supposed incidents occurred only rarely, we would be justified in dismissing them as honest (and occasionally dishonest) mistakes. But as a matter of fact they occur thousands of times a year in all countries and on all levels of society, and almost invariably to persons who never before had any belief in, or even knowledge of, them. Practically every witness whose story comes to public attention (and most witnesses, fearing ridicule, keep their stories to themselves) says something to the effect that "I never would have believed it if it hadn't happened to me."

Not that that helps any, since these things, however they might manifest themselves, are not supposed to exist, and to say that one has seen them —or that one believes that others have seen them— is to identify oneself as ripe for the booby hatch. Yet by now there is such an abundance of reports that, if everyone who says he has seen something out of the ordinary is nuts, we will have to hospitalize a good share of the population.

Ironically, in the end it comes down to a question of "common sense." While these manifestations may seem to defy common sense, the notion that untold numbers of apparently sane, responsible people have reported things that are not real constitutes an even greater affront to common sense. Any serious effort to explain away all these reported manifestations (and very few of the scoffers have any idea of the magnitude of the problem) demands the formulation of a new theory of the human mind, one which holds as a basic tenet that insanity is far more widespread than even the most pessimistic observers of human behavior have ever imagined. It would also have to explain the very selective operation of this insanity, showing us how the individuals in question could give, every appearance of sanity before the "sighting," and no further signs of derangement after it. It would also have to demonstrate that any number of people can collectively lose their grip on reality and imagine they were seeing the manifestation *at the same time*. And we would have to know how these hallucinations could leave peculiar tracks all over the landscape, or how animals could sense their presence and flee from them in terror.

On the other hand, acceptance of these stories creates other kinds of problems and some of the questions skeptics have raised are difficult indeed to answer. For example, if these things are real, why is there no conclusive proof of their existence? So far as reports of creatures—our main interest here —are concerned, why, if they are real, are there no bodies, no bones, no live specimens locked securely in zoos and laboratories? Why only certain kinds of physical evidence, invariably of a somewhat ambiguous nature—footprints, strands of hair or fur, possible feces samples, and not others? The "evidence" we have is always just enough to keep us from rejecting the reports as delusions but never enough to prove conclusively that unknown animals exist in our midst.

Elusiveness and ambiguity seem implicit in the manifestations. They refuse to be understood. The more closely we examine them, the more surely they escape our view. Just as soon as we think we have one of them isolated and categorized, it becomes something else, or suddenly shows up in what we presumptuously deem a thoroughly inappropriate context. Take, for instance, this bizarre little episode, cited by David Webb in his *1973— Year of the Humanoids:*

September 9, Savannah, Georgia: "Ten big, black hairy dogs" emerged from a landed UFO in Laurel Grove Cemetery and ran through the cemetery. The UFO turned out its lights after landing. Several youths made the report.

Confronted with incidents of this type, proponents of the theory of extraterrestrial UFOs (a theory which makes the common mistake of assuming that unexplained phenomena are not continuous with one another but the products of a variety of separate, unrelated forces) invariably speculate that the creatures are "test animals"—an astoundingly anthropomorphic notion if there ever was one.* Actually "black dogs" are nothing new to our terrestrial environment, as students of folklore and demonology will readily attest. Known widely in British and North American tradition, these supernatural beasts are considered demonic creatures and are sometimes called "the hounds of hell." (Conan Doyle got the inspiration for his classic *The Hound of the Baskervilles* from just such legends.) Their appearance is often associated with death. Thus it is fitting that in the present instance the witness observes them in a graveyard. We will have more to say about black dogs in a later chapter.

* John Rimmer remarks, "As ufologists we seem prepared to accept that such matters as UFO propulsion methods, alien physiology, and advanced technologies may be so far advanced beyond anything we are able to comprehend that they will appear to us as 'magic.' Yet, paradoxically, we also seem prepared to assume that the beings behind such marvels are going to behave exactly like us when we meet them face to face." (*Merseyside UFO Bulletin,* December 1970).

To read an account like the one just cited as evidence that black dogs are "UFO occupants" is to miss the point. The overwhelming majority of black dog stories do not involve anything remotely similar to UFOs. But such reports do suggest something about the "reality" UFOs and black dogs—and poltergeists and phantom cats—inhabit.

That reality is the "reality" of dreams, which constantly reshuffle the contents of the unconscious mind and manufacture ever-changing syntheses of those contents, with all manner of seemingly unrelated ideas and images coming together briefly, then splitting apart, then merging again in other, even stranger forms. The motifs of fairylore and UFO phenomenology therefore become so hopelessly entwined that in some cases the investigator cannot tell whether he is dealing with reports of "elves" or of "extraterrestrials." If he decides one way or another, he arbitrarily isolates the event—"freezes" it, in other words, when in fact it is fluid.

Borderland phenomena do not recognize boundaries. If we insist upon containing them, defining their territory, we are only fooling ourselves. We must be prepared to accept the bewildering fact that they can be any number of things at one time: real and unreal, objective and subjective, technological and supernatural. For example, in the following incident, investigated by veteran ufologist Len Stringfield, we confront a creature that is biological in appearance and mechanical in behavior.

The main witness, Mrs. H., who lived in a trailer court in the Covedale area of Western Cincinnati, Ohio, awoke around 2:30 a.m., October 21, 1973, and arose from bed intending to get a drink of water. But an intense light coming through the curtains attracted her attention, and when she opened the curtains she was startled to see a row of six individual lights forming an arc about six feet from her window. The lights were a vivid silvery blue, self-luminous (casting no light on the ground below) and four feet off the ground.

Mrs. H. then saw another bright light, this one farther out in the asphalt parking court beyond her trailer. A car parked a few feet from the trailer obscured the bottom part of the light, but she could see enough of it to observe an "apelike creature" inside. The light seemed to move toward the rear of the parked car and the witness had the impression that the entity was "maybe doing something to the car."

At that point she dashed into her son Carl's bedroom and tried to rouse him. When she returned to the window, as she would later inform Stringfield, "The creature appeared to be farther away from the car, maybe thirty-five feet away," and this time encased in a "shield of light . . . looking like a light in an operating room." The shield was shaped like a bubble umbrella and the light was contained within the shield. It was large enough, Mrs. H. thought, to contain several other creatures of the same size.

The creature, which seemed to be looking toward a warehouse building to the left of the trailer, was gray in color. Its face was "featureless" except for a downward-sloping snout. Its arms were moving up and down slowly and very stiffly. The elbows never bent. The whole effect reminded Mrs. H. of the movements of a robot. Though she could see no machinery inside the glasslike enclosure, she thought the creature might be moving some kind of invisible lever.

Mrs. H. picked up the phone and called the police, who did not seem to take her seriously. While she was talking, a "loud, deep *boom*" sounded and when she and Carl looked again out the window the strange phenomenon was gone. They were not sure if the *boom* and the disappearance of the UFO were connected, since they were not watching when they heard the sound. And by this time the owner of the car in the lot had returned with his girl friend to "jump" the vehicle. They thought it might be possible that the car had made the sound when it started.

Since Stringfield was unable to locate the young couple, we do not know the answer to that particular question. Nonetheless there are other instances in which UFOs have vanished in the wake of just such an "explosion."

Another series of creature reports describe something that seems to have assumed two presumably mutually exclusive identities.

One day in August 1970, three Rantoul, Illinois, youths on an early-morning fishing trip to Kickapoo Creek picked up in their headlights an upright creature as big as a cow. It seemed unbothered by the lights and continued ambling along the edge of the creek.

That same week another person saw it near the Heyworth-Kickapoo Creek area, followed it, and found a string of opened mussel shells and half-eaten minnows.

On the night of August 11, Steve Rich, 18, George Taylor, 17, and Monti Shafer, 20, were hiking through land belonging to Farrell Finger, about two miles northeast of Waynesville and half a mile from Kickapoo Creek. At 9:15 p.m. Rich called the others' attention to the "thing" standing atop a cliff. It was between seven and eight feet tall, slightly hunched over, but not so hunched over as an ape would be. Its arms were proportionately as long as a man's. One of the youths fired an arrow at it, but when they returned to the cliff the next day, they found only the undamaged arrow—no footprints. But they did discover piles of broken shells.

These stories, in common with many others, ask us to believe that a shadowy creature which does not leave prints and which is not affected by human weapons nevertheless eats solid food like a conventional animal. We seem to have here a phenomenon that is at once a ghost and a living creature.

"One measures a circle, beginning anywhere," Charles Fort wrote in a memorable phrase several decades ago. He was writing, as we have been, of a continuous universe in which all things, in varying degrees, are part of something else. One starts measuring, in other words, at an arbitrary point.

We shall start tracing our own circle in the Pacific Northwest.

CHAPTER TWO

The Bigfeet

1.

For some years now the Bigfoot, the legendary hairy giant of California, Oregon, Washington and British Columbia, has captivated the imagination of the world. Its occasional appearances to startled campers, lumberjacks and hunters have inspired numerous books, articles, television shows and movies. Several men, including Peter Byrne of the International Wildlife Conservation Society, have tossed all concerns aside, taken up residence in the wilds, and devoted all their energies to the problem.

And problem it is, and right now that's about *all* it is. For all their efforts, the investigators have produced nothing, such as a body or a live specimen, that would conclusively establish the beast's existence. There are, of course, a great many reports, but the people who make them can offer little in the way of proof beyond their own testimonies.

The other "evidence," what there is of it, is also

open to question. So far it includes footprints, hairs, droppings, odors (which may linger either at the site or on clothing and hair), injuries or fatalities to other animals, several low-quality still photographs, a 16-mm color movie, tape recorded cries, handprints, footprints, hairprints, blood, damaged or disturbed property, food remains, bones, and an alleged —and much disputed—body frozen in ice.

Some of this evidence, especially of the more conclusive variety (the bones and the supposed frozen body), has been allegedly lost or destroyed. Some of it is almost certainly faked. Some of it has proven to be not from any such creature as described. Much of it has not been examined by people qualified to study it.

Even the classic story of Jacko, an apelike creature reportedly captured in British Columbia in 1884, appears to have been a hoax, according to no less an authority than John Green, who first discovered and publicized the original news account from *The Daily British Colonist*. The case for Jacko's existence from the very beginning rested solely on the one newspaper article, and as Green dug for further evidence over the years, he finally discovered the story to have been nothing more than a journalistic fabrication. In any case, as primatologist John Napier had already noted in his *Bigfoot: The Yeti and Sasquatch in Myth and Reality,* "The description [of Jacko] would fit an adult chimpanzee or even a juvenile male or adult female gorilla." Of course, as Napier conceded, "it is difficult to imagine what an African ape was doing swanning about in the middle of British Columbia." Since Green's exposure of the hoax, the answer seems simple enough: The hoaxer patterned his creation after the model of real apes.

Like others, the authors possess a healthy fear of being made to look like fools, so let us state at the outset that we do not categorically reject the possibility that a physical creature prowls the Northwestern backwoods. If that sounds like cowardly bet-hedging—well, that's precisely what it is. But maybe some day somebody will walk out of the forest, Bigfoot in tow, and the issue will be settled once and for all. In fact, we frankly rather hope that will be the case, if only for the sheer joy of watching certain jeering skeptics sitting down before plates heaped high with cooked crow.

Nonetheless, as time has passed we have both struggled to contain a growing suspicion that, in common with a lot of other things, Bigfoot may be something other than what it's cracked up to be, that the case for a flesh-and-blood critter has been made at the expense of certain kinds of "unacceptable" data which have necessarily had to be suppressed.

To start with, for example, there is the frustrating matter of the footprints, about which Napier, by no means unsympathetic to the idea of Bigfoot, has complained, "There seem to be two distinct types of Sasquatch track, and the differences between them appear to go beyond the range of normal variation expected within a single species of mammal. This in itself is bound to make one rather suspicious." Napier concludes that one or both must be fakes.

"What I find a great deal more interesting," Bigfoot hunter Ken Coon writes in a privately distributed paper, "Sasquatch Footprint Variations," "are the *extreme* variations in foot form." Clearly, it would seem, Dr. Napier does not know the full magnitude of the problem.

Coon describes a track found in San Diego County, California, after a physician and his family made several sightings of a hairy apelike creature. "It was fourteen inches long, ten inches across the front of the foot, tapered to a very narrow heel, and had only four toes. It did not appear that a toe had been lost, as the arrangement was such that the foot appeared to be designed for just four toes . . . . [These] prints were in no way similar to what we expect a Sasquatch track to look like, yet the descriptions of the creatures, except for the size, are very similar to common Sasquatch sightings, the San Diego creatures apparently somewhat shorter in stature."

All primates have five toes. The idea of a four-toed primate is, as Coon notes, ridiculous. Even more ridiculous are the *three*-toed prints left by a Bigfoot in the Antelope Valley of California. Coon says that two fellow Bigfoot hunters to whom he showed these prints were almost frantic in their insistence that they had to be the product of a hoax or a bear. Coon, a skilled investigator and former sheriff's captain, points out in reply:

1. I personally interviewed several of the alleged witnesses in the Antelope Valley sightings and heard taped interviews of others. Several of them and one young lady in particular were among the most convincing of any interviews of my experience.

2.) The footprints like the one in my possession were found at various times and places in the same areas where the sightings were taking place. I have seen photographs of tracks (series of prints) wherein the creature displayed a stride of 55 to 60 inches and great print depth.

3.) The likelihood of their being bear prints is eliminated by the fact that there were very long toes evident, great stride, no evidence of a quadrapedal gait and no claw marks. This is in addition to the size (14 inches), larger than any black bear. I know that bear prints do not always show claw marks and that bears sometimes superimpose one print partially on another, creating a huge print. But all of the details of the print together eliminate the possibility that an outsized grizzly was walking around Antelope Valley on his hind legs. This, by the way, is desert country.

4.) The tracks *could* have been faked as is always possible unless someone sees them being made as the Sasquatch walks by. But I believe the circumstances surrounding them makes that no more likely than in the case of any other alleged Sasquatch prints found to date.

2.

The problem of Bigfoot's real identity grows even more acute when we consider the testimony of the Northern Athabascan Indians of the Canadian plains and Alaska, who have a longstanding traditional belief in the *Nakani,* also called "Bad Indians," Bushmen, and other names. In the early fall of 1970 Bob Betts and Jim McClarin flew into the remote Athabascan village of Ruby on the Yukon River to investigate the question firsthand.

Betts and McClarin discovered that the people of Ruby were unwilling to talk about the Bushman. But after the two researchers had lived in the village for a number of days, the villagers came to trust them and at last the two began to hear about the hair-covered, manlike being which supposedly still inhabited certain areas along the Yukon River.

The Indians said the Bushman is seen only in the fall of the year, just as the Alaskan night is starting to get truly dark but before the cold winter sets in. Villager Bill Captain took Betts and McClarin to see Paul Peters, an Athabascan who lived ten miles downriver from Ruby and who claimed to have observed a Bushman himself in the fall of 1960 on the north shore of the river near his fish camp.

Peters had been working in front of his cabin, which sat on the north bank of the river about a hundred feet back from the water. He kept his sled dogs chained on the beach near his boat. When they began whining and acting strangely, Peters stopped the work he was doing and looked up to see what was bothering them. About a hundred yards down the shore from where his dogs were tied, he saw something walking along the rocky beach toward the dogs. The "something" looked like a man but was quite tall and covered with black hair. A few seconds after Peters spotted it, the Bushman lumbered off into the dense brush along the river bank. It had appeared to the witness to be about six and a half feet tall and very stocky and muscular.

The Indians along the Yukon say the Bushman is usually nocturnal, although it will make an occasional appearance during daylight hours. Betts and McClarin were told it did not stay in any one place but that it would "travel around." No one could tell them where the Bushman spent the rest of the year, although some villagers suggested that perhaps it migrated south and others thought maybe it hibernated in caves or underground holes. They were convinced, however, that the Bushman lurks around villages and fish camps waiting to steal children. In fact, they often used the threat of the Bushman's presence to keep children from wandering too far away from camp.

The local informants thought that the Bushman came around the villages in the fall because it was then that the Indians hung salmon on the drying racks. They were sure the strange creature ate the fish because sometimes the salmon disappeared from the smokehouses and racks during the night. One man from Kobuk told Betts and McClarin he had spread loose dirt around his smokehouse to see what kind of animal was stealing his salmon and the next morning found large humanlike tracks in the dirt. The tracks were bigger than any he had ever seen before.

The Bushman also had the unsettling habit of throwing sticks or rocks at people who unknowingly entered an area it inhabited. The fear of Bushmen was so great that several villagers had actually abandoned productive fishwheels after having rocks tossed at them from the brush. One such incident supposedly occurred in 1949 to a man named Robert Kennedy, who ran a fish camp 22 miles downriver from Ruby.

Kennedy, who in 1970 was in his sixties, told the two investigators that he had been at the fish camp alone and was sitting quietly on the river bank watching his fishwheel when suddenly a large rock came sailing through the air only a few feet over his head. Startled and scared, Kennedy grabbed his .30-.30 and fired several shots in the direction from which the rock had come. A few moments later another rock was thrown at him from the thick brush. Kennedy unchained several of his big huskies, which dashed up the hill and into the brush. After a brief commotion they returned from the hill, frightened and whining, and resisted their master's efforts to get them to go back up. Convinced that it had been a Bushman in the brush, Kennedy gathered his things together and abandoned his camp the next morning.

While McClarin and Betts were in Ruby, Patty Nollnar arrived from nearby Nulato and, hearing that they were interested in the Bushman, said that he and six other Nulato villagers had encountered such a creature only a few days before while they were spending the night on the bank of the Koyukuk River. The seven Indians, who had been out trapping muskrat about twenty miles up the Koyukuk from its confluence with the Yukon, were lying around their small fire when suddenly a rock was thrown at them from the trees nearby. In response, the men fired their rifles into the trees and brush around the campsite. No more rocks were thrown but the party, certain that a Bushman had been responsible, threw their gear into the boats and left the area.

The local informants also commented frequently on the Bushman's high-pitched whistle. One man, an employee at an area Air Force base who claimed he had heard it as a boy, compared it to the high-pitched whine of a jet engine starting.

So far there is nothing in these reports to upset the conventional wisdom that, if the Bigfoot (or Bushman) exists, it must be some kind of flesh-and-blood animal. That, however, is not the view the Athabascans hold.

They believe that the Bushman cannot be caught or killed, and they told Betts and McClarin that if they did have the misfortune to encounter a Bushman, it would "freeze" them motionless before they could use the movie cameras they carried. It was evident that the Bushman was feared as much as an unknown being with supernatural powers as a physical threat. From childhood the natives are taught by their elders to avoid any meeting with the Bushman; if such a meeting should be unavoidable, one should look down at the ground and pretend not to see it. Above all, the elders impress upon the children that they must respect the Bushman as being more powerful, both naturally and supernaturally, than the Indian. To go out actually in search of one, as Betts and McClarin were doing, was thought not only disrespectful but highly dangerous.

When asked about the origin of the Bushman, many of the informants said they had no idea where it came from and would not discuss the matter further. Others said the Bushmen were once natives like themselves who, during an extended period of starvation a long time ago, had gone into the woods to live a primitive existence like the wild animals. While most of these Indians were said to have died, others had reverted to an animal state, growing hair all over their bodies and becoming larger and stronger. They had lost their ability to make weapons, clothing, or fire and could no longer communicate in the language they once knew.

We don't think we need take seriously the myth of the creature's origin, since it is clearly an attempt to account for an otherwise inexplicable presence. Still, it is interesting to note that the Athabascans see the Bushmen as related to man and both inferior and superior to him: inferior in the sense that the Bushmen have reverted to an animal state, superior in the sense that they have achieved supernatural powers. This theme of the peculiar union of opposites runs through much of the monster lore we shall be examining.

But how seriously are we to take the Athabascan notion that the Bushman/Bigfoot is somehow paranormal? Betts and McClarin tended to interpret that part of the story as a folklore embellishment growing out of the Indians' fear of a real, if elusive, creature. Maybe—but then maybe not, for other Bigfoot witnesses have maintained that there is something decidedly "unnatural" about the creature.

3.

For example, we have the story, printed in the July 16, 1918, *Seattle Times,* of "mountain devils" which attacked a miner's cabin at Mt. St. Lawrence near Kelso, Washington. Supposedly these hairy creatures, which stood seven to eight feet tall, could make themselves invisible. Unfortunately that is all we know about this alleged episode.

We know far more about the experiences of one Fred Beck, participant in an incident which has become a classic of Bigfoot lore. Or at least an *edited* version of that incident has become well known. The familiar version has been carefully bowdlerized by later writers who have cited it as further evidence that an unknown flesh-and-blood hominoid exists in the wilderness of the Pacific Northwest. Beck's version, on the other hand, suggests something rather different. The following is based upon Beck's own account as detailed in as obscure, out-of-print booklet, *I Fought the Apeman of Mt. St. Helens,* which Beck and his son R. A. Beck published privately in 1967.

One night early in this century two young brothers working in a logging camp near Kelso, Washington, heard a rustling sound outside their tent. Peering anxiously outside, they were terrified to see a huge, hairy, upright figure watching them. Finally the creature lumbered back into the woods.

The Beck brothers, who had never heard of the Bigfoot, then known only to the Indians, were perplexed by the whole episode. Finally, one of them convinced himself the thing had been a bear. But Fred, the other brother, was not so sure. He had seen many bears in his time and he did not think this was one of them. Later on, in July 1924 to be precise, Fred Beck's suspicion that he had seen something far out of the ordinary would receive spectacular confirmation.

For six years prior to that date Beck and his partner had been prospecting for gold in the Mt. St. Helens and Lewis River area in southwestern Washington. In the beginning, before they built a cabin, they lived in a tent below a small mountain called

Pumy Butte. Nearby a creek flowed, and along it there was a moist sand bar about an acre in size where the prospectors would go to wash their dishes and get drinking water.

Early one morning one of them came running to the camp and urged his fellows to follow him back to the creek, where he showed them two huge, somewhat humanlike tracks sunk four inches deep in the center of the sand bar. There were no other tracks anywhere nearby. Either whatever made them had a 160-foot stride, the men reasoned, or "something dropped from the sky and went back up."

As time passed, the miners came upon other, similar tracks which they could not identify. The largest of them was nineteen inches long.

After they had built their cabin, Beck and the four other miners working their gold claim, the Vander White, would hear a strange "thudding, hollow thumping noise" in broad daylight. They could not find the cause, though they suspected one of their number might be playing tricks on them. That proved not to be the case, since even when the group were gathered together the sound continued all around them. They thought it sounded as if "there's a hollow drum in the earth somewhere and something is hitting it."

Those were not to be the last strange sounds they would hear, either. Early in July 1924, a shrill whistling, apparently emanating from atop a ridge, pierced the evening quiet. An answering whistle came from another ridge. These sounds, along with a booming "thumping" as if something were pounding its chest, continued every evening for a week.

By now thoroughly unnerved, the men had taken to carrying their rifles with them when they went to the spring about a hundred yards from the cabin.

Beck and a man identified as "Hank" were drawing water from the spring when suddenly Hank yelled and raised his gun. Beck looked up and saw, on the other side of a little canyon, a seven-foot apelike creature standing next to a pine tree. The creature, a hundred yards away from the two men, dodged behind the tree. When it poked its head around the tree, Hank fired three quick shots, spraying bark but apparently not hitting the creature, which disappeared from sight for a short while. It reappeared 200 yards down the canyon and this time Beck got off three shots before it was gone.

Hurriedly, Beck and Hank returned to the cabin and conferred with the other two men there (the third was elsewhere at the time). They agreed to abandon the cabin—but not until daybreak. It would be too risky, they felt, to try to make it to the car in the darkness. The four got their belongings together in preparation for the move, then settled down for a good night's sleep which, as it turned out, they did not get.

At midnight they awakened suddenly to a tremendous thud against the cabin wall. Some of the chinking which had been knocked loose from between the logs fell on Hank, who was pinned underneath it. Beck had to help him free himself. Then, as they heard what sounded like many feet tramping and running outside, they grabbed their guns, prepared for the worst. Hank peered through the open space left by the dislodged chinking (the cabin had no windows) and spotted three "apes" together. From the sound of things, there were many more.

The creatures proceeded to pelt the cabin with rocks. Though terribly frightened (the other two miners were huddling in the corner in a state of

39

shock), Beck said they should fire on the creatures only if they physically attacked the cabin. This would show that the miners were only defending themselves.

But within a very short time the "apes" *were* attacking the cabin. Some of them jumped on the roof, evidently in an effort to batter it down. In response, Beck and Hank fired through the roof. They were also forced to brace the door with a long pole taken from the bunk bed, since the creatures were furiously attempting to smash it open. Beck and Hank riddled the door with bullets.

The attacks continued all night, punctuated occasionally by short quiet interludes. At one point a creature reached through the chinking space and grabbed an ax by the handle. Beck lunged forward, snatched the blade part and turned the ax upright so that the "ape" couldn't get it out. As he was doing so, a bullet from Hank's rifle narrowly missed his hand. The creature withdrew its arm and retreated.

Finally, just before daybreak, the attack ended. The embattled miners waited for daylight, then cautiously stepped outside, guns in hand. A few minutes later Beck spotted one of the creatures about eighty yards away, standing near the edge of the canyon. Taking careful aim, he shot three times and watched as it toppled over the cliff and fell down into the gorge 400 feet below.

As quickly as they could get out of there, the miners departed, heading for Spirit Lake, Washington, and leaving $200 in supplies and equipment behind. They never returned to claim it.

At Spirit Lake Hank told a forest ranger about the experience. After the group had come home to Kelso, the story leaked to the newspapers and caused a sensation. Reporters found giant tracks at the scene, but no other traces of the creatures the men believed they had shot at. The canyon where the episode allegedly occurred became known as "Ape Canyon" and still bears that name over fifty years later.

In his booklet Beck reveals that all his life, from his early childhood on, he had numerous psychic experiences, many of them involving supernatural "people." He says that they found the mine they were working in 1924 through guidance from two "spiritual beings," one a buckskin-clad Indian, the other a woman after whom they would name their mine (Vander White).

Of the "apemen," Beck writes, "they are not entirely of this world. . . . I was, for one, always conscious that we were dealing with supernatural beings and I know the other members of the party felt the same." Beck believes the creatures now known as Sasquatch or Bigfoot come from "another dimension" and are a link between human and animal consciousness. They are composed of a substance that ranges between the physical and the psychical, sometimes one more than the other, depending upon the degree of "materialization." Because of their peculiar nature none will ever be captured, nor will bodies ever be found.

Preposterous? The fantasies of an old man? Perhaps.

But we must note here that no one except those resolutely determined to reject *all* Bigfoot reports has ever questioned Beck's testimony about the Ape Canyon shoot-out. If we accept that much, then we cannot honestly reject the unpalatable portions, however much we might like to do so. And if we accept the reality of the isolated set of footprints, for instance, then we are forced to consider seriously Beck's contention that the Bigfeet "are not entirely of this world." Either this, or we must reject the Ape Canyon story entirely.

It is not our intention to deal at great length with the Bigfoot question, which has been adequately documented elsewhere. Our purpose is simply to point out certain paranormal elements in several of the reports and to suggest the possibility that the Bigfoot may not be significantly different from the "manimals" which are being sighted in increasing numbers throughout the rest of the country.

The considerable majority of Bigfoot encounters, in common with their eastern counterparts, are of very short duration, involving no more than a few seconds to a few minutes. Most are isolated events, free of obviously paranormal content, and it is not hard to understand why the stimulus for the reports has usually been assumed to be something purely physical. Most Fortean phenomena, however, also appear to occur in isolation and that is why, as we observed in the last chapter, UFOs, MAs and psi have seemed to be separate concerns. Our interest in this book is in that significant minority of incidents that tie the various classes of phenomena together and suggest that they are continuous with one another.

In that regard, let us consider four relatively recent Bigfoot cases.

Vader, Washington, winter 1970-71 and spring 1971: On December 4, 1970, Mrs. Wallace Bowers heard her children calling for her to come outside. Upon doing so, she discovered mysterious footprints in the inch-deep snow covering her farm yard. "The footprints were *very* large, measuring sixteen inches, and five to seven inches wide," she told an investigator. "The night before, it had snowed, freezing hard afterwards. In comparison of weight, my husband's pickup truck never even went through the snow and ice upon his leaving for work; he leaves around 5:30 a.m., as he is a logger. The morning we discovered the giant tracks, or footprints, alongside his truck in the drive, the prints were like black on white, as whatever made them was so heavy it took the frozen snow with each step, *plus* leaving one and a half-inch impressions in the frozen gravel beneath."

Mrs. Bowers recalled that the family dog had acted oddly the night before, as if sensing the presence of an intruder. Vader is in the middle of Bigfoot country and the tracks in the snow resembled those attributed to the creature.

At 7:15 a.m. three days later, on the seventh, the Bowers children again called their mother, this time to the window, where they were watching a "bright star" which was moving across the sky. The object flew closer to the witnesses and for ten minutes they were able to view it carefully.

Its center appeared to be a dome around which a larger circle seemed to be revolving. It was deep orange in the center, with the light diffusing toward the outer edge, but with a definite bright rim.

Mrs. Bowers said it seemed tipped sideways slightly, rather like an airplane banking, and then it hovered briefly over the nearby Bonneville power lines. After it left the power lines, it changed from orange to a bright, clear light, and at one time seemed to make one last sweep closer, again turning orange. The children thought they saw a "gray shape" drop away from the UFO just before it vanished in the distance.

During the sighting Mrs. Bowers switched on the intercom in the house, only to hear a peculiar "sharp" sound. "And the funny thing is," she said, "we tried to use the intercom the night before and got that same sharp sound."

But that was not to be all. Later in the week (the UFO sighting occurred on a Monday), Mrs. Bowers was putting a log in the living room fireplace when she saw the curtains moving in the boys' bedroom, which was visible from where she stood.

"All the children were in the living room with me," she said. "All I could think of was getting them safely out of there. So I loaded them into the car and we left, but I definitely saw a shape in the bedroom as we drove away." They returned only after Mr. Bowers had come home from work.

"I feel sure that was probably a prowler," Mrs. Bowers said. "We've had trouble in our neighborhood and I don't think it's related to the others. But the footprints and the saucer—I don't know . . ."

Nonetheless, the "prowler" was a strange one: He took nothing. He rummaged through the bedrooms but afterward the Bowerses could find nothing gone. While it is of course impossible to prove anything, we cannot help thinking of the mysterious "gray shape" the children thought they saw, and then of the long tradition of bedroom apparitions. Very shortly we will encounter another case of "prowlers" who took nothing.

Subsequently, according to Mrs. Bowers, "We had several months of strange noises in the night, something very heavy thudding across the yard, but we never saw anything. Our house is so well insulated it is hard for us to even hear a car come into our drive. So it was really strange to be awakened by this thudding jar going across our yard. Every night, it was around the same time. It would wake us up between 2:00 and 3:00 a.m."

Balls Ferry, California, late January 1972: Four teenage boys on their way to Battle Creek to fish on a dark, rainy night saw a brilliant glowing object swoop over their car. Later, as they parked at the

44

Battle Creek Bridge, they heard a noise, then a scream in the bush.

"We heard a blood-curdling scream," John Yeries, 16, recalled. "I threw the light over in the brush and there was this weird thing."

The beast was about seven feet tall, dark brown or green, had a large teardrop-shaped ear, and was hunched over. It appeared to have lumps all over its body, "like pouches in a flight suit." It turned and ran. So did the witnesses.

"I was wondering what it was," Darrell Rich, 16, said, "and at the same time I was turning to get out of there." James Yeries and Robbie Cross were already hightailing it back to the car. But when they got there, they were horrified to discover that it wouldn't start.* They had to push it before it would.

As they sped away, they all had the feeling they were being watched and followed. Soon thereafter, Darrell saw what looked like "firecrackers" going off on the pavement, only without the accompanying sound. John saw them out the rear-view mirror but soon their collective attention was captured by fiery

---

* Another creature-related car stoppage supposedly occurred in October 1960 in the Monongahela National Forest near Marlinton, West Virginia. While driving along a road behind a group of friends in a bus, W. C. "Doc" Priestley reportedly encountered an eight-foot hairy apelike "monster with long hair standing straight up." Just moments before he saw the thing, his car engine suddenly had ceased working. "I don't know how long I sat there," Priestley said, "until the boys missed me and backed up the bus to where I was. It seemed the monster was very much afraid of the bus and dropped his hair and to my surprise, as soon as he did this, my car started to run again. I didn't tell the boys what I had seen. The thing took off when the bus started."

Priestley and the bus resumed their journey. Soon, however, the car began to sputter again. "I could see the sparks flying from under the hood of my car as if it had a very bad short. And sure enough, there beside the road stood the monster again. The points were completely burned out of my car." The bus backed up again and the creature fled into the forest.

Priestley's was only one of a number of creature sightings made in West Virginia that year.

objects, blue and white, orange and red, seen moving erratically in the open fields on either side of the road. At one point two of the "glowing balls" came together in the sky while another time one shot straight up and disappeared. One of the glowing objects, weirdly enough, took on the appearance of a human figure beside the road. Strangely and suddenly, at the intersection of Deschutes and Dersch roads, the lights disappeared.

Racing back home, they told Darrell Rich's father, Dean Rich, of the incidents. The elder Rich, though somewhat skeptical, returned with the boys to the Battle Creek Bridge area and walked out into a nearby walnut orchard. All of a sudden they heard an odd "commotion" in the darkness in front of them. As Rich would later describe it, "It sounded like a real deep growl. It was a real weird type of sensation. It was something I've never experienced before." The boys abruptly fled and the father quickly followed suit.

The growling, a long, nerve-wrenching *eeeeaaaaaghhhrrr,* continued as Rich ran backwards to his car. Once there, he and the boys held a brief conference and concluded that the "thing" was warning them to depart from its territory. If it was trying to scare them, Rich said, "it succeeded."

The party went to the Anderson, California, police, who returned to the area but found nothing. However, the lawmen said they doubted the story was a hoax. One officer remarked, "They seemed completely sincere. There was no hint of the funnies or something else. They were really scared."

Summing up the group's feelings, Darrell Rich speculated, "I wonder if we saw something we shouldn't have."

King County, Washington, June 9, 1974: A man named Tony McClennan was driving through the evening darkness when suddenly he slowed to avoid hitting what he thought might be an injured dog. Then the "dog" stood up and McClennan gaped in astonishment at a hairy apelike beast with long, swinging arms and *glowing,* not reflecting, red eyes. It was about eight feet high.

When the police investigated, they came upon a freshly-made path something had made through the thick brush. Strands of dark hair four inches long were found on nearby branches.

Washington State, fall 1975: On October 1 three youths out hunting near Rimrock Lake heard noises in the woods around them. Feeling they were being followed, they began hiking back to camp, which they reached around 9:00 p.m. They built a fire and were sitting in front of it when they heard still more noises. One of the group, Earl Thomas, 18, beamed his flashlight across a small pond nearby and spotted a pair of greenish-yellow eyes staring back at him. Thomas and Tom Gerstmar, 17, returned to camp to talk the matter over.

Finally, all three carefully walked the short distance to the edge of the pond and shone the light again. This time they saw what the eyes were a part of: an eight- or nine-foot hairy creature with human-like features. The thing shied away from the light. Evidently, despite its size, it was a creature of retiring disposition. This, however, was not enough to keep the badly frightened young men from firing upon it seven times with their rifles. Immediately afterwards they fled back to camp and grabbed their provisions. As they were doing so, the Bigfoot commenced to scream, which only added to their sense of panic. Gerstmar nearly wrecked his jeep in his haste to get away.

When they got to Trout Lodge, they called the Yakima County Sheriff's office. Later Deputy Larry

Gamache interviewed the three youths and their testimony convinced him they had definitely "seen something."

But for Earl Thomas, that was not the end of the episode. Dick Grover, who interviewed all the witnesses and kept in touch with them for a time after their original experience, reports these bizarre developments:

"A two-tone green, four-wheel-drive Bronco with Oregon license plates had for two weeks followed the Thomases to town. The car has been seen driving by their house three to four times a day. The car had also been driven into their driveway. The driver was never seen leaving his car. [He] was described as a middle-aged man in his 50s or 60s, medium build, gray hair, crew cut. He keeps his car clean and appears to be very interested in the Thomases. This investigator had the opportunity to be shown the vehicle and driver when he was interviewing Earl Thomas.

"Earl Thomas also stated that threats have been made on his life. These threats were made via phone on two different occasions. On one occasion the caller, male, told [him], 'Don't step out your door. We'll blow your head off.' "

It is possible that a wealthy lunatic with a great deal of time on his hands decided to frighten Thomas for some reason, but that seems improbable in view of the fact that the harassment continued for several months after Grover made his report. Readers with a background in ufology will recognize this activity as strongly reminiscent of behavior associated with the fabled "men in black" (MIB), who reportedly have threatened some individuals who have had UFO sightings. Curiously, even the observation that the stranger "keeps his car clean" has precedents in MIB reports, for witnesses sometimes remark on the "clean" or "new" appearance of the vehicles these figures are said to drive.

More particularly it reminds the authors of another story we have heard. In November 1974, while Jerome Clark was on a field trip across midwestern America doing research on various Fortean phenomena, he talked at length with a bright, level-headed man who had conducted an in-depth investigation of reports of an apelike creature in the Sioux City, Iowa, area. The investigator confided to Clark —and his testimony was confirmed by a friend— that in the course of his work he discovered that two very strange men in a red compact car seemed to be keeping him and his apartment under surveillance. On one occasion he discovered that his apartment had been expertly broken into—he could find no evidence of how it could have been done—but nothing had been taken. *The intruders, however, had rifled through his files on the local creature sightings.*

The motif of "burglars" who take nothing takes us back, of course, to the Bowerses' mysterious intruder.

5.

So where does all of this lead us?

Perhaps we can sum it up thus:

1.) There are paranormal overtones to at least some Bigfoot encounters. UFO and psi phenomena figure prominently in certain of the cases.

2.) The best "physical evidence"—the alleged footprints—is ambiguous, inconclusive, and sometimes contradictory. The only unambiguous, conclusive, and noncontradictory physical evidence— bodies or bones—is notoriously nonexistent.

3.) The Bigfoot is more elusive than we could realistically expect a purely flesh-and-blood beast to be. After all, as Napier observes in his excellent book, "Is it really possible that a population of up to 1000 Bigfoot could exist in remote, but by no means untraveled, regions without being formally recognized by zoology? The American puma or mountain lion is widespread from British Columbia to Patagonia in quite large numbers. Yet it is so elusive that few people have seen it in the wild, and fewer still have been able to photograph it. Nevertheless, in spite of its retiring habits, the mountain lion is well known to science."

None of this constitutes conclusive proof that *all* Bigfeet are paraphysical in nature, but it is at least enough to raise some doubts about the popular notion of an unknown hominoid roaming the forests of the Northwest—especially when we discover that seemingly identical creatures are popping up all over the North American landscape in places where their presence is manifestly impossible.

CHAPTER THREE

The Manimals

1.

Our first account is not North American in origin, but it is the earliest one we have. We present it here because of its extraordinary interest.

The story is that one stormy day in the year 1161 English fishermen off the coast of Orford, Suffolk, caught a "wild man" in their nets. As Ralph of Coggeshall, a clerical historian of the early 13th century, has it, "All the parts of his Body resembled those of a Man; he had Hair on his Head, a long peaked Beard, and about ye Brest was exceeding hairy and rough."

The fisherman took the creature to the governor of Orford Castle, one Glanvill, who kept him for some time and allowed his soldiers to torture him in an effort "to make him speak." The wild man was fed on raw meat and fish, which he "pressed with his hands" before eating. Finally, one day he was taken out to the sea "to disport himself therein."

But he broke through a triple barrier of nets and escaped.

Yet not long afterwards he returned to the castle and voluntarily reentered captivity. But at last, "being wearied of living alone," he went back to the sea and was heard of no more.

While—as we shall see presently—our manimals have certain aquatic habits, there is no precise modern parallel to this fascinating old folk tale. The nearest thing we have to it is an August 21, 1955, incident from near Dogtown, Indiana.

Late on the afternoon of the day in question, Mrs. Darwin Johnson and Mrs. Chris Lamble, both of Evansville, were swimming in the Ohio River, about fifteen feet from shore. Suddenly something came up behind Mrs. Johnson and grabbed her left leg. She could see nothing—the attacker was under water— but she could feel large claws and a furry palm gripping her knee. The thing, whatever it was, yanked her under. She kicked and fought and managed to come up once more. Again she went under.

Though she wasn't being attacked, Mrs. Lamble, who was safely in an innertube four feet away, proceeded to kick and scream on the theory that this might scare "it" away. In the meantime, Mrs. Johnson lunged for the innertube and hit it with "a loud, hollow thump." It was then, she said, that "whatever was around my legs loosened its grip."

The two women quickly headed for shore, where they treated Mrs. Johnson's leg, which had begun to sting, with alcohol. But for several days afterwards a green stain with the outline of a palm remained just below the knee. The woman became hysterical from the experience and her husband, who was called from work, had to summon a doctor to give her sedatives.

No one ever saw the creature, but Mrs. Johnson said, "Whatever this thing was, it had a strong grip and it was very furry . . . All I know is that I will never go swimming in the river again."

After the story was published in the *Evansville Press* the next day, several persons came forward to say they had observed a "shiny oval" a few hundred feet above the river at about the time the alleged incident had taken place.

A short time later an Air Force colonel is supposed to have called upon the Johnsons and interviewed them at some length. He urged them not to discuss the matter publicly any further.

Perhaps Mrs. Johnson had encountered the same critter a Saginaw, Michigan, man is reputed to have sighted one day in 1937. He was fishing on the banks of the Saginaw River when a manlike "monster" climbed up the bank, leaned upon a tree, and then returned to the water. The witness allegedly suffered a nervous breakdown from the experience.

Charles Buchanan may not have had a nervous breakdown, but his own experience shook him considerably. On November 7, 1969, Buchanan, camped out on the shore of Lake Worth, Texas, awoke about 2:00 a.m. to find a hairy creature that looked "like a cross between a human being and a gorilla" towering above him. Buchanan had been sleeping in the bed of his pickup truck when the thing suddenly jerked him to the ground, sleeping bag and all. Gagging from the stench of the beast, the camper did the only thing he could think of: He grabbed a bag of leftover chicken and shoved it into the long-armed creature's face. It took the sack in its mouth, made some guttural sounds, then loped off through the trees, splashed in the water, and proceeded to swim with powerful strokes toward Greer Island.

Another creature from the black lagoon—or from

some place—first appeared shortly after midnight on June 25, 1973, and was seen by Randy Needham and Judy Johnson, who were parked on a boat ramp to the Big Muddy River near Murphysboro, a town in southwestern Illinois. The couple, who had been startled by a cry "about three times as loud as a bobcat, only deeper," emanating from the nearby woods, looked up to see a huge biped lumbering toward them, still shrieking but now in altering tones. It was not a human sound.

Randy and Judy agreed the thing was about seven feet tall, white, its short body hair matted with river mud. They were not interested in examining it at close range, and by the time it had got within twenty feet of them, they were roaring away from the scene, bound for the Murphysboro police station.

Officers Meryl Lindsey and Jimmie Nash checked the area and found "impressions in the mud approximately ten to twelve inches long and approximately three inches wide," according to the report they filed later. To Jerome Clark, Needham later described the impressions as "something like a man with a shoe on would make—only the thing wasn't wearing shoes." He suggested that toe prints may not have registered in the mud.

At 2:00 a.m. Nash, Lindsey, Needham and Deputy Sheriff Bob Scott returned to the scene. This time they discovered fresh tracks, similar in general appearance to those they had seen an hour earlier, but deeper and smaller. The police report noted an especially strange detail: "The prints in the mud were very irratic [sic] in that no two were the same distance apart and some were five to six feet apart. Also prints were found very close together."

Officer Lindsey left to get a camera to take pictures of the prints, and while he was gone the other three followed the tracks. While they were bending over to examine some of them, there came "the most incredible shriek I've ever heard," Nash recalled. Apparently the creature was hidden in the trees less than a hundred yards away. The trio didn't stick around to find out. They beat a hasty retreat to the squad car. In the hours that followed, the officers scoured the area in pursuit of an elusive splashing sound but found nothing.

When daylight came, things got quieter, but with darkness the creature returned.

The first to see it this time was four-year-old Christian Baril, who told his parents he had seen "a big white ghost in the yard." They didn't believe him, of course, but ten minutes later, when Randy Creath and Cheryl Ray saw something very much like that in a neighboring yard, parents and police reconsidered the youngster's words.

About 10:30 p.m. Randy and Cheryl were sitting on the back porch of the Ray home when they heard something moving in the trees just beyond the lawn. They saw the creature standing in an opening in the trees, quietly watching them through glowing pink eyes. Cheryl insisted, in an interview with Jerome Clark, that the eyes were glowing, not reflecting, since there was no nearby light source that could have caused the effect.

The creature was either the same one the other young couple had seen the night before or one similar to it. It was white and dirty, weighed close to 350 pounds and stood seven feet tall. It had a large round head. Cheryl thought its arms might be "ape-length," although she wasn't certain because it was standing in waist-high grass.

Randy went down to get a closer look while Cheryl went inside to turn on the yard light. The light did not reveal much more of the creature than they had already seen.

Finally the thing ambled off through the trees,

making considerable noise. Later, investigators found a trail of crushed weeds and broken brush, as well as imprints in the ground too vague and imperfect to be cast in plaster.

Cheryl's mother, Mrs. Harry Ray, called the police. While waiting for them to arrive, they suddenly began to smell a "real strong odor, like a sewer," Cheryl said, but it lasted only a short time.

Soon Officers Nash and Ronald Manwaring pulled up in their car. What happened then is recounted in their report given to Loren Coleman:

Officers inspected the area where the creature was seen and found weeds broken down and somewhat [sic] of a path where something had walked through. Jerry Nellis was notified to bring his dog to the area to see if the dog would track the creature. Upon arrival of Nellis and dog [a German shepherd trained to attack, search buildings, and track] the dog was led to the area where the creature was last seen. The dog began tracking down the hill where the creature was reported to have gone.

As the dog started down the hill, it kept stopping and sniffing at a slime substance on the weeds; the slime appeared periodically as the dog tracked the creature. Nellis put some of the slime between his fingers [and] rubbed it and it left a black coloring on his fingers. Each time the dog found amounts of it, the dog would hesitate.

The creature was tracked down the hill to a pond, around the pond to a wooded area south of the pond where the dog attempted to pull Nellis down a steep embankment. The area where the dog tracked the creature to was too thick and bushy to walk through, so the dog was pulled off the trail and returned to the car. Officers then searched the area with flashlights.

Officer Nash, Nellis and the dog then proceeded to the area directly south of where the dog was pulled off the tracks. The area was at the end of the first road to the west past Westwood Hills turnoff. The area is approximately one-half mile south of the area of the pond behind 37 Westwood Lane.

Nellis and the dog again began to search the area to see if the dog could again pick up the scent. Nellis and the dog approached the abandoned barn and Nellis called to Officer Nash to come to the area as the dog would not enter the barn. Nellis pushed the dog inside and the dog immediately ran out. Nash and Nellis searched the barn and found nothing inside. Nellis stated that the dog was trained to search buildings and had never backed down from anything. Nellis could find no explanation as to why the dog became scared and would not go inside the barn. Officers continued to search the area and were unable to locate the creature.

The Murphysboro creature was reported twice more in 1973. During an evening July 4th celebration in a city park near the river, carnival workers said they had seen it watching the Shetland ponies. And on July 7th Mrs. Nedra Green heard a shrill piercing scream from near the shed on her isolated farm. She did not go out to investigate.

The creature supposedly made brief return appearances in July 1974 and July 1975.

So what was it? The authorities frankly admit they have no idea.

"A lot of things in life are unexplained," Police Chief Toby Berger concluded, "and this is another one. We don't know what the creature is. But we do believe what these people saw was real. . . . These are good, honest people. They are seeing something. And who would walk through sewage tanks for a joke?"

Those creatures we shall call "manimals"—the hairy things of varying sizes reported outside the Northwestern Bigfoot/Sasquatch territory—have a long history in this country, if we are to lend some credence to a body of remarkably consistent folklore.

The Indian tribes of what one day would be the eastern states spoke frequently of cannibalistic giants which, except for their reputed taste for human flesh (our modern manimals are actually quite timid, for the most part), sound like the things we are coming to know so well.

Some examples:

The Micmac, a tribe located in New Brunswick and Nova Scotia, refer in their traditional lore to the *Gugwes,* who, Elsie Clews Parsons wrote in a 1925 *Journal of American Folklore,* "have big hands and faces hairy like bears. If one saw a man coming he would lie down and beat his chest, producing a sound like a partridge." The gray partridge of southeastern Canada makes a one-tone whistle; such a whistle is cited among other tribes as the creatures' characteristic cry. The Micmac have three other names for the beasts: *Kookwes, Chenoo* and *Djenu.*

The Penobscot Indians of Maine know of *Kiwakwe,* another cannibalistic giant, which is similar to the Huron and Wyandot *Strendu.* "Half a tree tall" and larger than men, they are covered with flinty scales, which ties them to the Stone Giants of upper New York, about which Hartley B. Alexander writes:

The Iroquoian Stone Giants, as well as their congeners among the Algonquians (e.g. the *Chenoo* of the Abnaki and Micmac), belong to a widespread group of mythic beings of which the Eskimo Tornit are examples. They are . . .

huge in stature, unacquainted with the bow, and employing stones for weapons. In awesome combats they fight one another, uprooting the tallest trees for weapons and rending the earth in fury ... Commonly they are depicted as cannibals ...

The Algonquians call these ogres the *Windigo* (or *Witiko, Wendigo, Wittiko,* and other variants) —creatures known widely in the folklore of eastern and central Canada. "The *witiko* wore no clothes," the Rev. Joseph E. Guinard noted in an article in *Primitive Man.* "Summer and winter he went naked and never suffered cold. His skin was black like that of a negro. He used to rub himself, like the animals, against fir, spruce, and other resinous trees. When he was thus covered with gum or resin, he would go and roll in the sand, so that one would have thought that, after many operations of this kind, he was made of stone."

Among the Passamaquoddy, Cooper wrote in 1933, ". . . a similar habit is ascribed to the . . . *Chenoo* who used to rub themselves all over with fir balsam and then roll themselves on the ground so that everything adhered to the body. This habit is highly suggestive of the Iroquoian Stone Coats, the blood-thirsty cannibal giants, who used to cover their bodies carefully with pitch and then roll and wallow in sand and down sand banks."

Windigos have a frightful, menacing mouth with no lips. Often a sinister hissing is made by them, or a noise described as strident, very reverberating, and drawn out is accompanied by fearful howls. The *Windigo,* a huge individual who goes naked in the woods and eats people, probably is the same creature the Grand Lake Victoria Band of Quebec call the *Misabe,* a long-haired giant.

Among the Ojibwa of northern Minnesota, there were, according to Sister Bernard Coleman, "the

Memegwicio, or men of the wilderness. Some called them a 'kind of monkey' . . . about the size of children of 11 or 12 years of age . . . faces covered with hair." To the Tingami Ojibwa the *Memegwesi* are "a species of creature which lives in high remote ledges," Frank G. Speck recorded in 1915. "They are small and have hair growing all over their bodies. The Indians think they are like monkeys judging from the specimens of the latter they have seen in picture books." The Cree of the James Bay area viewed the *Memegwicio* as diminutive human beings covered with hair and having a very flat nose.

By the 19th century, when white people began to settle the central regions of the continent, the stories got more specific but, interestingly enough, rather less credible.

In 1834 we come upon vague references to hairy "wild men" reportedly seen in St. Francis, Poinsett and Green Counties in Arkansas. Twenty-two years later one such creature supposedly roamed the Arkansas-Louisiana border near Fouke, Arkansas, home of the now well-known "Fouke Monster" which inspired the popular movie *Legend of Boggy Creek.* Tracked by a search party, the "wild man" was finally cornered, but escaped by throwing one of the posse off his horse, severely mangling him in the process, hopping on the animal himself, and galloping off into the sunset. Well . . .

Slightly more believable are the stories of the Giant of the Mountains, allegedly observed "many times in the remote mountains of Saline County during the years after the Civil War," according to Otto Ernest Rayburn's *Ozark Country.* The being in question was a naked white man with long, thick hair, who seemed to reside along the Saline River. Finally, the story goes, he was captured, but escaped not long after, never to be seen again, though local people did find some "enormous tracks."

Assuming these tales to have any factual foundation at all, we still have no business jumping to conclusions, since it is distinctly possible that these were in fact wild *men,* not manimals. After all, the frontier did attract some awfully strange types, some of them individuals of a reclusive nature who may have gone more native than the actual natives (the Indians) themselves. Certainly the curious insistence that the Saline County giant was a "white man," when that sort of identification of a true manimal would be meaningless, suggests this might well be the case.

Further evidence for this possibility comes from another Arkansas "wild man" story. During the fall and winter of 1875, a number of Pulaski County residents asserted, no doubt to the considerable amusement of their contemporaries, that they had seen someone covered with long, bushy, black hair who looked like a "half-wild animal." In early December of that year, he was captured and taken to Little Rock, where an *Arkansas Gazette* reporter, who saw him in the county jail, described him as "the wildest, greasiest, ugliest-looking, half-clad specimen of humanity it was ever our lot to behold." When interviewed—this "wild man" was capable of speech—he proved to be an apparently mentally-deficient railroad worker who four years earlier had wandered into Arkansas from St. Louis.

We are more impressed with the 1869 reports along the Osage River of Missouri and Kansas, where in the latter state's Crawford County residents claimed to have seen a "wild man" or "gorilla." The creature had a stooping gait, very long arms and immense hands. Then, as is often the case in our time as well, local opinion held that the thing was a gorilla or large orangutan which had escaped from a menagerie.

Our favorite story, though, comes by way of our friend and fellow Fortean Brad Steiger, who, in

Mysteries of Time and Space, recounts an 1888 episode which a correspondent claims to have discovered in his grandfather's journal. The grandfather supposedly had accompanied an Indian friend to a cave in the "Big Woods Country" of Tennessee where a "Crazy Bear"—a hairy, apelike creature—was being fed regularly on raw meat. The Indian explained that this was only one of a number of similar beasts which had been left by "skymen," who would land from time to time in "moons." The "skymen," who were basically human in appearance, wearing short hair and shining uniforms, would always wave in friendly fashion to the presumably amazed onlookers. The Indians believed the Crazy Bears had been sent to bring them "powerful medicine."

Readers who wish to accuse us of being unduly skeptical are free to do so, but somehow this story has always struck us as being a little too good to be true. That, of course, is purely a subjective impression on our part. But recently, when we read the following in Slate and Berry's *Bigfoot,* we could not help thinking of the Crazy Bears and their powerful medicine:

My folks used to tell me of this legend which was passed on to them by their parents about a large man with red eyes who came to live with the tribe [a Yakima Indian fire guard told W. J. Vogel in August 1974]. Whenever any of the Indian people became sick, he would heal them. One day, when he knew he was dying, he asked the Indian people to take him to a particular location so that he might be there when he died. This they did. Shortly after he died, a large flying object came down from the skies, put his body aboard and flew off into the sky.

The first manimal tale with which we are fully satisfied is also our first from the 20th century.

One rainy night in July 1901, three 'coon hunters from Chester County, Pennsylvania, had the displeasure of encountering an "impossible" something that frightened the hell out of them. Milton Brint, his brother Taylor, and Tom Lukens were carefully making their way through Stewart's woods in Pensbury township. The only light they had emanated from a dim bull's-eye lantern. Ahead of them their hunting dogs scurried through the underbrush barking madly.

Suddenly the hounds were silent. The hunters paused, surprised and perplexed. The next thing they knew, the dogs were flying out of the woods with their tails between their legs, whining and growling in terror. They huddled near their masters and would not go back into the trees.

"I never saw dogs so scared in all my life," Milton Brint said later, "and I have been 'coon hunting now for nearly forty years. It appeared to me as if the critters had just escaped from a catamount [cougar or mountain lion]. Presently they led us forward in the direction of a cedar tree. We turned the bull's-eye into the limbs time and again, but it availed us nothing. We were at a loss to discover what had frightened the dogs so badly. While we were yet standing there trying to discover the cause of their fright, a low dismal sound came from the tree top. We were startled. By and by the top of the tree began to shake as if some living, moving object were descending.

"It had not gone far when it let go its hold. Straight as an arrow it came tumbling down to the ground. It all happened so sudden and unexpectedly that it was impossible to tell precisely just what it was, for strange to say, every bull's-eye was instantly extinguished by the impact of the fall. We were

63

left in total darkness. I got a faint glimpse of the thing before it struck the ground, however, and while its head and neck bore every semblance to a man, it had the body and legs of a wild beast. I am not naturally a timid man, but I was scared that night. I looked about me for Taylor and Lukens. They were nowhere to be found. They fled the moment the weird object began its unexpected descent.

"The dogs ran like craven curs and I was shortly seized with the same fear. I struck out as fast as I could, not knowing which way my steps were carrying me. I became so badly bewildered that instead of going toward home I ran in an entirely different direction. I brought up in the neighborhood of Kennett Square so badly exhausted that I could not go any farther.

"I did not see Lukens again for several days and Taylor came to my house on the morrow to make sure that I had turned up. When he found that I was all right, he went away again without mentioning the happening of the night before. It was nearly a week before the dogs put in an appearance in a nearly half-starved condition. We have tried several times to continue hunting in Stewart's woods, but it's of no use. The dogs won't hunt in the woods. The place is haunted and we will give it a wide berth in the future."

Not long after, two other men, Lewis Brooks and Jack Murphy, were riding one night in a wagon along a path through the woods when something with a manlike head and an animal-like body crossed the road directly in front of them. It was walking on four feet. Murphy, who would later call the phenomenon "spectral-like," saw it pass directly *through a fence* and disappear into the forest. Brooks emptied a revolver into the thing but with no apparent effect.

We have here some of the first hints of what will

become familiar motifs of MA lore: their capacity to terrify other animals, such as dogs; their apparent lack of normal physical substance; their immunity to bullets; and the occasional failure of machines and instruments (in this case lanterns) in their presence.

Around 1915 a young man named Crum King, who lived just southeast of Wann, Oklahoma, was returning home from a dance one night when he saw something near the gate of his house. "It was about five or six feet tall and it stood with its arms stretched out," King recalled in 1975. "It was about four feet wide in the chest and hairy all over. It was like a bear or something, but it stood up like a man."

Terrified, King fled. He told no one of the strange encounter.

On January 21, 1932, while passing through an area five miles north of Downingtown, Pennsylvania, John McCandless heard a moaning sound in the brush. There he spotted "a hideous form, half-man, half-beast, on all fours and covered with dirt or hair." After others told of seeing the figure, McCandless and a group of friends armed with rifles and shotguns plowed through the trees and fields every day for a week, but by this time the thing had disappeared.

This letter, signed by Mrs. Beulah Schroat of Decatur, Illinois, was published in the *Decatur Review* on August 2, 1972:

In reference to the creatures people are seeing, I am 76 years old. My home used to be south of Effingham. My two brothers saw the creatures when they were children. My brothers have since passed away.

They are hairy, stand on their hind legs, have large eyes and are about as large as an average person or shorter, and are harmless as they ran away from the children. They walk, they do not jump.

They were seen on a farm near a branch of water. The boys waded and fished in the creek every day and once in a while they would run to the house scared and tell the story.

Later there was a piece in the Chicago paper stating there were such animals of that description and they were harmless. This occurred about 60 years ago or a little less.

My mother and father thought they were just children's stories until the Chicago paper told the story.

During the summer of 1941, the Rev. Lepton Harpole was hunting squirrels along the Gum Creek bottom near Mt. Vernon, a small city in the southeastern Illinois county of Jefferson, when "a large animal that looked something like a baboon" leaped out of a tree and walked upright toward the startled hunter. Harpole in turn struck the creature with his gun barrel and then frightened it away by firing a couple of shots into the air.

In the months that followed, rural families would report hearing terrifying screams at night in the wooded bottom lands along the creeks. Hunters sometimes found mysterious tracks. By early spring of the next year, after the killing of a farm dog near Bonnie, large parties of volunteers scoured the creek bottoms, some with rifles and shotguns, others with nets and ropes. But the creature easily evaded them (perhaps because of its reputed ability to leap twenty to forty feet in a single bound), and in fact appeared as much as forty or fifty miles from the site of the original sighting, in Jackson and Okaw

Counties. Finally it disappeared and was not seen again—for a time, at any rate.

In its March 1946 issue *Hoosier Folklore* noted:

About 25 years ago, a 'coon hunter from Hecker one night heard a strange beast screaming up ahead on Prairie duLong Creek. Hunters chased this phantom from time to time all one winter. Their dogs would get the trail, then lose it, and they would hear it screaming down the creek in the opposite direction. It was that kind of creature: you'd hear it up creek, but when you set out in that direction you'd hear it a mile down creek.

3.

From a relatively sparse prehistory we enter the modern period and we discover manimals crawling, and walking, out of the woods in staggering numbers, beginning particularly in the 1960s and proliferating at an incredible rate into the 1970s. There seems little doubt that, while manimals are not exactly a new phenomenon, they are appearing now in larger numbers than ever before, and in the future we expect them to be nearly as frequent as UFOs, in whose company, as we already have observed, they sometimes manifest themselves.

There is not a state in the union which by now has not logged its share of reports. Where once the situation seemed safely confined to the inaccessible Northwest, today it has escaped such confinement and is completely out of hand. A full recounting of all known incidents would prove not only tedious but pointless. For our purposes it should suffice to cite manimal activity in three representative states—

Illinois, Indiana and Oklahoma—and then to take note of parallel events in other places.

Illinois

In Marion County during the last three weeks of May 1970, 24 hogs disappeared. In the three preceding months "hognappings" had occurred frequently at Salem area farms. In the central part of the state near Farmer City three sheep turned up dead in the early spring. Officials assumed—until July 9, anyway—that it was the work of "wild dogs."

On that date Don Ennis, Beecher Lamb, Larry Faircloth and Bob Hardwick, all 18, decided to camp out on a wild ten-acre buffalo grass-covered piece of land a mile south of Farmer City near Salt Creek. Their campsite, often used as a lovers' lane, was very isolated. Before the night was over, they would realize just *how* isolated.

About 10:30 p.m., as they sat around the campfire, they heard something moving in the tall grass. When "it" moved between them and their tent, Lamb decided to turn his car lights on. The thing, with widely-separated eyes gleaming at them, was squatting by the tent. Then it ran off—on two legs. The young men left in such a considerable hurry themselves that one of them ran on one leg—Ennis, who had one foot in a cast because of a broken ankle, left his crutches behind.

Soon word about the Farmer City "monster" spread. On Friday, July 10, more than ten persons said they had seen a pair of glowing eyes near the site of the first sighting. And on the 12th and 14th at least fifteen persons swore they had seen a furry creature in the same area. Witnesses told Loren Coleman that it seemed to be attracted by the sound of loud radio music and by the light of campfires.

68

Police Officer Robert Hayslip of Farmer City decided to check the stories of the monster. He went out to the campsite/lovers' lane area early in the morning of July 15, between two and three o'clock. Hayslip heard something running through the grass. Then, he said to Coleman soon after the sighting, "out of the corner of my eye I could see these two extremely bright eyes, just like it was standing there watching me." As he turned toward it, it disappeared.

Hayslip returned to the site about 6:00 a.m. He found that the heavy steel grommets in a tent that had been intact at 3:00 a.m. now were ripped out. A quilt lying nearby was torn to shreds.

The Farmer City police chief, who earlier had expressed the curious view that the so-called monster was nothing more than a Shetland pony (evidently one of the bipedal variety), now decided to lock the gate that led to the ten-acre area.

The creature apparently moved on.

A couple driving near the Weldon Springs State Park on the afternoon of July 24 spotted a "bear" near the Willis Bridge on Salt Creek. Stopping at a farmhouse, they asked the residents to notify the Dewitt County Sheriff's office. The Sheriff and State Conservation Officer Warren Wilson found several tracks with definite claw marks around the water's edge, and on a sandbar in the middle of the creek. Wilson said the tracks were more like a large cat's but definitely not a bear's.

This little episode is hopelessly confusing and we place it here in the manimal category for purely arbitrary reasons. It is clear from the evidence of the footprints that the creature in question was *not* a bear, or at least a conventional bear. Imperfectly-seen or briefly-glimpsed manimals are sometimes mistaken for bears (the opposite, of course, occurs occasionally as well). But, to complicate matters further, at the same time (as we shall see in the next chapter), Illinois was undergoing an invasion of mysterious catlike animals whose prints, unlike those of conventional panthers, *Felis concolor,* characteristically contained claw marks. Yet it is unlikely that anyone would mistake a "cat" for a "bear." *However,* in the 1970s we have seen some evidence that a new kind of MA, a "bear" which may leave ambiguous prints in its wake, is beginning to appear on the Fortean scene.

Soon after the Willis Bridge incident, during the first week of August, Vicki Otto sighted something near the Ireland Grove Road three miles southeast of Bloomington. She saw a pair of eyes reflecting her automobile headlights as she approached what she at first thought was a dog. Then, she said, "I saw this ape running in the ditch. The thing I saw was the size of a baboon."

Around 9:30 p.m. on August 16, while driving on Route 136 approaching the Kickapoo Creek bridge north of Waynesville, Dan Lindsey and Mike Anderson encountered a similar creature. "My first thought was a tall man or maybe a bear or a gorilla," Anderson said. The manimal stood six feet five inches tall, was all brown and had stooped shoulders. Walking on two legs and illuminated by the car lights, it more or less trotted across to the west side and along the creek's edge. Then it was gone.

Manimals came back to Illinois during the summer of 1972, though far more dramatic events were going on just across the border, in Louisiana, Missouri, where a smelly, red-eyed creature dubbed "Momo" (for "MO. MOnster") had arrived in the company of UFOs, disembodied voices, religious visions and poltergeist phenomena.*

The *Peoria Journal-Star* for July 26 of that year relates the claim of Randy Emert, 18, who reportedly saw a "monster" two different times over the previous two months. Emert said the thing resembled Momo in most particulars, although its height was between eight and twelve feet and it was "kind of white and moved quick." When it appeared, it brought with it Momo's rancid odor and also seemed to scare the animals living in the woods near Cole Hollow Road. Emert said, "It lets out a long screech —like an old steam-engine whistle, only more human."

Emert asserted that a number of friends had seen either the creature or its footprints. "I'm kind of a spokesman for the group," he said. "The only one who has guts, I guess."

Mrs. Ann Kammerer of Peoria corroborated Emert's story, stating that all of her children, friends of Emert's, had seen the thing. "It sounds kind of weird," she admitted. "At first I didn't believe it, but then my daughter-in-law saw it."

According to Emert, there was an old abandoned house in the woods with large footprints all around it and a hole dug under the basement. Emert thought this might be where the creature was staying. Interestingly enough, Edgar Harrison, the chief personality in the Momo affair, believed his creature might be residing temporarily in an abandoned building. Readers will recall the abandoned barn near Murphysboro and the tracking dog's curious reluctance to enter it. Was it, too, a manimal dwelling?

* Those readers not familiar with this much-written-about episode are referred to our *The Unidentified,* pp. 12-14. A fuller account appears in our article, "Anthropoids, Monsters and UFOs," in England's *Flying Saucer Review,* January/February 1973.

On July 25 a Pekin resident reported seeing "something big" swimming in the Illinois River, which also flows through Peoria. On the night of the 27th "two reliable citizens" told police they had seen a ten-foot something that "looked like a cross between an ape and a caveman." According to a UPI dispatch, it had "a face with long gray U-shaped ears, a red mouth with sharp teeth, [and] thumbs with long second joints . . ." It smelled, said a witness, like a "musky wet-down dog." The East Peoria Police Department said it had received more than 200 calls about the creature the following evening.

Leroy Summers of Cairo saw a ten-foot, white, hairy creature standing erect near the Ohio River levee during the evening hours of July 25. The Cairo police found nothing when they came to investigate and Police Commissioner James Dale warned that henceforth anyone making a monster report would have his breath tested for alcohol content.

The following year, when creatures descended upon White County in southeastern Illinois, Sheriff Roy Poshard, Jr., took an even sterner stance: He threatened to arrest the key witness.

Whatever it was that Henry McDaniel of Enfield saw, it was not a classic manimal—or for that matter classic anything we have ever heard of. Nonetheless, an undoubted manimal was observed during the resulting "monster scare."

McDaniel claimed that late in the evening of April 25, 1973, he heard something scratching on his door. Upon opening the door, he did a double take, for the "something" looked as if it had stepped out of a nightmare.

"It had three legs on it," he said, "a short body,

two little short arms coming out of its breast area, and two pink eyes as big as flashlights. It stood four and a half to five feet tall and was grayish-colored. It was trying to get into the house."

McDaniel, in no mood to entertain the visitor, grabbed a pistol and opened fire.

"When I fired that first shot," he said, "I know I hit it." The creature hissed like a wildcat and bounded away, covering 75 feet in three jumps, and disappeared into the brush along a railroad embankment that runs near the McDaniel home.

State police, summoned to McDaniel's home soon afterwards, found tracks "like a dog's except that [they] had six toe pads." McDaniel told Jerome Clark that two of the prints measured four inches around while the other measured three and one-quarter inches.

Loren Coleman further discovered that ten-year-old Greg Garrett, who lived just behind McDaniel, had been playing in his back yard half an hour before when the creature approached him and stepped on his feet, tearing his tennis shoes to shreds. The boy had run inside, crying hysterically.

On May 6 at 3:00 a.m. McDaniel was awakened by the howling of neighborhood dogs. Looking out his front door, he saw the creature again.

"I seen something moving out on the railroad track and there it stood," he said. "I didn't shoot at it or anything. It started on down the railroad track. It wasn't in a hurry or anything."

Referring to one of the explanations offered for his sightings, McDaniel told Clark, "I've been all around this world. I've been through Africa and I've had a pet kangaroo. This was not a kangaroo. I've never seen this type of creature or track before.

The publicity McDaniel's report received brought hordes of curiosity seekers, newsmen and serious researchers to Enfield. Among them were five young men whom Deputy Sheriff Jim Clark arrested for hunting violations after they said they had seen and shot at a gray hairy creature in some underbrush. Two of the men thought they had hit it but the thing had sped off, running faster than a man. The incident is supposed to have occurred on May 8.

Another witness was Rick Rainbow, news director of radio station WWKI, Kokomo, Indiana. On May 6 he and three other persons saw a strange creature beside—note—an old abandoned house near McDaniel's place. They didn't get a good look at it because its back was to them and it was running in the shadows, but they later described it as apelike, about five and a half feet tall, grayish and stooped. Rainbow taped the cry it made.

Investigators Loren Coleman and Richard Crowe did not see the creature but they did hear a high-pitched screech while they were searching the area around McDaniel's home.

About a month later Edwardsville police received and checked three reports of a musty-smelling, red-eyed, human-sized being said to be lurking in the woods on the eastern edge of town. The creature reportedly was more than five and a half feet tall and broad-shouldered, with eyes that apparently were sensitive to light. It made no sound when it walked. The witnesses said the thing chased them and one man told police the creature had ripped his shirt and clawed his chest.

The summer months of 1973 were taken up, as we have seen, with the events at Murphysboro. The monster season ended on the night of October 16, when four St. Joseph youths—Bill Duncan, Bob Summers, Daryl Mowry and Craig Flenniken, all but Summers high school seniors—supposedly encountered a hairy "gorilla-like" creature on a road south of the town. They had stopped their car to investigate what they thought was a campfire near the bridge on the Salt Fork. One of them lit a match and they all saw the creature, approximately five feet tall, about fifteen feet away. They did not linger to investigate further.

"None of us believe in that outer space stuff," Duncan told the *Champaign-Urbana Courier*. "I wondered if I was nuts or something. I thought it was a bear at first, but I really couldn't say."

This account raises a number of interesting questions which unfortunately we cannot answer, since our efforts to contact the alleged witnesses were unsuccessful. However, there are two obvious questions: What was the nature of the mysterious light the boys at first took to be a campfire? And more to the point, how could a match struck in an outdoor setting generate enough light to reveal a presumably dark object fifteen feet away?

Indiana

On the evening of May 18, 1969, a power blackout blanketed a small rural area outside Rising Sun. For two hours the home of Mr. and Mrs. Lester Kaiser was without electricity. The Kaisers did not connect the blackout with sightings of mysterious lights along a nearby ridge which had been made in previous weeks.

The next evening, around 7:30, the Kaisers' son George was walking through the farmyard on his way to a tractor, when he was startled to see a weird figure standing about 25 feet away.

"I watched it for about two minutes before it saw me," young Kaiser said later. "It stood in a fairly upright position, although it was bent over about in the middle of its back, with arms about the same length as a normal human being's. I'd say it was about five-eight or so and it had a very muscular structure. The head sat directly on the shoulders and the face was black, with hair that stuck out of the back of its head. It had eyes set close together, and a very short forehead. It was covered with hair except for the back of the hands and the face. The hands looked like normal hands, not claws."

When Kaiser, who had been standing transfixed, moved, the creature made "a strange grunting-like sound," turned, leaped over a ditch, and disappeared down the road running at great speed. Subsequently, investigators made plaster casts of footprints found in the dirt by the ditch. These casts show three toes plus a big toe.

The following evening, around 10:15, neighbor Charles Rolfing watched a glowing, greenish-white object for eight minutes as it maneuvered in the sky above him.

For two weeks in August 1970, people in the Winslow area, in the southwestern part of the state, reported seeing a "ten-foot-tall creature covered with hair [which] appears to walk on hind legs, top speed sixty miles per hour." The state police, which investigated, described the witnesses as "reliable."

One night in June 1970 a farmer, whose initials are D. K., was visiting his future wife, who lived in nearby Sharpsville, when suddenly both were struck with a feeling of intense dizziness, coupled with sensations of moodiness and fear. They decided to drive out to the farm in hopes of shaking the "attack."

The night was dark and little patches of fog dotted the road. As they drove down the country road, they came upon an even darker area, which seemed to extend upward. When they entered it, they were perplexed to find that their headlights did not seem to extend very far ahead and that the air around them was strangely warm.

"We got home and was walking up to the house," D. K. told Don Worley and Fritz Clemm six years later, when "Zipper [the family dog] attacked us twice. I had to almost break his head to keep him off us. The dog felt it. He had known me since he was a pup and had never been hostile to me before. But he did try to attack us twice. Both of us were pretty shaken up."

A year after that, the creature appeared on the scene.

"One night around 10:00 or 10:30 p.m. in June or July, all the dogs started barking," D. K. recalled. "I went outside to investigate and there was my dog [Zipper] lunging at a thing that was standing in a low spot. It was still taller than I was." When the witness stepped out the door, the "thing," about 25 feet away, turned around and looked at him.

It was, he said, "big, real big . . . The head wasn't shaped like an ape's and I don't think that it looked like a man's head either. It looked like a helmet but it was furry. It didn't look natural to anything zoological on earth. It just didn't look right for the ape-looking body that it had. It didn't look like an ape's head or a human's head. It was dark and I couldn't see too well for all the details."

There was, however, no mistaking its "rank and sickening" odor. "The smell of it almost made you want to barf," D. K. said. It was something like a "decaying meat and vegetable combination."

The creature, nine feet tall and covered with stringy, "dirty" hair, was stooped over like an ape, with no neck and long arms. It was growling in a "deep rumbling manner."

"It would swing at the dog," he said. "It was funny the way it swung. Kind of like it was slow

77

motion. Its strokes were coming close to the dog . . . It wasn't like a prizefighter throwing a haymaker at an opponent. It was, you know, more like a slow motion type of thing. . . . The dog would run up to it and lunge, teeth and paws out, but seemed like before it got there, it would hit the ground and jump back. And before it jumped back, the thing would swing and barely miss it. And this went on for two or three minutes."

D.K. thought the creature acted rather confused and uncertain, "like an animal or a human that was put on a spot and really didn't know what to do."

When he recovered his senses, D. K. dashed inside, searched frantically for shells to put in his shotgun, and ran out again in time to see the creature lumbering off in the direction of the creek. Though he realized the weird intruder was by now too far away for it to do any good, he fired twice in its direction.

Immediately after that, he called the sheriff, who openly laughed at the story, and though the manimal would return five times more over the space of the next year, D. K. never again notified the authorities.

The manimal reappeared around midnight three or four weeks later. The witness, who was inside watching television, was alerted to its presence when he heard the dogs barking wildly. D. K. grabbed his shotgun and followed Zipper, who seemed to be tracking the thing, to the cemetery. Suddenly the dog stopped as if he had lost the scent but he apparently found it again on the other side.

"When I got down to the creek," D. K. said, "the dog started running up alongside the creek, barking and looking down in it. I couldn't keep up. The dog wasn't in the water but along the side of the creek. I heard splashing in the water and again the smell was there. I knew the creature had to be a few yards ahead of him. I proceeded to follow him. I followed him clear back to Beatty's woods and then I turned around and came back. . . . The dogs were restless part of the night, probably an hour or so afterwards."

The third appearance was later that same year. This time D. K. was sleeping—it was around 4:30 a.m.—when the dogs again alerted him to the presence of something unusual. Looking out his bedroom window, he saw the creature moving down by the creek. By this time, D. K. was determined to kill it so that he could prove to skeptical friends, some of whom had sat up with him long nights on his assurances that they might get to see the thing themselves, that it existed. He ran outside, shotgun in hand, and tracked the manimal until it got lost in the thick woods. He did not know until later, when his mother, who had been watching all of this, told him so, that *the thing had doubled back and was now trailing him.* It followed him for a short while before disappearing back into the trees.

That winter D. K. was rabbit-hunting when he discovered that a small pond had mysteriously dried up. Next to it was a thirty- or forty-foot circular area with dead, crushed weeds and grass laid down in a perfect counterclockwise swirl pattern. He had no idea what might have caused it. To ufologists this sounds suspiciously like a "flying saucer nest"—ground traces like these have been noted all over the world and are usually associated with UFO landings. And this is hardly the first time we have heard of dried-up ponds left in the wake of such touchdowns.

One evening in the spring of 1972, D. K. and his brother, both now married and living with their wives at the farmhouse, went out for an evening on the town. When they got back, they found the two women in an hysterical state. The wives said they had heard the thing trying to pry open an aluminum storm window not long before.

The brothers went out with guns and flashlights and examined the window. They could smell the manimal's characteristically foul odor, which lingered at the site. But what puzzled them was the fact that, though one corner of the window had been pulled out, it "wasn't pried out," as D. K. would put it. "There were no marks on it. The screen on the inside wasn't cut or anything. It didn't look like anything had happened using a tool—no marks on the wood around the frame. That's what led me to believe it had to be something super to do it. No marks on the window and it got me shook up again."

A week or two later, at 11:30 p.m., D. K. heard the dogs barking and he knew "it" was back. He looked out his bedroom window and there it was, moving along the creek in the same direction it always went. D. K. decided to let it alone this time.

In the fall it came back for the last time.

"I don't know the month on it," he told Worley and Clemm, "probably September. It was before the first major frost, I know that. The only time it seemed to come around was when it was fair weather. I never saw it after a major frost or before a good summer yet. It didn't appear in cold weather.

"I had taken the gun out again when I heard the dogs raising thunder and went after it, but I never did get a shot at it this time either. Seems like every time I'd try to shoot . . . why, it always got something between me and it. I consider myself good on running shots and I've shot dogs and deer but—it knowed that I was after it. It was cunning. It just knew how far to keep away from me and what to keep in front of me to keep me from firing on it. . . .

"This last time I chased it, it went through the cemetery. I was by myself, no dogs, and I again chased it up toward the woods. Then I doubled back to the cemetery and waited, but it never did come back."

A month before D. K.'s final encounter, and fifty miles directly southwest, a similar creature had caused such a fright that some people in the village of Roachdale thought the Day of Judgment might be at hand. (Before you smile too indulgently at that, wait until we have examined a certain very strange episode from Pennsylvania later in these pages.) Since we have already recounted the Roachdale creature scare in our earlier book,* we will not treat it in detail here.

Briefly, the manimal showed up after a mysterious glowing object had exploded silently over a cornfield. Two hours later the thing was heard just outside the field in a young couple's yard, and for the next two or three weeks made regular nightly appearances. The manimal, which resembled an enormous apelike animal, left no tracks even when it ran, on all fours, over mud, and once the wife thought she could see *through* it. Almost forty persons saw the creature before it disappeared, including a farm family, the Burdines, who lost 170 chickens, which were ripped apart but not eaten. The Burdines fired on the manimal without any apparent effect.

By the last week of August the Roachdale reports had subsided. But just what appeared three weeks later in Parke County (north of Roachdale's Putnam County) no one seems to know.

Shortly before 11:00 a.m. Wednesday, September 20, Parke County Sheriff Gary Cooper broadcast a bizarre warning to authorities in other counties: "Attention all counties surrounding Parke County. Be on the lookout for a ten-foot-tall monster. It is covered with fur and its feet are 21 inches long."

* *The Unidentified*, pp. 14-19.

Cooper explained that he had received several calls from the Lodi, Tangier, Howard and Sylvania area, a sparsely-settled, heavily-wooded region near the Parke-Fountain County line. The creature had been seen on Tuesday night.

"One lady came to my office with the story, and I have had at least three other persons call in sightings," Cooper said. He would not release any of the witnesses' names.

Two 'coon dogs and a pig were killed by something that had slashed them across the stomach. Cooper thought a badger might have done it but he wasn't sure. "I'm not ruling out anything at this point," he said.

"Apparently," the *Crawfordsville Journal and Review* concluded, "this monster, just as the the creature from Roachdale, will be listed as another of West-Central Indiana's UFOs (unidentified furry objects)."

In early October 1973, a manimal appeared near Galveston. The first person to encounter it was Jeff Martin, who was fishing at a lake with two companions. His friends had gone off to another part of the lake when Martin heard something behind him. He turned and saw, about twenty feet away, an ape-like figure watching him. At least Martin *thought* it was apelike, since it was dusk and visibility was poor. Frightened, he called to the being, which did not respond. For some reason, though, Martin felt better about the situation, and was almost sorry when the thing slipped away.

A few minutes later something touched his shoulder. Martin, who was sitting, whirled his head around and saw a sandy-colored anthropoidal creature—evidently the one he had just observed. The manimal ran away with amazing swiftness, Martin in hot pursuit. It moved in running leaps, "like a man on a rope being pulled too fast by a car," Martin later would say. As it crossed the road, the witness could hear its feet slapping on the blacktop. It turned around one last time, leaped over a ditch, and disappeared into the woods. Shortly afterwards a glowing bronze object shot out of the trees and into the sky, fading away so quickly that the whole series of events seemed nearly instantaneous.

The next day Martin returned to the scene but saw nothing. The following evening he, his fiancée Nellie Floyd, father-in-law-to-be Gene Floyd, and two friends drove to the spot, trailed all the way by a white, glowing starlike light. The object disappeared near a bridge not far from where Martin had seen the manimal. When they got to that spot, the creature was waiting for them.

The thing, about eight or nine feet tall, was standing in tall weeds. The observers turned their flashlights on it and noticed a very curious detail: The beams seemed somehow "weaker" on the creature, which stood motionless, almost as if in a trance, giving off a "musty" odor. Oddly, its presence did not seem to disturb the crickets, frogs, or other wildlife, which the witnesses thought most unusual. They yelled at the creature but, getting no response, decided to hurl some rocks at it. They could not tell whether the rocks had missed, bounced off or gone through the thing, but, whatever the case, they could not get it to move in any way.

Finally, the appearance of an approaching automobile forced the three remaining witnesses (the other two had fled to the safety of the car) to move their own vehicle from the road. When they returned, the manimal was gone.

Perhaps significantly, Gene Floyd, one of the witnesses, already had an eight-year history of dealings with strange phenomena. Since 1965 he had had a dozen UFO experiences. On one occasion, a peculiar impulse had led him outside, where he saw an orange glow in the sky. An "unspoken command" told him to shine his flashlight up at it, and when he did, flashing the light three times, the glow blinked three times in reply.

Floyd also had a vivid "dream" in which he stood aboard a UFO conversing mentally with a humanoid figure with a large bald head. Since that time, like other contactees (if that is what Floyd is), he seemed to acquire a noticeable degree of psychic ability.

In mid-September 1975 both types of UFOs— a flying one and a furry one—showed up on a farm near Waterloo.

At 3:00 a.m. a farmer on his way to the bathroom happened to look out his upstairs window and noticed a red light the size of an auto headlight in a soybean field about seventy-five yards away. He also saw, at the edge of an area illuminated by a dusk-to-dawn light, a large, bipedal "animal" walking toward the object with a forward swaying motion. Suddenly the red light changed into a brilliant magnesium-like light for five seconds, then vanished. When it did so, the creature disappeared, too.

That morning, when the farmer went out to examine the area where he had seen the mysterious light, he found a thirty-foot circle of browned soybeans. As time went by, he realized that the beans had stopped growing, though the plants outside the circle remained unaffected.

The farmer told Don Worley that in 1966 he and his wife had seen a cupola-shaped UFO hovering over his cornfield. In the nights that followed, he said, he had heard a strange sound like a "baby crying"—a sound often associated with manimals as well as poltergeists.

One night in November 1968, Roger Boucher of Oakwood was returning home from nearby Canton when a "gorillalike" animal ran across the highway in front of him.

Two months later, in that same general area, Deward Whetstone found tracks measuring 10½ inches long and four inches wide. The plaster casts he made suggested that whoever or whatever made them was primatelike. The tracks showed a deep split between the first two toes, and the weight of the body apparently placed most pressure on the outside edge of the foot. At the time he found the prints, said Whetstone, the ground was soft due to a spell of wet weather.

"There were tracks all the way across the road. I followed them to where whatever made them jumped the fence. There have been a number of sightings of a strange animal in this area."

On Friday, February 26, 1971, C. Edward Green and his wife were driving home along Lake Avenue in Lawton about 11:00 p.m., when they saw a strange figure walking beside the road.

"He was walking bent over like a gorilla," Green recalled not long after in a interview with Jerome Clark, "but not on all fours. He wore black pants that were cut or torn off at the knees and he had a big beard—it began higher up on his face than beards usually do—and long hair, very unkempt."

When the Greens reached their apartment shortly after seeing the strange creature, they called the police. They assumed they had seen a mentally disturbed person.

A few minutes later, at 11:15, the sound of police sirens brought Green to the window of his second-floor apartment. He pulled the curtains aside and found himself staring into the face of the figure he had seen on the road.

"He was crouched still upon the walkway," Green reported, "and while I was startled myself, I noticed that the person, as I say, was either extremely frightened or not oriented to his surroundings. There was a glazed expression in his eyes as if he didn't quite understand where he was.

"His hair and beard were very black, and he himself was darked-complected. He was barefooted—his feet looked normal—and he stood at least six feet tall. Nothing about his body seemed disproportioned.

"When he saw me, he jumped to the gravel below. Now that's about a fifteen-foot jump, but it didn't seem to bother him. He must have been very strong. I didn't stay to watch him run away."

Green was not the only Lawton resident who reported seeing the creature that night. Just before his experience at the window, a group of passersby had seen a "monkeylike" figure running down a street not far away, dodging cars, hiding behind bushes, and then running on. And fifteen minutes after Green's second encounter, several Fort Sill soldiers, leaving a grocery store three blocks away, saw a similar strange creature amble past.

Almost exactly 24 hours later the creature appeared again, and this time it nearly caused a man to have a heart attack.

Donald Childs, a 36-year-old television technician with a history of heart trouble, stepped into his back yard at 11:00 p.m., having heard a noise outside. He thought it might be a prowler. Instead he came upon someone or something "real huge, way over six feet tall. He was trying to get a drink out of the pond," Childs said, "but the pond was empty.

"He had long hair all over his face. Maybe he had a beard, too. I don't know. It was dark and I couldn't tell for sure. He was wearing dark-colored pants that were way too little, and a plaid jacket that was kind of too small. His legs, what I could see of them, seemed hairy. Like I said, it was dark and I couldn't swear to it.

"All of a sudden he saw me, and he was as scared of me as I was of him. He didn't even stand up or get any kind of running start—he just sprung from his squatting position and jumped clear over the pond. The next day I measured it and that pond is twelve feet across!

"He could really run awful fast. He ran kind of hunched over like an ape in a Tarzan movie. He wasn't running on all fours. It was definitely a man. I'm sure he was somebody, you know, mentally off. I've heard that people like that have strength that normal people don't have."

Childs suffered a heart seizure from the excitement and spent the next few days recovering from it.

Later, a police officer told Childs that the department had received about twenty calls from persons who reported seeing a similar person, or animal, between Friday and Monday but the story of the sightings did not appear in the Lawton newspapers until the next Tuesday, March 2. Then the local press gave the reports headline treatment.

After the publicity, Childs heard from a farmer three miles south of Lawton who had an odd problem, one neither the sheriff nor the Cattlemen's Association, to whom he had appealed, could help with.

About once a month for the last year, he said, he had been finding either a calf or a full-grown cow lying dead in his field with one of its legs ripped off. The rest of the carcass was never wounded or marked. It seemed as if someone possessing incredible strength approached the animals, tore off a leg, and left the beasts to die. But no footprints were ever found that might offer a clue to the nature of the attacker.

Maybe the culprit was the same creature which had plagued a farm in the El Reno area. One morning in December 1970, according to an Associated Press story dated February 27, 1971, a farmer found the door to his chicken coop ripped off and lying on the ground. On the surface of the door and inside the coop itself were strange handprints about seven inches long and five inches wide. When he saw that several of his chickens had disappeared without a trace, he called the local state game ranger.

The door was shipped to zoologist Lawrence Curtis, Director of the Oklahoma City Zoo. After a study that included comparisons with the hand- and paw-prints of human beings, apes, monkeys, bears, and other animals, Curtis confessed his bafflement. "I don't know what this is," he said. "It resembles a gorilla but it's more like a man." According to Curtis, the creature's thumb 'crooked inward as if deformed or injured.

"It appears that whatever made the prints was walking on all fours," he said, judging from prints on the ground outside the coop. Unfortunately these were not preserved.

"We've shown it to several mammalogists and wildlife experts in Oklahoma and some passing through," Curtiss told Jerome Clark. "All agree it is the print of a primate. These were made by some sort of man." The man, if such he was, was barefooted.

Curtis added that he had heard from a man in Stillwater and a woman in McAlester who had discovered similar prints.

Let us return for a moment to the curious events at Lawton and compare them with several unusual reports from elsewhere.

For example, from near the Eel River above Eureka, California, about 1950 or 1951, when a ten-year-old girl, who nine years later would recount the experience to the late Ivan T. Sanderson (who in turn reprinted her letter in his classic *Abominable Snowmen: Legend Come to Life*), allegedly encountered a red-eyed, hairy creature "with the strangest-looking fangs that I have ever seen . . . However . . . the strangest and most frightening thing of all . . . [was that] he had on clothes! . . . They were tattered and torn and barely covered him, but they were still there."

In late September 1973, a family living in a mobile home four miles north of Tabor City, North Carolina, claimed to have had a number of sightings of two "space creatures" which roamed the neighboring woods. Though these creatures were not described as precisely manimal-like, nonetheless, according to witness Rose Williamson, "They are about seven or eight feet tall with big red eyes that glow in the dark. They are dressed in brown shirts *with black pants which are ragged at the bottom.*"

In *Strange Creatures from Time and Space,* John Keel cites a number of instances in which percipients have reported seeing apparitional figures wearing "checkered shirts," perhaps reminiscent of the "plaid shirt" the Lawton witnesses saw.

Just as interesting is Edward Green's observation that the manimal "was either extremely frightened or not oriented to his surroundings"—echoed by Donald Childs' parallel remark that "he was as scared of me as I was of him."

In 1967 Hembree Brandon, editor of *The Winona*

[Mississippi] *Times,* received this letter from an Atlanta man who signed himself "J. H.":

This letter I am writing will be hard to write. But being it concerns an object and in an area east of Winona on the highway to Europa, I feel like someone in that area should know what me & my brother seen.

The date was about 7th of Nov. [1966], the time one or one thirty appx. A.M.

We were traveling east to Marietta Georgia in Chevrolet pickup when my headlights picked up an object running down a steep hill on my left, on its two legs, as if to run out and stop our truck. Then my headlights was on this creature. It size was liken that of a huge Kodiak Bear. But it was running on two legs not four. Its eyes were bright red appx two inches in diameter. On its body was hair appx 1½" long. Its weight was 5 to 700 lbs. Its height was appx 7 ft tall or more. Its left arm was held up like waving goodbye or giving a stop signal to us. The expression in its eyes was like a human in mortal terror. And my brother & I both agreed it (the expression) was like a person saying "Please help me."

The face of the object was like a person gone wild or crazy. Its shoulders were appx 4 ft wide with narrow waist line.

The object then tried to hide behind the shoulder of the road.

If this object was scared, which no doubt in my mind it was, well I was a hellva lot scardier and I have camped in some of the west's wildest places, seen many bears & mountain lions, which didn't excite me in the least. For I am a prospector, that's my hobby. And I am usually alone in the high Sierra of California or the high country of some other state.

Many a time I have laughed at the stories of

"Big Foot" of northern Calif., a person that picks up 60 gals. of oil & gas & smashes a tractor or catapiller with it. Now after seeing this object I just can't doubt anything anymore. For it was that big. I believe it could've turned over my truck easily. My brother & I was cold sober not even one can of beer all evening or that night.

So I advise all people living in the hill country between Winona & Europa to lock their door at night until some one can explain this. I think it could possible be a huge man gone wild, then I don't know for it looked both human & animal. But no doubt it was pleading for help. But why? . . .

Why indeed?

This whole business gets even weirder when we consider that one of the Tabor City witnesses claimed that one of the manimal-like humanoids had scrawled a cryptic message in the dirt: "Help no." She thought the second word might have been incomplete. Whatever the case, during the "Momo" scare in Louisiana, Missouri, the seven-year-old son of a family which had experienced many of the strange phenomena that had converged on the town came home with two pieces of paper with writing on them. He explained to his mother that "something in my head told me" to pick them up and take them with him. The messages, while somewhat incoherent, were written by someone who said he was "lost & forlorn." They seemed to be some kind of plea for help.

Let us return now to complete our survey of Oklahoma manimals.

Nowata County is located in northeastern Oklahoma along the Kansas border. In late July 1974, Mrs. Margie Lee, who lived in the Watova settlement just outside the town of Nowata, saw a six-foot "Bigfoot" (as she would come to call it) from the decidedly uncomfortable distance of only six feet. She admits she was "scared silly."

For the next two weeks, during which she saw the thing repeatedly, her jangled nerves got little chance to rest and she went practically without sleep as she waited for the thing to reappear, which it inevitably did once darkness had set in. Eventually, when she realized the thing meant no harm, she lost some of her fear.

The "Bigfoot" was young, Mrs. Lee believed, and the several other witnesses, including members of her own family and two deputy sheriffs, concurred. It was male, with arms rather longer than a normal man's, and covered with brown hair about an inch long, though on the underside of the arms the hair was considerably shorter. It had five fingers on its hands, whose undersides seemed devoid of hair. "The hair," she told Jerome Clark, "was in those places where it would be on a man, only more so."

She saw it running a number of times. "You wouldn't believe it," she said. "It could go as fast as or even faster than a deer." It ran quietly, making a sound reminiscent of "moccasins over gravel." It exuded an odor so foul that sometimes Mrs. Lee almost got sick from it.

From its eyes, which looked "curious," Mrs. Lee inferred it meant no harm. The eyes were "normal," not self-luminescent.

Its behavior could best be described as timid, but it did exhibit a certain peculiar interest in women, to the extent that it bypassed houses where only men resided. It certainly appeared to be more interested in Mrs. Lee than it did in her husband, John, and from all this the couple concluded the strange visitor was looking for a mate.

Whatever the case, the Lees developed a sort of

affection for their "Bigfoot," and once engaged in a little game with it. They had noticed it kept putting their feed pail in front of the barn door, blocking the entrance; every day they would remove it and every night the creature would put it back. Finally, they took to hiding the pail, but the beast inevitably would sniff it out and put it back in front of the barn door.

"That's how we found out it had a sense of humor," she recalled. She also heard it laugh once, the only sound she ever heard it make.

On the whole, though, it was something of a pest. A neighbor lost a chicken to it, and occasionally it would go into the Lees' barn and thrash around. One evening Mrs. Lee heard it doing just that and ran outside to chase it away. She heard it crash through a window laced with chicken wire and flee into the night.

By this time two sheriff's deputies, Gilbert Gilmore and Buck Field, had been called in, and the two of them saw the thing repeatedly. They were there the last night it appeared, when they blinded it with car headlights and opened fire on it. Weirdly, the creature showed no sign it had been hit as it dashed toward the woods and safety. The next day a thorough search uncovered no tracks, blood, or hair.

It made its last call on Mrs. Lee that morning just as she, by now utterly exhausted from too many nights with too little sleep, was bathing. Suddenly she heard a loud *thump!* against the outside wall. Grabbing a robe, she sped outside, but the creature was already gone—for good this time.

A year later other strange visitors appeared at Noxie, a few miles north of Nowata. The man who had the largest number of sightings, farmer Kenneth Tosh, first encountered one of the things on the evening of September 1, 1975, when he and a friend heard it clawing on the screen door of a dilapidated house twenty feet from the Tosh residence.

"We walked over by that house," Tosh told Clark, "and it was standin' there watchin' us. I don't know how long it had been there. We walked towards it and it started growlin' at us.

"I'd say it was seven or eight feet tall. It had hair all over its body, a dark brown, blackish-brown color, anywhere from an inch and a half to two inches long. It had hair all over everything but around its eyes and its nose. That was the only part where I could see the skin on it.

"The eyes glowed in the dark, reddish-pink eyes. You don't need light or anything to shine on 'em like most other animals. They glow without a light bein' on 'em.

"We was about ten feet away from it. We just ran away and it ran, too.

"About two hours later we seen it again. It was over by the barn, on top of the barn, across the road from me. And then we seen it two nights later after that and it was about every other night we seen it for positive. It was about a week or two and then people got so busy comin' out here that we didn't see it there for a while, and we thought it was gone and then about two weeks later we spotted it again. It was still there."

Another witness was Marion Parret, a friend of Tosh's. Parret saw it for the first time one night when he was sleeping and "it poked its face in the window above the door," he reported. "It looked like someone's face shaved high on the cheekbone."

Parret actually shot at the manimal on three occasions with a .30-.30 hunting rifle. He was sure he had hit it each time, but the creature's only response was once to swat at its arm as if brushing away a mosquito.

"I was in Vietnam thirteen months," Parret said, "and I'm more scared here than I was over there. At least over there I knew what was out there. Here I don't."

Tosh, like Parret and the deputies before him, had the same problem trying to bring down the creature. Once, he claims, he and two companions opened up on it with two shotguns and a .22 rifle. "I didn't see how we could miss," he said, "but it didn't even holler. It just ran off." It left no blood in its path, either.

From all indications the creature had been in the Noxie area some months before it appeared to significant numbers of locals and attracted media attention. Researcher Hayden Hewes, who came to Noxie to investigate reports, maintains that he talked with 24 persons who said they had seen or heard the thing. Gerald Bullock of Noxie realized he had been hearing the creature for about six months after he encountered it one Sunday night near Tosh's place.

"The sound," he said, "is like a kid screamin'. Anyway that's how it sounded to me. It was probably about fifty to seventy-five yards out there and we just seen the eyes of it. They [the eyes] looked like they was kinda reddish, an inch apart, like a couple of little old flashlight bulbs hanging out there in the air. It kinda smelled like dead fish to me.

"We had another gentleman drive in there about fifteen minutes after we seen it. He come in and his lights shined on off the road there and he seen it crossing the road about fifty yards from where about as far as your headlights will reach.

"I still hear that noise, you know, right now. I heard it last night [October 11, 1975] when I came home. But for a long time you know I didn't know what it was. I heard that thing probably a long time before they ever said anything about it, going back probably six months or so. There's people living

95

south of us and I'd thought maybe it might have been one of their little kids. But I guess it wasn't."

Bullock lived half a mile from the Tosh place. A small creek separated their land.

Everyone who saw it remarked on the manimal's awful stench. "It's hard to place just what it smells like," Tosh said. "It smelled like rotten eggs or sulphur. Or it was like somebody left a bunch of dirty diapers, wet, for a while."

The only physical evidence the creature left was a print which Tosh examined before the hordes of gun-toting, beer-guzzling curiosity seekers descended on the scene and destroyed it. Tosh recalls that it "was about eight inches across the toe, about two inches across the heel, and flat-footed. It looked like maybe it had only three toes."

Tosh's final sighting, which took place late in September, was by far the strangest. While it raised all kinds of new questions, it did at least clarify one aspect of the mystery: why the Toshes and other witnesses were hearing different kinds of monster sounds.

"The first time we heard it," he said, "it was growlin'. And then one time we heard it and it sounded like a woman hollerin' or screamin', and then a real strange whistle. Then we heard it and it sounded like a baby bawlin'. And then my sister-in-law and them, they said they was hearin' it last week [week of October 5-11]. They said it hollered and it sounded like it was laughin' real loud. It was such a sound that it was enough to give you a headache if you listened to it and it was close enough to you."

It developed that the reason for all this was that there were at least *two* creatures in the Noxie area.

"My brother-in-law was out and we was lookin' around," Tosh said. "We heard one. Then about that time there was another one out behind us and they was callin' towards each other. That's when we knew that there was two of 'em.

"One of 'em had red eyes and the other had yellow eyes. They was about 300 yards away from each other, just callin' to each other, I guess.

"Their sounds was a little different. One of 'em, the one with red eyes, was more like a woman screamin'. The other one sounded more like a baby bawlin'.

"The one with the yellow eyes was more of a grayish color than the other one. And it was about half a foot shorter. They probably weighed between 300 and 500 pounds."

In an October 12, 1975, interview, Tosh told Clark that his sister-in-law had seen the creature—or one of the creatures—just several days before, but he said she was unwilling to discuss it with outsiders because of all the ridicule the family have been subjected to. Tosh did say, however, that "she was in her bedroom gettin' ready for bed when she got this real weird feelin'. She started lookin' around the room and she looked over to the window. She had the curtains open a little bit and she could see the eyes lookin' in at her, and about a night or two later she seen 'em again.

"Then they started to hear 'em hollerin'. And she and my mother-in-law both could tell there was two of 'em because they could hear 'em hollerin' back and forth at each other."

They did not see anything, probably because of the darkness.

4.

No study of the manimal phenomenon would be complete without a summary of the Uniontown, Pennsylvania, incident, by now a classic—and for good reason, since it is beyond doubt the single most fascinating such report on record.

The episode began at around 9:00 p.m., October 25, 1973, when "Stephen Pulaski"* and at least fifteen other persons observed a red ball of light hovering high above a field just outside Uniontown. Pulaski, 22, grabbed a 30.06 rifle and drove to the scene with two ten-year-old boys, fraternal twins. As they approached, they noticed the UFO slowly descending toward the field. While it did so, the car's headlights dimmed mysteriously.

Pulaski brought the vehicle to a stop, and he and the two boys walked over the crest of a hill. Looking down at the field, they saw the UFO, now bright white in color, resting on or just above the ground. About a hundred feet in diameter, "it was dome-shaped," Pulaski recalled, "just like a big bubble. It was making a sound like a lawn mower." In addition, the three heard "screaming sounds" emanating from somewhere near the object.

Just then one of the boys yelled that there was something walking near the fence. From the light given off by the UFO, they could see two large ape-like creatures with glowing green eyes. A smell like that of "burning rubber" filled the air. Pulaski, who was not wearing his glasses at the time, thought the creatures were bears. To make sure, he fired a tracer slug directly over their heads. This did not seem to affect them in any way, but now Pulaski could see they were something very strange indeed.

Both had long, dark gray hair, and arms that almost reached the ground. The taller one, about eight feet in height, was running its left hand along the fence. The shorter, which stood slightly over seven feet tall, seemed to be hurrying along to keep up

---

* A pseudonym given the percipient by psychiatrist Berthold Eric Schwarz in his article "Berserk: A UFO-Creature Encounter," *Flying Saucer Review,* Vol. 20, No. 1 (1974).

with its companion. Both were making a whining sound, like a baby crying, and apparently were communicating with each other via this strange noise.

By this time one of the twins had fled the scene. But Pulaski stood his ground. He raised his rifle again and fired three times directly into the larger creature, which emitted a whine and reached its right hand toward the other creature. Suddenly the UFO vanished from sight and the noise it had been making ceased.

The manimals turned slowly around and returned to the woods. As they did so, the two remaining witnesses noticed that the area where the UFO had landed was glowing now a brilliant white color, so bright, in fact, that one could easily read a newspaper by it.

Pulaski and the boy noticed that their eyes were troubling them. They made their way to a telephone and called the police.

At 9:45 a state trooper arrived on the scene with Pulaski. The luminous area, about 150 feet in diameter, was still glowing, though less intensely than before. The farm animals, horses and cattle, would not go into the area but would stop just outside it.

When the two men approached the area where the creature had appeared, they heard crashing sounds in the woods, as if something were following them. When they stopped, the sounds stopped. Whatever was making the noise, the two knew it had to be something large—something that could break down trees as it walked.

About this time Pulaski was getting thoroughly hysterical, forcing the officer to abandon his plan to go over to the lighted area to examine it more closely. As they started back to the patrol car, the sounds in the trees started again. Pulaski swore that a "brown object" was moving toward them and fired off his one remaining bullet.

By now Pulaski's manner was beginning to un-
nerve the officer as much as the weird events going
on around them. Suddenly he screamed that something was coming out of the woods toward them,
and both jumped into the car and drove about fifty
yards before the officer realized he was in the safety
of his car. He stopped, turned the vehicle around,
and shone the headlights into the trees. He saw
nothing, not even the glowing area, which had
disappeared.

The officer phoned Stan Gordon, head of the
Westmoreland County UFO Study Group, an organization which had worked with the local police
forces in the investigation of other creature sightings
in the area. At 1:30 a.m. Gordon arrived in the
company of four other members of his group. While
the twins stayed behind in Pulaski's truck, Gordon's
crew, along with Pulaski and his father, searched the
area for evidence. The glowing ring was long gone
and there were no markings on the hard ground.
The radiation level was normal.

At 1:45 the Pulaskis, who were standing by the
truck, shouted that the nearby farmhouse area had
suddenly lit up with a glow. The group checked out
the scene but found nothing unusual.

Dr. Schwarz describes the incredible events that
followed:

The team and the two Pulaskis walked up
from the truck towards the area where the creatures were observed. It was about 2:00 a.m. Suddenly the bull (in a nearby field) was scared by
something. Stephen's dog also became alarmed
and started tracking something. The dog kept
looking at a certain spot by the edge of the
woods, but the group didn't see anything.
George Lutz was asking Stephen some questions
when all of a sudden Stephen began rubbing his

head and face. George Lutz asked him if he was
OK, and Stephen then began shaking back and
forth as if he were going to faint. George Lutz
and Mr. Pulaski, Sr., grabbed Stephen. Stephen
. . . is over 6'2" tall and weighs around 250
pounds. He then began breathing very heavily
and started growling like an animal. He flailed
his arms and threw his father and George Lutz
to the ground. His dog then ran towards him as
if to attack, and Stephen went after the dog.
The dog started crying. George Lutz and Mr.
Pulaski were calling to Stephen to come back,
that it was all right, and that they were returning to the car.

Then Dennis Smeltzer suddenly said, "Hey,
Stan, I'm starting to feel lightheaded." Dennis
became very weak and felt faint. His face was
pale.

Dave Baker and Dave Smith went over to
help Dennis. Then Dave Baker began to com-
plain about having trouble breathing.

During all this, Stephen was running around,
swinging his arms, and loudly growling like an
animal. Suddenly he collapsed on his face into
a heavily manured area. Shortly afterwards he
started to come out of it and said, "Get away
from me. It's here. Get back."

Just then Stephen and Stan, as well as the
others, smelled a very strong sulphur or chemi-
cal-like odor.

George Lutz said, "Let's get out of here."
Then he and Mr. Pulaski, Sr., were helping
Stephen along when, suddenly on the way down
the hill, Stephen pointed and yelled: "Keep
away from the corner! It's in the corner!"

Stephen kept mumbling that he would protect the group. He also mumbled that he saw a
man "in a black hat and cloak, carrying a
sickle." He told Stephen, "If Man doesn't

straighten up, the end will come soon." He also said, "There is a man here now, who can save the world." Stephen also said that he could hear his name—"Stephen. Stephen."—being called from inside the woods. When he collapsed, Stephen's glasses fell off.

On the way down, as Stephen was coming out of his confused state, his father handed him the glasses and Stephen asked whose they were. Stan asked if he could see OK and he said, "Just fine."

Subsequently Dr. Schwarz conducted psychiatric interviews with Pulaski, finding that the percipient had no past record of such dissociative, disoriented behavior. Nonetheless there was a history of violence and unhappiness in his life, which Schwarz thought may have caused Pulaski to react as he did. That is certainly possible but it really doesn't explain the dog's reaction (so reminiscent of another dog's at Sharpsville, Indiana), or the foul odor that surrounded him during the period of the trance—unless, of course, all of this was psychokinetically generated.

During the interview Pulaski would drift in and out of trance states. Recalling his vision of the man in black, he said:

Was it a dream? I heard a crying noise. I could see a man in a black robe, carrying a scythe. Behind this man was fire and in front of him was a force, and in this force were the creatures. They were calling, "Stephen! Stephen!" One was laughing. It was a tantalizing laugh, and making me mad. My hands were clenched tight. Behind us was a big light. In this light something was telling me to go forward. "Go forward. Come on!" It was edging me. I could see myself as crazy, as a man so powerful that I wasn't

102

scared of anything. The creatures kept calling me and the light kept saying: "Go, my son, you can't be hurt." I think of a mother sheep calling to her little lambs. As I walked to the edge of the woods, the creatures kept wailing. I looked at them and all I could think of was death and the faceless form in the black robe who was commanding these things to kill me—it was hate . . . a hatred for everything. I knew that these things came from this force and if they got to the light they would be destroyed. The tension was so terrific that I passed out. Then I heard, "He is here—He is here." But who is He? Somebody was putting a puzzle in my head. My hands and ankles were hurting. Somebody was telling me that these people are going to destroy themselves. I kept seeing the date 1976—1976. It popped out of my mouth: "If these people don't straighten out, the whole world will burn" . . .

I'm living in hell now. What I'm telling you happened before. This is how the world was destroyed. It will be very soon, and this world will be gone. Somebody better find out before long or the world will end. We're destroying the world. What's the fire? What's going to happen is burning. Is there someone smarter than us that is playing upon us, laying a picture or puzzle out for us? It seems stupid but it seems like I *have* to tell the President of the United States, because somebody else has to know. It seems that somebody else is also being told at the same time, but they're not going to do it. They're scared. I don't know what happened in the field, or what these guys told you, but I felt like an animal. If you could find the one who would believe me—1976 is not far off. I don't believe America is going to live to be 200 years free, because that's been getting to me, too. And the world will go. Man will destroy himself.

Pulaski's "vision" is a strikingly interesting one, and as we already have seen, this is not the first time apocalyptic ideas have been associated with the appearance of a manimal. The fundamentalist population of Roachdale, for example, saw the creature's presence as proof that the Day of Judgment was at hand.

Even more specifically, however, we have the vision of California psychic Joyce Partise, who, handed a sealed envelope containing the photograph of a Bigfoot print, announced (according to B. Ann Slate's "Gods from Inner Space," *UFO Report,* April 1976), "This envelope is like a death certificate! I foresee an impending disaster . . . I keep getting the name John . . . What could that mean? I see people gathered together, frightened and praying. Some think it's spiritual, those craft in the sky. Some think it's the so-called Second Coming, but God help them!"

Mrs. Partise saw the Bigfoot as subterranean creatures somehow associated with UFOs, and UFOs as associated with the impending doom of the human race.

Her mention of "John" in this context is extraordinarily revealing. In *The Unidentified* we discussed in detail the remarkable contact claims of Paul Solem, an Arizona man who seemed to be able to produce UFOs on command, and the witnesses to these UFOs were not just credulous types but included skeptical newspaper reporters as well. On one of these occasions, as *Prescott (Ariz.) Courier* editor Joe Kraus watched, Solem went into a trance and repeated words allegedly received through mental communication with a being aboard the ship.

"Great sorrow and fear will be coming to this planet very soon," the "Venusian" supposedly said, "and few will escape it. Our leader as spoken of in Hopi prophecy is already here on Earth in mortality and is known as the Apostle John, the same as in the New Testament. The white brother shall be introduced by a huge fire and the earth shall quake at his arrival."

Pulaski's "voices" told him "He is here," and apparently the answer to the percipient's question, "Who is He?" is "John." Pulaski's vision is right out of St. John's Book of Revelation in the New Testament. The man in black is the devil, who traditionally appears from time to time in the company of bizarre creatures. Men in black (MIB), of course, have long been a part of the UFO phenomenon, going back at least as far as 1905 and that year's sighting wave in Wales, which came in the midst of a hysterical religious revival.* According to the *Barmouth Advertiser* of March 30, 1905:

> In the neighborhood dwells an exceptionally intelligent young woman of the peasant stock, whose bedroom has been visited three nights in succession by a man dressed in black. This figure has delivered a message to the girl which she is frightened to relate.

Years later, during the post-1947 Flying Saucer Era, other persons would claim encounters with menacing men in black, some of whom would impart messages "too frightening to relate." These messages usually would involve prophecies of the earth's imminent destruction.

Such visions are also a staple of contactee lore. In these cases, the benevolent space people seem to lament our fate and hold out the hope that we can straighten ourselves out before it's too late. The malevolent MIB, on the other hand, apparently feel that we have it coming to us.

We are not prepared to take these gloomy visions

* *The Unidentified*, pp. 116-19.

literally, since human history is littered with failed prophecies about the end of the world. But clearly these mean *something* and Pulaski is certainly right when he says that "someone . . . is laying a picture or puzzle out for us." But what is it?

5.

Any summing up of the data we have examined so far must necessarily be filled with qualifications, since the sole universal feature of these reports is the general description of manimals as hairy, heavy, and hominoid—and even that will come into question shortly. Nonetheless, these points can be made:

1.) In many of the incidents the creature's eyes are self-luminous. The color of this light is most often red, and sometimes green or yellow.

2.) It usually emits a foul odor, often compared to decaying meat, rotting garbage, or sewage.

3.) It is invulnerable to bullets.

4.) It is usually retiring in its behavior, although sometimes destructive to livestock and wildlife.

5.) It makes a variety of sounds, the most frequent of them a low growl or a high-pitched screech which may remind percipients of a baby crying or a woman screaming.

6.) It usually does not leave tracks. When it does, such tracks may be: two-toed, three-toed, four-toed, five-toed, and even six-toed. Even prints which have the same number of toes may have dramatically different shapes in different cases.

This much said, unsatisfactory as it may be, we enter an even denser thicket of uncertainty, and it begins to look as though we are the victims of some cruel cosmic joke. Far from knowing answers, we may not even know the questions. In the case of the Uniontown episode, for example, to whom shall we turn—the ufologist, the biologist, the psychologist, or the demonologist?

The incident at Uniontown was only one of many creature reports being made in western Pennsylvania during 1973 and 1974. Some were of classic manimals, several appearing in the company of UFOs. In one instance, three women driving in a wooded area supposedly came upon a landed rectangular object, from whose door a ramp was lowered and three apelike creatures emerged, disappearing into the trees. In another, two teenage girls reported seeing a manimal with white hair and glowing red eyes; it was, they said, "carrying a luminescent sphere in its hand." In yet another a witness is said to have fired on a creature, which then vanished in a flash of light.

Absurd, all of it, but the observers of these occurrences were so numerous, and so many of sterling character, that the authorities were forced to take them seriously, even if individually or collectively the stories made no sense.

When Allen V. Noe of the Society for the Investigation of the Unexplained probed the mystery, puzzled by the sudden influx of reports of what he thought to be an "eastern Bigfoot," he ended up noting in *Pursuit,* the SITU journal, "We are unnerved, to put it mildly, to think that there might be five types wandering about in western Pennsylvania." Actually, as Noe himself would come to realize, that was an extremely conservative estimate. Some of the creatures resembled nothing so much as—if you will pardon the expression—"werewolves."

Not that werewolf reports are anything particularly new, even in modern-day America. During July and August 1972, a number of people in Toledo and Defiance, Ohio, swore they had seen something which appeared to be "human, with an oversized, wolflike head, and an elongated nose," and between six and eight feet in height. Witnesses said it "had huge hairy feet, fangs, and ran from side to side, like a caveman in the movies." It also possessed glowing red eyes. A trainman working along the tracks near downtown Defiance claimed that the thing had sneaked up behind him in the early morning darkness and clobbered him with a two-by-four board.

"We don't know what to think," Police Chief Donald Breckler said, "but now we're taking it seriously."

In the meantime, during the second week of August, people living near Cleveland's Brookside Park were seeing a more conventional manimal, this one huge, black-haired and apelike. Again the authorities conceded that the witnesses were probably telling the truth. "These people seem very sincere about what they saw," investigating officers said. "It scared the bejabbers out of them." Richard Merrill of the Cleveland Zoo denied that either of the two resident gorillas had escaped.

The final werewolf sighting took place in southwestern Ohio (Defiance is in the northwestern, Toledo in the northeastern parts of the state) one night late in October. Mr. and Mrs. Ed Miller of Carlisle had driven out into the countryside between Carlisle and Germantown to look for a license plate that had fallen off the car earlier. Mrs. Miller happened to look across a field and she noticed a black, partially erect figure running on two legs. "It turned and came at us," she told the *Middletown Journal,* "and then it crouched down and was almost crawling. I screamed for my husband to take me home. I was scared to death."

When the Millers returned home, they told three teenage friends about their experience. Excited, the youths jumped into a car and raced out to the scene, where they observed the same creature and the same behavior. They, too, decided to get out of there.

"Then we went back out," Mrs. Miller said. "But

we still couldn't get a close look at it. It would start to run toward the car, standing up, but then it would crouch down and hide in the weeds. And it howled at us, a loud snarling, hissing sound."

Mr. and Mrs. Gary Moore of Carlisle went separately to the area. Because of the darkness they could not tell how tall the thing was but they could see that it was "wide." They were certain it was not a man. Its eyes, which were huge, "glowed like fluorescence in the light of the car." Its face and body were very hairy.

There is a long tradition of werewolf lore among the Navaho Indians of Arizona and New Mexico, and in modern times the entire question gets hopelessly confused with manimal and UFO phenomena.

In *Flying Saucer Occupants,* for instance, Coral and Jim Lorenzen relate a story told by a friend, who said that around midnight on June 9, 1960, she had seen a little broad-shouldered, long-armed figure in the headlights of her car. It appeared to have no mouth, nose, or ears on its pumpkin-shaped head, but two yellowish orange-glowing eyes were visible.

In the fall of 1965, Roger Heath saw something quite similar. In a letter to Loren Coleman, he wrote:

I was driving north from Winslow, Arizona, toward the three mesas of the Hopi villages. Nearer the 2nd Mesa end of the road than the Winslow end, and I would guess in the vicinity of Little Jedito Wash, I saw what I first thought was a man charred from an auto wreck crawling from a wash onto the road. I realized almost at once that it would have to be an awfully small man with long arms. I had a gun, an over and under, in the car. I stopped, in short order did the following: rolled down my window, poked the gun out same, turned around and went back. I saw this thing in a kind of hand scramble headed out the same side, the east, of the road from where I assumed it had come. I did not fire.

Heath described the being as about three feet tall, shiny black (probably fur, he thought), without apparent ears, and having a roundish "harmless-looking face." It departed with a kind of hop, scrambling with its hands. The only detail on the face he clearly recalled was a reddish area over the eyes.

He showed drawings of the thing to the Hopis and Navahos. The Navahos identified it as a "skin-walker"—their name for the werewolf.

A "skin-walker" showed up in the South Valley section of Albuquerque, New Mexico, during October 1966. On the 14th of that month the *Albuquerque Journal* reported that the Clifford McGuire family had complained to the deputy sheriff about "a monster about five feet tall, hairy, and with a small blank face and crying like a baby [that] has roamed through their backyard several times in the past three weeks." The McGuires' eighteen-year-old son went out one night and was struck by something which knocked him unconscious. When he awoke, he found fork-shaped footprints near him. Thereafter, every time the creature reappeared, the McGuires' radio would stop playing, and the young man would feel a pain in the chest. Police officers, taking the stories seriously, said the family was "pretty rational about it—there's something out there." The "monster" was reported fifteen to twenty times in the following week, though apparently a prankster dressed in a costume was responsible for some of the supposed sightings. One informant told the *Albuquerque Tribune* that during the late 1930s and early 1940s residents in the same area had seen the same or a very similar creature.

In January 1970 four Gallup, New Mexico, youths —Clifford Heronemus, Robert Davis, Carl Martinez and David Chiaramonte—claimed to have seen a "werewolf" near Whitewater. They saw a "hairy thing with two legs" pacing their car, which was going about 45 miles per hour.

"It was about five foot seven, and I was surprised it could go so fast," Heronemus said. "At first I thought my friends were playing a joke on me, but when I found out they weren't, I was scared!

"We rolled up the windows real fast and locked the doors of the car. I started driving faster, about sixty, but it was hard because that highway has a lot of sharp turns. Someone finally got a gun out and shot it. I know it got hit and it fell down, but there was no blood. It got up again and ran off. I know it couldn't be a person because people cannot move that fast." *

Tony Zecca passed the same spot earlier in the evening. He also saw something, but he didn't think it was a werewolf, but rather a man from a flying saucer. He did not mention whether or not he had seen the saucer.

6.

One of the creatures observed during the Pennsylvania monster scare was something that looked more like a cross between a human being and a cat than the by now "commonplace" human/ape blending. Another beast resembled the "conventional" manimal in all ways except that its hair was *tan*. We are about to take an even deeper plunge into the abyss of the absurd.

* Four decades ago anthropologist William Morgan talked of the human-wolves with a Navaho named Hahago, who said, "They go very fast." "How fast?" Morgan asked. "They can go to A. in an hour and a half," Hahago replied. Morgan noted, "It takes four hours by automobile." ("Human-Wolves Among the Navaho," *Yale Publications in Anthropology*, XI, 1936.)

We can start with an undated clipping (ca. 1964) in our files, citing the testimonies of two young campers on Mt. Tamalpais in Marin County, California, who were disturbed on three occasions during July by a very strange animal—or actually *two* very strange animals, since on one occasion they heard it "chittering" back and forth with another, which apparently was hidden in the bushes.

Speaking of the one they were able to observe, Paul Conant said, "Its head was close to its body and below the shoulders it was very muscular. No ears could be seen." Neither did it possess a tail. It seemed to weigh around 200 pounds *and its tracks indicated that it walked on two feet.*

All unlikely enough, to be sure, but on November 9, 1968, a Mr and Mrs. Cataldo of Lorain, Ohio, reportedly encountered a similar phenomenon.

At about 5:45 a.m. a loud *bump* on the roof of their house awoke the couple. The bump was followed by the sound of something moving near their bedroom window. When they looked up at the window, they saw a huge face staring down at them. The thing's two front paws or hands were resting on the windowsill.

Mr. Cataldo leaped out of bed and frantically searched for his gun, but by the time he located it, the creature was gone from the window. Running on two legs, it dashed around the east side of the house, weaving from side to side like an ape (a detail we have heard before), crossed two streets, and disappeared into the woods.

The Cataldos said the creature stood about six feet tall. Its front side was a light grayish brown, the rest of the body a darker shade of the same color. It resembled, they stated, "a large lion of around 600 pounds." Lions, as we all know, are quadrapedal.

The palm prints found on the windowsill looked humanlike, except that "the prints were reversed

112

and ran in a straight line." Interestingly, the creature seen at Latrobe, Pennsylvania, in September 1973 (the incident alluded to in the first sentence of this section) was described as having hands that were *turned backward.*

That same year—1968—a logging crew in British Columbia had several run-ins with an equally weird creature. They first became aware of the presence of something out of the ordinary when they heard "hooting sounds" unlike anything they were familiar with. They also found footprints that were somewhat "catlike" but still decidedly unusual.

Not long after that, the foreman, a man named Woods, was walking through the Cedar Swamp when he heard the hooting so closeby that it terrified him, and he ran for the safety of his Caterpillar. From that time on, he took to carrying a pistol with him on his rounds.

Finally, Woods got to see the thing. He was driving the Caterpillar one day when he heard something behind him. He turned around to see a creature (which he first thought was a mountain lion because of its tawny color) leap from the trees, land on its back feet, stretch out, and jump across the skid into a tree on the opposite side. It all happened in one quick moment.

Woods was stunned. What he had seen resembled some kind of bizarre cross between a cat and an ape.

Veteran Bigfoot hunter Rene Dahinden went to the scene and spent ten days investigating. Though he himself heard nothing unusual, he did interview buck-bush pickers (buck bush is used in wreaths) who had. They told him they had found an unusual bed which they thought might be connected with the creature in some way.

Dahinden examined the bed, which was situated on an old skid trail overgrown with small (seven- to ten-foot) trees. It was the only sunny spot there.

The ground was covered with snow two and a half feet deep, but there was no snow on the bed, which was three to five feet long, three feet wide and one foot high. Nearby and underneath a dead tree was a hole about a foot and a half in diameter with a nest in it. Around this nest something had carefully placed a number of broken branches with the stems outward and the soft material arranged in the middle.

He found two or three different types of teeth marks on the bark, but the animal or animals responsible did not eat the bark. From these scratch marks Dahinden inferred that a bear could have been the cause, but the other evidence—most notably the fact that all the little twigs from around the bed were cleared away and in little piles—made him question that theory. Two old wolverine trappers, intimately familiar with the area, told him they had never seen anything like it; for that matter, neither had Dahinden, a longtime woodsman himself.

Across the lake from Salmon Run, where the loggers had made their sightings, Dahinden heard stories about monkeylike creatures which apparently were different from the Bigfoot. One woman related that once her daughter had run home frightened, saying she had seen a little hairy man carrying a bundle of moss.

It appears from all this that we are seeing one type of MA (the manimal) shading off into another (the phantom panther). Already we have seen the shading in the "opposite" direction, toward sometimes robotlike "UFO occupants." But for the moment we are adrift in a twilight zone of ambiguity.

Our last series of cases comes out of southwestern Kentucky, where in the fall of 1973 farmers around the town of Albany were confronted with an impossible beast, its mate and its cub.

The "male" reportedly stood over three feet tall

at the shoulders when on all fours; it was also bipedal, and when on two legs it reached six feet. Its hair was dark brown or black, its tail, which it carried like a cat's, was long, bushy, and black. According to one witness, its head was shaped "like an ape/human with a flat face and nose with large nostrils. Its ears are like mule ears and will perk up."

We first heard of the affair when witness Rick Hall wrote the Indianapolis Zoological Society about it. The Society's Education Director, Richard G. France, referred Hall to Loren Coleman. Hall subsequently gave Coleman the following information:

This animal is very cunning, agile and strong. It can toss a 300-lb. sow around with ease and can leap over fences, with a good distance between foot tracks—10 ft. to 15 ft. It has wiped out two herds of pigs and has been said to have killed a calf and a dog. At night when it is in the area the livestock all start running the pens, while all the wildlife seems to have disappeared from the local area. The grandfather of the girl I'm engaged to owns the mountain, and it's supposed to be loaded with wildlife. But since the sightings the wildlife has moved, and I'm not sure why.*

We tried to track this animal with several dogs, but after they caught its scent, they wouldn't track it, acted scared . . . [The tracks were three-toed and distinctly manimal-like.]

The farmers have seen this animal watch them as they work in the fields as well as engineers who are building a new road in the area. My

* "The woods where the cries [of an Ohio manimal] were heard seems to be dying, and many trees have fallen. There appears to be an almost complete absence of birds or animals in this woods, yet across a field there is another wooded area where everything is lush and green, and where animal and bird life abounds."— Allen V. Noe, "And Still the Reports Roll in," *Pursuit*, January 1974.

girl's aunt went home one evening and found it just outside their back door eating old table scraps. She shot at it six times with a pistol & 17 times with a .22 rifle and she says she missed it [?]. But the animal ran about 100 yards and sat at the edge of the woods & cornfield, sat on its haunches and watched her, but disappeared when her husband went after it.

Hall himself claimed to have seen two adults and one "cub"—presumably a "monster family." He and other local folk believed the creatures dwelt in caves and abandoned mines in the area.

In late October eighteen-year-old Gary Pierce allegedly was chased off the mountain by the creature and subsequently had to be placed in the hospital, for hysteria, rather than any physical injury.

Finally, a farmer named Charlie Stern caught it prowling around his barn. He opened fire on it and apparently wounded the creature, which he then tracked to a cave that he chose not to enter. Sightings subsided after this incident.

In many ways this is a classic creature story. We have here the destruction of livestock, the beast's enormous strength, the ability to jump great distances, the capacity to terrify other animals (primarily dogs)—all integral parts of what might be called the Monster Archetype.

And this takes us inevitably to the Phantom Cats and Dogs.

CHAPTER FOUR

Phantom Cats and Dogs

1.

On Friday, April 10, 1970, Mike Busby of Cairo, Illinois, was driving on Route 3 to Olive Branch, Illinois, to pick up his wife. At about 8:30 p.m., a mile south of Olive Branch, on the dark, mostly deserted road that parallels the edge of the vast Shawnee National Forest, Busby's automobile quit running. He got out of his car and had begun to release the hood latch when he heard a noise on his left. He was startled to see two quarter-sized, almond-shaped, greenish-glowing eyes staring at him.

Before he had a chance to move, the strange form, six feet tall, black and upright, advanced on him. Without warning it hit him hard on the face with two padded front feet, and they rolled over together to the left side of the road. "It" remained on top of Busby as the two tumbled about. Shredding his shirt to pieces, it inflicted wounds on his left arm, chest and abdomen with dull two-inch claws. Busby desperately held its mouth open at arm's length. Certain that it was trying for his throat, he tried to keep clear of its long yellow feline teeth.

While unable to see its features very well (and probably not much interested in the question just at that moment), Busby did feel something "fuzzy" around the mouth which he took to be whiskers. Its general body hair or fur was short and wiry ("like steel wool," he told Loren Coleman) to the touch, and although it was dry it smelled like wet hair. The creature emitted deep, soft growls unlike anything Busby had ever heard before.

Soon a diesel truck passed. Busby now saw clearly that the thing's color was a slick shiny black. He also could see the "shadow of its tail." The truck's headlights apparently scared the creature, and with "heavy footfalls," Busby said, it loped off across the road.

Dizzy, his body aching, Busby crawled back to his car. It started without trouble.

The truck driver, John Hartsworth, was waiting for Busby in Olive Branch. Hartsworth explained that he had been unable to brake his truck and stop for help. From what he had seen in his headlights, however, he said the thing looked like a big cat.

Mike Busby was treated in St. Mary's Hospital in Cairo by a Dr. Robinson, who gave him two inoculations, one for tetanus, another for the relief of pain. Busby's brother Don told Coleman that in the days following the encounter Mike required aid in walking, was often dizzy, and fainted once.

Mike Busby was by no means the first person from extreme southern Illinois to claim an encounter with a "black panther." Four years earlier, in April 1966, the *Cairo Evening Citizen,* recounting the most recent of a long series of reports, asked, "Does the black panther really roam the Shawnee Forest wilderness in Alexander County?" On April 13 Joseph Moad and his wife had gone outside to see what was disturbing the livestock on their farm near Elco. "I turned on a floodlight and could see his eyes shining," Moad told Game Warden Peter Clarke. "He screamed and it was the keen scream of a panther, not the coarse scream of a bobcat or cougar." Moad, who had a deer rifle with him, got off one quick shot before the animal got away.

Commented the *Evening Citizen*:

One popular version of the black panther in Alexander—still not known to be true or not—is that many years ago a circus train or truck was wrecked in the area and some black panthers escaped into the hills and were never found.

Thomas Coleman, Cairo IVC service officer and a native of Elco, recalls that in his youth frequent search parties were organized to tramp the hills looking for the black panther after someone had reported seeing one.

"We would take our guns and go out in large parties looking for them," Coleman said. "We never were able to see one or find a trace of them."

Deputy Sheriff Gene Rambeau is positive that when he was a child and living in rural Alexander County, he and others saw a black panther that had gone inside a house.

"It dashed out the door and streaked off fast as greased lightning," Rambeau said.

There are others in the county who will vow that they have seen the elusive beast.

Conventional zoology, unfortunately, does not allow us to accept stories like these—and there are a great many more just like them. To begin with, there are no panthers, or pumas, or mountain lions— all popular names for the same animal, known scientifically as *Felis concolor,* in Illinois, where they have been extinct since 1850. In fact, except for isolated groups in the Florida Everglades, there are supposed to be no panthers east of the Rocky Mountains, though some zoologists now concede that a small number may have survived in several far eastern states and provinces.

For another thing, New World panthers are not, except in very rare instances, black. In 1843 a melanistic (i.e., black) puma supposedly was killed in the Carandahy River section of Brazil. It is not known what became of the body. There have been several so far undocumented reports of a black subspecies of the Florida panther, but to date no one has photographed, captured, or exhibited a black puma.

The bobcat (*Lynx rufus*), a native of North America, has a range overlapping most of the areas where black panthers have been seen. Bobcats are smaller than pumas, and melanistic bobcats do exist. But they are so rare that only two have ever been caught, at different times in the same place, Martin County, Florida.

Melanism in the *Felidae,* the family of cats, runs the highest, zoology tell us, in the moist tropics and subtropics. The most frequent numbers of black mutations occur in the jaguar (*Panthera onca*) of Latin America and the leopard (*Panthera parus*) of Africa and Asia.

In summary, the likelihood of black panthers in North America, even a tiny handful of them, is slight. Yet reports of them are so persistent and widespread that exasperated zoologists and game wardens have taken to calling them the "flying saucers of the animal world"—an identification whose true significance we shall examine later.

Finally, panthers, whatever their color and whatever their reputation, do not usually attack people. As the late Ivan T. Sanderson observed in *Living Mammals of the World,* "The Puma is the great coward of all the great or not so great cats. Despite voluminous fictional tales and innumerable accounts published as fact, the number of authenticated cases of deliberate attacks upon human beings by these animals is so paltry as to be almost nonexistent and most of these are open to some doubt. The animal is a retiring beast . . ."

Well, then, just what did attack Mike Busby? And just what are the people of Alexander County and other places seeing anyway?

That is not an easy question to answer. We have here the bare hints of an enigma so vast and so impenetrable that, unlike UFOs and Bigfeet, it has remained virtually invisible to society at large. Even Forteans, with a few rare exceptions (Charles Fort being one of them), have failed to recognize its significance or even its occurrence. But what we seem to be dealing with, as will become apparent, are thousands of accounts, spanning at least two centuries and six continents, of unexplained, large, and often dangerous catlike creatures whose appearance and behavior are not really those of any known animal. We are confronted with sightings of "animals" that should not be, doing things they are not supposed to do, in places they should not roam, and doing them in patterns that repeat themselves with discomforting regularity. The sheer volume of these reports leaves us with only two alternatives, neither of them a very happy one: either we reject them all as hoaxes and mistakes, or we forget everything we know about conventional zoology and search for answers elsewhere.

2.

Let us begin our search with an event reported in the August 3, 1823, issue of the Boston-based *New England Farmer.*

The account has it that, not long before, people near Russelville, Kentucky, had begun seeing a "tiger of a brindle color with a most terrific front— his eyes are described as the largest ever seen in any animal." Four men, two of them armed, got a close view of the beast. The two with guns

> fired on him at the distance of 50 yards without forcing him to move from his stand; a furious look and appalling brow frightened the two men without guns who fled to town. Experienced marksmen continued to fire, and on the 12th shot the beast put off at full speed. . . .
>
> When the news reached Russelville about 40 gentlemen repaired to the spot, and had a full view of the ground. The print which the paws of this animal made in the earth corresponds with the account given of his great bulk by those who had an opportunity of viewing him at a short distance for several minutes. . . .
>
> The above Tiger was seen a few days after braving a dozen shots and making its way into the state of Tennessee, and there is still a prospect of its being taken. . . .

But it never was, even though it is difficult to understand how "experienced marksmen" were unable to kill the beast, which was both large and still, at such comparatively close range.

We are reminded of a much more recent tale from Atlanta, Georgia, where in April 1958 two patrolmen emptied their service revolvers into a "black panther" as it charged "like a bullet" from a wooded area they were searching. "Both of us were firing at point-blank range," Officer J. F. Porter said. "I don't see how we could have missed it"—a complaint we have heard before from other Mystery Animal observers. The yellow-eyed creature ran between them and disappeared, uttering not a sound.

One night in December 1877, a badly frightened man appeared at the door of his employer, a wealthy farmer named Hunt, and blurted out an amazing story. At first Hunt did not believe him, but later events were to force him to change his mind.

Earlier in the evening, the young man, a member of one of two tenant families working for Hunt and living on his land, had gone to the village of Rising Sun, Indiana. On his way he had passed through an area midway between the farm and the village called "Halfway Place," a spot where Hunt's fence divided the cleared land from the woods which were locally called the "Black Forest" because of the height and thickness of the trees.

All this had taken place routinely and without incident. But it was on his way back, about 9:00 p.m., that something happened for which he was not prepared. "Some monstrous animal," he said, had come crashing out of the woods and pursued him down the road, clearly, he felt, intent on killing him. He felt that he barely had escaped with his life.

Several evenings later a young woman named Mary Crane was visiting a family on Hunt's farm and someone told her of the young man's experience. She laughed it off, but the story impressed her at least enough to insist someone accompany her when she left. No one was willing to oblige, so she went next door and got another young man to escort her to the village, just a mile away. The two set off in the dark.

As they entered the blackest part of the Black

Forest, Miss Crane and her companion suddenly heard a peculiar shriek from deep among the trees. Mary Crane whirled around to see two glowing eyes descending from the branches of a poplar not more than forty feet away, and to hear the sound of claws scraping against bark.

Deciding to get out of there fast, they sped off down the road and then stopped briefly to look behind them. For a moment they saw nothing—until the animal, "big as a good-sized calf, with a tail as long as a door," leaped onto the fence. Running along the rail of the fence, the creature moved rapidly toward them. The couple started to run again and had begun to outdistance the animal, when it bounded to the ground to follow them down the road, quickly gaining on them.

At this point the young man, who had had about all he could take, let go of Miss Crane's hand and dashed the short remaining distance to the village to sound the alarm—in the meantime leaving his companion to the mercy of the thing that had been stalking them. Soon Mary Crane felt the animal's claws ripping at her dress. She collapsed in a faint, awakening moments later to find herself pinned to the ground, and something licking her face. Knowing she could do nothing else, she lay motionless and prayed.

Shortly afterwards she heard voices. The animal perked up its ears, rose, and growled menacingly, looking for a moment as if it were going to charge the approaching villagers. Instead it let out a piercing shriek, jumped over the fence, and disappeared. The deeply shaken Miss Crane had to be carried to the village where she was treated with stimulants.

The next morning, a large party of men with hunting dogs tracked the creature for half a mile until its footprints, which measured over six inches across, were lost in the high ground. The hunt continued for the next two days to no avail.

As the *New York Times* observed, "The whole affair is wrapped in mystery, which the inhabitants of that region would like to have solved."

So would we. *Felis concolor* supposedly has been extinct in Indiana since 1850. Of course, one might argue, it is possible that one may have wandered back into its old haunts, but that would not explain the creature's ferocious behavior. After all, as puma authority Herbert Ravenel Sass once wrote, "Ninety-nine times out of a hundred a panther, meeting man, woman, or child in the woods, will flee as though from the Evil One himself." We also wonder about those "glowing" eyes. The eyes of a standard panther reflect light but are not luminous in themselves. We already have examined other reports of creatures with glowing eyes (Busby's the most recent example) and the Rising Sun incident may be another of these. Certainly the original account does not mention any light source which the eyes could have been reflecting. But we don't have enough information to arrive at any firm conclusions.

As the reader may have inferred by now, all mystery felines are not black. Some of them even look like conventional giant cats, and some of them undoubtedly are just that. For example, after numerous Minnesotans had reported sighting a mountain lion over a six-year period between 1945 and 1951, two conservation officers conducted an intensive investigation and determined that one or two panthers had meandered down from Canada into the northeastern and southwestern parts of the state.

But what interests us are sightings of catlike creatures that do not behave as large cats are supposed to behave. We are also concerned with reports of things that may resemble known varieties of cats

125

but are woefully out of place—such as the African lion that terrorized central Illinois all through the month of July 1917.

3.

They called her "Nellie the Lion," an oddly affectionate nickname for a creature whose nasty temper made her anything but lovable.

Nellie, or her male companion (there seem to have been two giant cats, not just one), first managed to draw attention to itself by attacking Thomas Gullett, a butler at the Robert Allerton estate southwest of Monticello, while he was in the garden picking flowers. Gullett suffered only scratch marks, but the incident touched off a furor that didn't abate for weeks.

The affair had actually begun around Camargo a few days before, but the Monticello report was the first to receive press attention. It led to the forming of a 300-man posse which spent most of July 15 tramping through the thick woods near the Allerton place. While the hunters were engaged in this fruitless endeavor, the lion nonchalantly reappeared a quarter-mile away from the Allerton house and Mrs. Shaw, the chief housekeeper, got a good look. Unfortunately, she was one of the few persons in the vicinity not carrying a gun at that moment. Like Gullett she referred to the animal as an "African lioness."

On July 17 searchers discovered tracks five inches long and four inches wide near Decatur. Two fourteen-year-old boys, Earl Cavanaugh and Glyan Tulison, claimed to have seen the beast that day walking along Allen's Bend on the Sangamon River, a short distance east of Decatur.

As public hysteria mounted, residents of central and northern Illinois outdid themselves in silly behavior. On a number of occasions they mistook collie dogs for the lion, and one farmer distinguished himself by shooting a hole through the radiator of an approaching car; he had mistaken the headlights for the beast's shining eyes. The papers, of course, had a good time with this, and it must have helped casual readers dismiss the other reports as jokes.

But the families of Earl Hill and Chester Osborn of Decatur were not amused when the lion pounced on their car in an apparent attempt to get at them. The attack took place at 10:30 p.m. on July 29 as the two men and their wives motored west on the Springfield road. Hill and Osborn, sitting in the front seat, first caught sight of the big animal standing in the weeds alongside the road. Suddenly it leaped a distance of twenty feet and crashed into the car, which was traveling twenty miles an hour. The women in the back seat screamed as the creature struck the side of the vehicle and slid off onto the highway.

Osborn, who was driving Hill's car, turned around and headed back to Decatur to tell the police. Two officers and the two male witnesses immediately returned to the scene, to find the creature still there. When it saw them, it disappeared over a bank and the policemen, lacking heavy firearms, elected not to pursue it. At 1:30 a.m. two car loads of police returned with high-powered rifles to search the spot, but after some hours returned to town with nothing to show for their efforts.

On July 31, at about 3:00 p.m., James Rutherford, a farmhand, was driving a hay wagon past a gravel pit when he spotted a "large yellow, long-haired beast." As he gaped in terror, the animal regarded him without interest, then wandered off into a clump of bushes near a small creek. When the inevitable armed posse rushed to the scene, they found only its tracks, which, strangely enough, had claw marks in them. This extremely odd detail should have alerted the searchers to the fact that they were chasing something decidedly out of the ordinary, since virtually all members of the cat family possess retractile claws that do not customarily show in the prints. At any rate, continuing their search into the evening, they came upon the remains of a calf which its owner said had been missing four days.

After that, "Nellie" vanished as mysteriously as she had arrived, leaving behind her innumerable stories of mind-boggling events which the locals chose to forget as quickly as possible. And who can blame them? After all, who would want to try to explain what African lions were doing in Illinois?

Or on Long Island, for that matter? On June 20, 1931, police in Malverne, New York, took a call from Mrs. E. H. Tandy saying that a "lion" was walking around in her back yard. When officers arrived at the scene, the animal was gone; it had jumped over a fence, Mrs. Tandy explained. The lawmen were skeptical, but within the next couple of days two other Malverne residents had called with a similar story.

But that was not to be all. On the afternoon of the 24th, at nearby Albertson Square, Mr. and Mrs. George Ballis and their children saw a "monkey about half the size of a heavy-set man" drop from a tree and dash into bushes alongside the road. About ten persons eventually viewed the creature and agreed it was large, hairy, and had a long gray face.

4.

1948 was the year of the "varmint"—or the "varmints," depending on whose stories you choose to believe. At least four distinctly different animals figured in the reports of the witnesses. Two of the creatures sometimes worked as a pair. Another seems not to have been a member of the cat family at all. One bore enough of a resemblance to a conventional tan-colored puma to convince some individuals, though by no means all, that that in fact was what they were seeing. Most observers, perplexed, confessed they had no idea what it was. One even thought it might be a "wolf with yellow spots"!

The Great Varmint Scare began in the fall of 1947 when weird screeching cries disturbed the sleep of Fountain City people and, as a contemporary news account puts it vaguely, "cattle, sheep, and horses acted in an unusual manner." A group of citizens late one night saw a huge catlike beast in a roadway.

Richmond policeman Louis Danels had the most detailed sighting but did not make it public until months later. "It was so strange," he said, "that I just didn't mention it to anyone at the time. But now that other folks are seeing things and talking, I guess I can talk, too."

He and his family had been out on a casual Sunday afternoon drive along a road southwest of Centerville. "Suddenly," Danels related, "the strangest, most vicious-looking thing walked toward my car down the center of the road. It had long front legs, a large head with small pointed ears, and small glittering eyes."

Its back sloped down in an odd manner, and its body narrowed at the hips, ending in back legs considerably shorter than the front two.

"We got to within ten feet of it and it ran off the road into the weeds," Danels continued. "We all remarked that it was the most ferocious, evil-looking thing we ever had seen."

He thought it might be a hyena. Or anyway, he said, that's what it looked like to him.

It was only when the varmint started killing livestock, though, that the Hoosiers got riled. In mid-

July 1948, farmer Dorten Moore, who lived a mile southeast of Fountain City, complained to Sheriff Carl Sperling that something had slaughtered seven of his small hogs, eating their hearts and livers. Shortly thereafter Sheriff Sperling and three other law officers kept a vigil at Moore's place from dark to 3:00 a.m., but saw nothing.

A night or so later neighbor Harold Erskine heard a "strange caterwauling noise" over in Moore's fields, grabbed a gun, and scooted over to rouse Moore. They set out after whatever made the sound but it already had vanished, leaving in its wake still another butchered hog.

Another neighbor, Lewis Swain, heard a "strange whining call" on several occasions, and found a wide path through his wheatfield as if cut by the animal on the prowl. "Just like the one they found last year in the cornfield," he said. One farmer, unnamed, supposedly got chased out of his barn by an unidentified something.

The night of August 1, Clifford Fath, a game warden, and Charles Cornelius, a county conservation officer, testified they had encountered a varmint on the road between Quakertown and Roseburg. It was sitting in the middle of the road, and Fath had to swerve his car in order to avoid hitting the animal, which looked as though it might weigh close to 350 pounds. Frightened, it lunged at the car and crashed against its side, then fled off into the woods.

Fath and Cornelius hurriedly organized a posse. With the help of dogs they tracked the animal to a tree in whose branches it was hiding. Members of the group opened fire, but all they heard was the sound of something leaping into another tree deeper into the forest.

The next night a farmer near Liberty discovered the carcass of a 1000-pound bull in his pasture, one of many such accounts pouring into Fath's office.

Angry and unnerved farmers gathered in bands and beat through the backwoods, but the varmint eluded them easily.

One thing not hard to find was its tracks, which stretched along the sand at Silver Creek and measured six inches in length. "Such tracks are not those of any of the wildlife living in this section of the country," the *Richmond Palladium-Item* noted.

Three days later, during the evening hours of the fifth, an "African lion" rushed a fishing party at Elkhorn Falls south of Richmond. The party consisted of four adults and two children. According to Ivan Toney, who lived nearby, "About 7:30 p.m. a man came to the house and wanted to use the phone to call the sheriff. He said he and another man, along with their wives and two children, were fishing along the banks of the pool at the foot of the Elkhorn Falls. Their car was parked on the road near the gate to the lane leading to the Falls.

"He said the animal came up the stream from the south. When they sighted it, they started running for the car. They reached it, but the animal lunged at the car, then plowed through the fence into the sandy bar along the stream's edge."

The creature "looked like a lion with a long tail," the witnesses asserted, with bushy hair around the neck. Deputy Sheriff Jack Witherby, who examined the tracks it had left, described them as like "nothing I have ever seen before."

The morning of the 7th two farmboys, Arthur and Howard Turner, sixteen and fourteen, saw a strange shape while walking to the barn at 5:30. It appeared near a plum tree not far from the gate leading into the barnyard. To its right another animal stood on a rise of ground not 200 feet away. Arthur, who like other rural people in the Richmond area had taken to carrying a gun with him on his rounds, raised the rifle to his shoulder and fired

131

away. The creatures wheeled around, jumped a gate, and escaped.

Curiously, the animals, while generally similar, were not identical. The first had the "appearance of a lion": large-headed, "shaggy," and brownish in color. The other, said the boys, "had more the appearance of a panther and was black."

The following afternoon farmers northeast of Abington, in Richmond's Wayne County, watched two varmints similar to the ones the Turners had seen, and the morning after that others sighted identical beasts in the same general locations. At 4:30 in the afternoon a "long black animal" crossed the Robert Martin farm near Middleboro. Police searches proved unproductive except for the usual discovery of five-toed tracks made by animals clearly weighing in excess of 300 pounds. (Ordinary panthers generally weigh no more than 200 pounds and they leave four-toed tracks.) Art Lecamp showed officers a spot in a ravine where apparently some large animal had bedded down for the night.

With panic growing and rumors spreading uncontrollably, many people were ready to shoot at anything that moved. Unfortunately for those trying to stem the rising tide of hysteria, the varmints were moving in closer to houses, even ones in town. One story had it that a giant cat had run a woman into her home. James Leo of Pennville, a little town west of Richmond, nearly fainted when he found a strange animal on his back porch on the morning of the 11th. With nothing to defend himself with but a butcher knife, he was considerably relieved when it sauntered away.

That evening police got a call from Robert Martin, who said he had fired at a varmint through the screen of his bedroom window. "I know I hit him," Martin insisted, "but I'm too scared to go out in the yard to see what I hit." A police check uncovered nothing, though Martin stuck to his story that the animal "reared up" after the second shot and fled in the darkness.

On the 12th a 100-man posse led by Deputy Witherby and H.B. Cottingham, a state conservation official, plowed through a cornfield and the woods near Middleboro. Earlier in the day, Cottingham, after studying the tracks near the Test Bridge south of Richmond, had expressed "an opinion only" that these were from "some type of wildcat." Other tracks, specifically those from Abington and Middleboro, were "different" and much larger.

Suddenly varmints were in other parts of Indiana as well. At Bedford, in the central part of the state, two lions were seen lying in a field near the Crane Naval Ammunition Depot on the 10th. One witness, Andrew Street, said he had hunted mountain lions before and knew one when he saw one. Armed Marine patrols were put on alert and ordered to shoot if they saw the animals. And at Gosport, over forty miles northwest of Bedford, William Sterwalt lost a 400-pound calf to something observer Keith McGinnis described as "long in body, black in color, with short perked-up ears and a long tail." It resembled a panther, he said. The same week Eugene Myers' dogs treed a screeching animal, but in the darkness Myers could not see exactly what it was.

Near Greenville, Ohio, twenty miles northwest of Richmond, Darke County Game Protector Robert Wiegand was investigating large tracks "definitely not made by a dog." After receiving several varmint reports, he interviewed George Royer, who at noon on the 19th watched a strange animal from a distance of twenty feet as it passed by the Slagle gravel pit. "I could not have mistaken it for something else," Royer said. "It was a black panther."

On the 22nd Orris Tate, a farmer in the Sand Creek, Indiana, area, found one of his pigs with claw marks four inches deep and several inches long over its right shoulder and with a hole under each of its front legs; miraculously it was still alive, though it died later in the day. In the ground nearby were mammoth five-inch tracks.

Near Peppertown on the morning of the 28th something jumped Henry Ferguson, Jr., from the rear while he was topping tobacco on a farm. He didn't get a good look at the animal, but it succeeded in tearing his trousers and shirt and cutting his arm before it streaked away. Ferguson's story started a flood of sightings in the area, about thirty miles southwest of Richmond. Most were of a big catlike creature dark yellow in color. There were more posses, now bigger than ever, and some shots got fired, but the prey never had any trouble escaping unscathed.

September 11 marks the last recorded 1948 appearance of the varmint. Harry Rodenberg and Ed Raffe, working on a roof at the Rodenberg farm, observed an animal "about the size of a wolf and having yellow spots." It did not harm any livestock.

For the time being Indiana had shaken itself of its nasty varmints. In January 1951, three persons at a farm near Noblesville in the central part of the state saw a giant panther, "five feet long and pitch black," which left tracks as big as the "palm of a woman's hand." It disappeared into a thicket along Stoney Creek after David Simons took a shot at it.

5.

Certain patterns begin to emerge, even though we have examined only a tiny fraction of the mystery cat reports in our possession. We have seen, first of all, the strange elusiveness of the beasts, shown in the absolute inability of even skilled hunters and trackers to kill or capture them (inevitably recalling Ivan Sanderson's dictum about Fortean phenomena in general: "we'll never catch them"). We have also noted their frightening hostility to human beings, and we have touched on the puzzling matter of clawed footprints.

With the 1948 Indiana varmints something new and extraordinarily significant emerges: a certain element of ambiguity enters the picture and we discover that reports don't quite "add up." Not only do we have sightings of three different kinds of unknown cats, we also have reports of a "hyena" and a "wolf with yellow spots." We will find that, the farther we pursue our Mystery Animals, the more difficult to follow the trail becomes.

Rather than detail the entire history of phantom cats in North America, an effort that would prove pointless and repetitive, let us consider a few representative incidents from the last three decades:

Abesville, Missouri, June 1945: A woman sitting with a baby in a shack near the town heard a scratching at the door. Opening it, she was terrified to see a huge catlike beast standing upright and staring at her. It had a long tail and big teeth, and in general did not look like anything she wanted to let into the house. She slammed the door and spent the next few minutes listening to it trying to break in. The following night it returned and again attempted to enter. When it left, she notified the neighbors, and dozens of them scoured the hollows trying to find it. Several of them got brief glimpses and one even got a shot at it.

For several weeks after, the locals lived in terror, hesitating to go out at night for fear of getting jumped. One person who did, a man named Warren, reported that it sprang at his truck and crashed against it several times trying to get in.*

Santee River, South Carolina, autumn 1948: Sam Lee, manager of the Rice Hope Plantation, and a companion, Troy T. Rogers, out looking for nighttime poachers, stopped at the White Oak Swamp about 10:30, got out of their truck and abruptly heard a "queer sound." Lee switched on his flashlight and saw a huge cat, "like a maneless lion," rear slowly upward and stand erect on its hind legs, staring eye level at the startled Lee, who was armed with only a small .22 rifle. Rogers was already back to the truck by the time it occurred to Lee to follow suit.

Queens County, New Brunswick, Canada, November 22, 1951: In yet another report of an erect panther,** we have this account from Herman Belyea, cited in Bruce S. Wright's *The Ghost of North America:*

> I was returning home about 6:00 p.m. I came to a pole fence and before crossing it hit it with my axe . . . within seconds I heard five loud yells off in the woods. . . . I walked about 100 yards further . . . when I heard four or five more yells. I looked back and saw it coming leaping. I ran a short way when it overtook me, so I had to stop and face it. When I stopped it stopped and stood up on its rear legs with mouth open and

---

*In a 1955 issue of *Missouri Conservationist*, Chief Biologist Dunbar Robb of the Conservation Commission's Mammal Unit, after noting that "reports of 'panthers' have persisted through the years from many parts of the state," conceded "at least a half-dozen sightings were unquestionable. . . . The return of the big cats [cougars: extinct in Missouri since 1927 and rare long before that] should not alarm anyone. They are not considered dangerous to humans. . . . Unfortunately, many people are obsessed with the idea that a cougar or a panther, as it is often called, has to be black. The truth is quite the contrary. . . ."

** Conventional panthers, we might note, do not stand erect.

"sizzling" and with forepaws waving it charged. I swung the axe at it but it jumped back and I missed, so I ran for it and whooped. It leaped off in the woods and I ran for the house but didn't run very far before I saw it coming again and had to stop and swing the axe at it. It jumped to one side so I ran for it and it ran off in the woods again. . . . It repeated the same thing over and over five or six times until I came to a field where I could see the lights of the houses; then it leaped off and never came back.

The animal was black or dark grey in color. The tail was at least two and one-half feet long, and the animal was at least six feet long.

Decatur, Illinois, September-October 1955: On October 25, Game Warden Paul G. Myers shot at and thought he had wounded a black panther near the central Illinois city. Panther stories had been circulating in the area since September 13, when a woman saw one slinking along the road. The next evening two truck drivers spotted it in the vicinity of Rea's Bridge. Other persons reported hearing its scream in the night. According to the *Decatur Review,* "The animal has been described as long, low-slung and jet black with gleaming eyes."

Monument City, Indiana, June 1962: A large tan-colored animal jumped farmer Ed Moorman and clawed him on the face one day as he was hunting in the woods. Moorman fired a quick round and the thing ran off. Later, after seeing it twice more in the distance, he called Sheriff Harry Walter, who quickly organized a search party. Finding nothing, the group went home.

Several days passed and on the morning of the 25th Moorman discovered ten of his pigs lay dead, the blood sucked from their necks, their sides ripped open so that the attacker could devour their hearts and livers. He called the sheriff again.

In the meantime "blood-curdling howls" in the night were keeping locals on their toes. One man, Everett Widmeyer, a student of wild animals and their habits, theorized that a 400-pound "African lioness," presumably escaped from a circus or zoo, was the culprit. At any rate, that was his impression from Moorman's description and from an examination of claw marks on a wooden fence gate.

When the lion made its last well-publicized appearance near Huntington, several farmers, Moorman among them, were waiting with rifles. Unfortunately two excitable city slickers, employees of an Indianapolis television station, opened up before the animal got in range and it fled out of sight.

Joliet, Illinois, July-August 1964: The Joliet panther actually appeared first one evening in April 1963 at a gravel pit near the DuPage County line. Two nights later, when it returned, it was observed by watchman Emmett McKaney and described as a "huge black leopard."

During July of the next year something hairy resembling a lion, "only larger," began prowling the outskirts of Joliet between the hours of midnight and 1:00 a.m. On one occasion it killed a large dog, and on another, as it passed a cemetery, J.J. Smith shot at it several times.

Suddenly everyone was seeing the creature, and within two days a full-scale panic was on. Joliet police reported taking hundreds of calls from individuals who claimed they had seen the thing. A ripped-open rabbit carcass was found on Joliet's Midland Avenue amid tracks of an animal evidently six feet long which a high school biology teacher asserted had to be a dog. Not long afterwards a "huge black animal, larger than a German shepherd," stepped out of the bushes of Midland Avenue and growled menacingly at two teenage boys. Hal Finkle told police he then threw a piece of pipe at it and the beast screamed and fled into West Park.

The next day City Manager Aaron Marsh, who had been doing everything in his power to stem the mounting public alarm, announced, "The case of the phantom panther is closed. The wild animal expert who was in Joliet identified the tracks as those of a large dog." As if to confirm the unnamed "expert's" claims, that evening Victor Gul was attacked in his barn by what he called a "boxer dog with a long tail."

On the 30th the *Joliet Herald-News* noted, "Although Joliet's case of the black panther was closed officially last week with the identification of tracks left in the vicinity of West Park as those of a dog, reports persist of continued sightings of an unidentified animal." The accounts came from outlying areas of the city, where witnesses saw a "big animal with black, smooth fur."

In mid-August officials dismissed the dog explanation after state police got a look at the animal themselves. They sighted the panther one night on a road near New Lenox (less than ten miles east of Joliet), did a double-take, and called in an airplane on the chase. The panther got away but at least authorities knew what it was—whatever it was.

Lamar County, Texas, 1965: Near the tiny village of Direct there were persistent reports of a Mystery Animal something like a panther. An article in the *Paris News* in July 1965 quotes a woman from Direct:

"We can expect it in the last part of June and again in October just before deer season begins. We figure it migrates through here yearly."

139

Direct residents called it a "manimal"* and said that it left tracks like a cat's except the claws showed. The prints were so large that a man could put both hands in one track.

The "manimal" made a sound that at first resembled the cry of a' wildcat, but soon the voice would begin to deepen and take on the quality of the screams of a man in pain. "Its wail is guaranteed to raise goose pimples," Direct citizens said.

The tracks indicated that the beast weighed about 190 or 200 pounds and ran on all fours in eight-foot leaps. In June it moved westward and in October it reversed direction and came back east.

A Direct woman described her first encounter with the "manimal":

"One evening as I was walking around the house with a flashlight, I turned at the corner of the house and I must have startled the thing as much as it startled me. It made one tremendous jump and left the yard. I hurried back into the house and called my cousin. We stood at the window and watched it as it crossed a fence and then stood on its hind legs staring back at us. It stood about six feet, two inches tall. Finally it walked away on all fours."

Illinois, 1970: Mike Busby's April encounter in Alexander County was only one of several strange phantom cat reports to take place in the state that year.

The first of these occurred in January, when an employee of the Macon Seed Company, west of Decatur, saw a large black animal he described as a "cougar." William F. Beatty told Loren Coleman that he himself had found tracks left by the animal. He also claimed that the thing twice tore down his electric fence. But not until two days after Beatty

* Obviously their use of the expression is different from ours.

had made his report did Game Warden James Atkins bother to investigate. Atkins concluded somewhat imaginatively that the animal was a beaver. A most unusual beaver, to be sure, since the footprints Beatty discovered were "very large" and had claw marks.

A month later and 75 miles away to the southeast, in Jasper County, Mrs. Donald Miller saw what she later described as an all-black cat as large as her German shepherd. Although not as tall as her dog, the cat was longer and had a tail at least as long as its body. The cat came within less than 150 yards of her house and she was surprised that *the dog continued to lie near the house and watch without even barking.*

Late in May, in eastern Winnebago County in the northern part of the state, astounded residents reported what one state trooper described as "a male African lion about eight feet long with hair growth at the end of its tail and a mane." One group of young men said it ran alongside their Volkswagen.

The weirdest incident of all happened on September 19. Six passengers moving along a highway near Pana encountered something they could neither explain nor comprehend. Alongside the road, a small tannish-gray pumalike animal suddenly appeared as if, in the words of A.V. Hamm, who saw it, "it just fell out of the sky." Later Hamm would attempt to convince himself that it had leaped out of a clump of bushes and only *seemed* to have materialized a few inches above the ground. But there was no way to account for the fact that *not everyone in the car could see it* even though it should have been clearly visible to all of them.

Fairfax County, Maryland, February 1971: A black panther prowling through the suburbs of Washington, D.C., killed three dogs and a horse, and

141

avoided an ambush set by two residents, George Correll and Lonnie Dennis, who hung a slab of deer meat on a pole and spent several fruitless nights waiting in hiding with high-powered rifles. The creature left four-and-a-half inch prints with claw marks in them.

Chippewa County, Michigan, November 21, 1972: About 7:30 a.m. Walter Wegner was hunting in the Munuscong Bay region when he heard what sounded like buck deer fighting in the brush. Soon the noises stopped. Three hours later Wegner examined the site and was amazed to discover the body of a 200-pound, ten-point buck, its bones stripped clean. Only the head and rack remained, except for teeth marks on the skeleton.

"There is no animal on the North American continent that can kill and eat a deer that large in such a short time," Conservation Officer Harold Hammond told the *Detroit News*. "A pack of animals might be able to do it, but we found no tracks."

A few days before, Wegner said, he had found panther tracks in the area.

The *News* remarked, "Stories of a mystery killer cat or some other animal have circulated for almost twenty years. . . . The mystery animal . . . has been sighted about a hundred times since 1954 in the area, the last time in 1969 about five miles from Wegner's Chippewa County cabin."

6.

Before we move on to explore the curious question of the "Surrey puma," let us consider briefly one final North American feline MA, this one from Mexico, where an elusive melanistic cat reputedly dwells in the western highlands. Robert Marshall treats the subject fully in his 1961 book, *The Onza*.

The onza, we discover, sounds amazingly like a member of the phantom panther troupe. Said to be about the length of the puma, it is a dark "smutty-gray" with a "dark chocolate streaking" along the spine. As with other mystery cats, the onza "has a foot that is not round, the foot being longer than broad, and . . . the claws are not entirely sheathed; the ends of the claws show in the tracks." It supposedly has been seen over a wide area of Mexico's great Sierra Madre Occidental by modern locals and the Spaniards for over three centuries.

Back in the 1770s Friar Baegert wrote that the onza had invaded his neighbor's mission while he was visiting and had attacked "a fourteen-year-old boy in broad daylight and practically in full view of all the people; and a few years ago another killed the strongest and most respected soldier in California."

Earlier in this century Dr. George Parker found the onza well known to the natives in the districts of the state of Durango. These people, who greatly feared the creature, described it as possessing "yellow eyes that look like balls of fire in the night"— again, the luminous eyes we have noted earlier. Parker called the onza "the most dangerous animal in the mountains."

Although Robert Marshall argues convincingly that another cat besides the jaguar and the puma is being sighted in western Mexico, he is unable to supply us with real physical confirmation to substantiate the claim. Marshall's examples of "slain onzas" seem to be nothing more than pumas. Like others before him, he fails to realize that he is dealing with something other than a conventional animal, and eagerly seizes upon dubious evidence to prove his case. Yet the truth appears to be that our mystery felines cannot be caught or killed, that in fact their elusiveness is basic to their nature.

7.

The history of British MAs is a long one and stretches back into the rich folklore of the Isles. We will deal with these earlier tales, which raise some complex questions, later in this chapter. For now, however, we will borrow from Fort, whose first British account is dated May 1810, when some unseen animal in the Ennerdale area, near the English-Scottish border, went on a rampage and proceeded to slaughter seven or eight sheep a night, biting into the juglar vein and sucking the blood.

Fort also tells us that over a four-month period in 1874 an animal leaving catlike tracks, complete with claw marks, roamed Ireland and killed as many as thirty sheep in a single night.

And during the winter of 1904-05, an incredible season when a hysterical religious revival, a rash of poltergeist infestations, a series of "spontaneous combustions," and a UFO flap all competed for space in the newspapers,* an unknown animal preyed on sheep along the River Tyne. Another appeared in Kent in March. This one was thought to be a jackal, and one was actually shot there about the same time. "There is no findable explanation, nor attempted explanation, of how the animal got there," Fort observed. At any rate, the attacks continued.

A year later, in March 1906, 51 sheep died in one night near Guildford, about seventeen miles from Windsor. Not long afterwards a "panther" grabbed a woman in a field. In October 1925 a creature

* See *The Unidentified,* pp. 116-19.

"black in color and of enormous size" slaughtered sheep in the district of Edale, Derbyshire, "leaving the carcasses strewn about, with legs, shoulders and heads torn off; broken backs, and pieces of flesh ripped off. . . . People in many places are so frightened that they refuse to leave their homes after dark, and keep their children in the house." *(London Daily Express,* October 14, 1925.)

Almost forty years later, we have the sorely-misnamed "Surrey puma," a creature or series of creatures which range far from the area that gave them their name, after a particularly well-publicized wave of sightings in that county in September 1964. As zoologist Maurice Burton, self-appointed debunker of the phenomenon, has written with understandable exasperation, "It was reported from places as far apart as Cornwall and Norfolk, over an area of southern England of approximately 10,000 square miles. It has even been seen in two places many miles apart at the same time on the same day. It seems to have been particularly disturbed during one week when its presence was reported from ten different places in half as many days."

The problem, of course, is that there are no pumas in Britain—a fact numerous witnesses blithely ignore as they continue to report seeing large catlike animals, while the "experts" pull their hair and scream "impossible." The much-beleaguered Burton assures us that the "puma" is actually a feral dog or cat— or otter, badger, fox or deer—as perceived by the hysterical and the imaginative.

Pardon us as we stifle a yawn and note simply that behavior that is unusual for a real feline is normal for our phantom friends. Burton is right, up to a point: We quite agree that *Felis concolor* does not exist in Britain. But it does not therefore follow that all reports of one are mistakes. Burton, like the people in the Illinois Department of Conservation who foolishly try to tell us that "the 'black panther' of Illinois is a black Persian cat, a Labrador retriever or a black Angus calf," is dealing with matters outside his area of expertise.

Perhaps the only real expert on the British mystery felines is our friend R. J. M. Rickard, editor of the excellent *Fortean Times* (formerly *The News*), to whom we are indebted for the information which follows.

The first known written account of what would become known as the Surrey puma appears in the September 1962 issue of the Mid-Wessex Water Board house magazine, where we are told that in August and September something "like a young lion cub—definitely not a fox or a dog" appeared near the Heathy Park Reservoir in Hampshire. Apparently these were not the first sightings in the area. In any case reports persisted through the end of the year.

Then on July 18, 1963, at Oxleas Wood, Shooters Hill, London, a lorry (truck) driver saw a "leopard" leap from the road into the park some time before dawn. Later that day four policemen reported that a "large golden animal" had jumped over the hood of their squad car and into the woods. A huge search involving 126 police officers, 30 soldiers and 21 dogs and covering 850 acres failed to produce anything but large footprints. The *London Evening News* for July 19 noted that this was not the first report of an MA in the area, and that a woman recently had seen a "wandering boxer dog with a curious spotted appearance." (Compare this with Victor Gul's Joliet, Illinois, report of a "boxer dog with a long tail" mentioned earlier. The story also calls to mind the 1948 Indiana animal "about the size of a wolf and having yellow spots.")

A "wild cat" was seen again in Heathy Park in September and October of the same year, and on

February 14, 1964, a "huge" animal with razor sharp two-inch claws left large prints sunk two inches deep into firm ground. The same month people in Norfolk were seeing a creature variously described as a "tiger," a "puma" and a "cheetah."

In September the Surrey flap began, with sightings spilling over into neighboring Sussex, Hampshire and Berkshire of the same or a similar beast, a gold- or ginger-colored giant cat with a long tail. A typical report came from West Sussex in early October, when a woman walking her dogs in the woods encountered a "puma" six feet long and three feet high, "fawn gold" in color. Her dogs chased it into the woods and the witness heard "spitting and screeching sounds." It left prints which showed clear claw impressions.

A stranger, certainly less typical "puma" appeared at Farley Mount, near Winchester, Hampshire, and was shot at by a gamekeeper, who called it a "black slit-eyed animal." A police search failed to uncover anything. At least that much is typical.

In August 1964, according to Burton, "an employee of a dairyman at Crondall . . . reported his minivan had run over 'a strange catlike animal,' which bent the front number plate, rolled under the vehicle, hit the underneath part of the car forcibly, and was then seen to bound over a hedge into a field of uncut barley." Burton, of course, finds this story thoroughly unacceptable; after all, no animal the size of the reported creature could have passed under the minivan, "which is flush, with no space for axles, and only five inches off the ground . . . and survived to leap a hedge."

This tale reminds us somewhat of the car/creature collision at Salem Heights, Ohio, mentioned in Chapter 1.

In the meantime, it is worth noting that throughout the area that fall something was killing and partially eating deer, sheep and cattle, leaving claw marks either on or near the carcasses.

By January 1965 there had been so many "puma" reports in Surrey that the police issued warnings to the public that such an animal might be wintering in the 4000-acre Hurtwood Common. On February 3 a "huge animal" leaped out of the bushes at Ashurst, New Forest, Hampshire, and was seen by a girl on a bicycle. She first thought it was a horse, but after recovering from the initial shock realized that it was "like a leopard" and had "ferocious eyes."

Sightings continued throughout 1966. The most curious of these occurred on September 1, when a woman farmer driving near Chiddingfold, Hampshire, stopped her Land-rover "for some unknown reason," got out and walked through a thistle patch, where she stepped on the tail of a "puma." The animal reared up and hit the woman in the face with both paws. She in turn struck it with a stick, causing it to run up a tree. She went for assistance, but by the time she returned, the thing was gone. A Ministry of Agriculture and Fisheries official found no tracks, just some hair.

On November 23 someone reported seeing a "lion" on a road near Coulsden, Surrey, but a subsequent police search failed to come up with anything.

The number of reported sightings diminished during 1967 and 1968, but by the fall of 1969 Englishmen were seeing panthers, some black, some brown. In December 1970 a "puma," which a number of Kent people claimed to have seen, was held responsible for the killing of four sheep near Dover.

The next year numerous persons, at least two of them police officers, encountered a pumalike animal in various parts of England. Since then sightings have continued unabated and it seems likely that the "Surrey puma" will remain as much a part of British life as UFOs. Rickard tells us that a Godalming police file contains over 350 reports from that area alone. If that is so, there must be thousands of sightings, of which only a comparative few have become public knowledge.

Three different types of cats figure in the reports. Rickard summarizes them thus:

a) Lynxlike: pointed tufted ears; doglike body; short tail; mottled markings.

b) Pumalike: heavy muscular body; small head; large paws; long thick tail; flat catlike face; sandy/mustard color, lighter chest and belly; round ears.

c) Pantherlike: much like above, but black or dark color, face less flat.

All of this, as we shall see presently, is only generally true. Meanwhile we note a couple of problems. Victor Head writes in an article in *Field* (April 18, 1965):

The puma is a big eater, generally resting up for two or three days between kills. Some authorities in the U. S. believe that it needs to consume one mule deer (300 lbs.) or its equivalent in other foods each week. As this is five times the average weight of a British Roe deer, a fully grown puma would need to kill 250 each year to live comfortably and free in Surrey.

And Burton writes:

Altogether, from September 1964 to August 1966, the official records show 362 sightings, and there were many more, possibly as many again, claimed but not officially reported. In other words this animal, declared by American experts to be "rarely seen by man," was showing itself on average once a day for a period of two years. The police . . . reckon that some 47 of the 362 are "solid" sightings. Even this means that this animal belonging to a species characterized by its highly secretive nature was showing itself about once a fortnight throughout a period of two years. In two years it was reported from places as far apart as Cornwall and Norfolk, over an area of southern England of approximately 10,000 sq. miles. It has even been in two places many miles apart at the same time on the same day. It seems to have been particularly disturbed during one week when its presence was reported from 10 different places in half as many days.

8.

On October 25, 1969, the occupants of a car driving down Exeter Road in Okehampton saw a "Great Dane" appear in front of them. Before they could stop, they had driven right *through* the "animal," which then disappeared.

At dawn one day late in April 1972 Coastguard Graham Grant, at watch over the harbor entrance to the beach at Great Yarmouth, noticed something out of the ordinary. "It was," he told the *London Evening News* (April 27, 1972), "a large, black hound-type dog on the beach. It was about a quarter of a mile away from me. What made me watch it was that it was running, then stopping, as if looking for someone. As I watched, it vanished before my eyes. I kept on looking for a time but it did not reappear."

Because bulldozers had recently leveled the beach, there was no place the dog could have disappeared.

Two years later, in April and May 1974, residents of Hampshire and Cheeshire reported a mysterious doglike animal. Some said it was "half cat, half dog."

We have here modern reports of a supernatural MA well known to students of folklore: the black dog, which is apparently a prototype of today's black panther. The black dog, however, is more clearly paranormal and has never been mistaken—for very long, at any rate—for a conventional zoological phenomenon. It figures prominently in the literature of witchcraft, in which Satan takes the form of a dark hell-hound with glowing eyes. To see it is to know that one is damned.

The most frightening of the early accounts is preserved in a report prepared by one Abraham Fleming, who claimed not to be repeating a folk tale but to be recording something he himself had witnessed—an event, he conceded, "which to some will seem absurd."

The incident supposedly occurred on Sunday, August 4, 1577, at Bongay, a town ten miles from Norwich, during a violent storm. Inside the local church the congregation sat in almost total darkness, the only light coming from frequent "fearful flashes of lightning."

Immediately hereupon, there appeared in a most horrible similitude and likeness to the congregation then and there present, a dog as they might discerne it, of a black colour; at the sight whereof, togither with the fearful flashes of fire which then were seene, moved such admiration in the minds of the assemblie, that they thought doomes day was already come.

This black dog, or the divel in such a likeness (God hee knoweth al who workcth all), runing all along down the body of the church with great swiftnesse, and incredible haste among the people, in a visible fourm and shape, passed between two persons, as they were kneeling uppon their knees, and occupied in prayer as it seemed,

151

wrung the necks of them bothe at one instant clene backward, insomuch that even at a momet where they kneeled, they strangely dyed.

This is a wonderful example of God's wrath, no doubt to terrifie us, that we might feare him for his justice, or pulling back our footsteps from the pathes of sinne, to love him for his mercy.

To our matter again. There was at ye same time another wonder wrought: for the same black dog, still continuing and remaining in one and the self-same shape, passing by an other man of the congregation of the church, gave him such a gripe on the back, that therewith all he was presently drawen togither and shrunk up, as it were a piece of lether scorched in a hot fire; or as the mouth of a purse or bag drawen togither with a string. The man, albeit hee was in so straunge a taking, dyed not, but as it is thought is yet alive; whiche thing is mervelous in the eyes of men, and offereth much matter of amasing the minde.

Moreouer and beside this, the clark of the said church being occupied in cleansing of the gutter of the church, with a violent clap of thunder was smitten doune, and beside his fall had no further harme: unto whom beeing all amased this straunge shape, whereof we have before spoken, appeared, howbeit he escaped without daunger: which might peradventure seem to sound against trueth, and to be a thing incredable; but let us leave thus and thus to judge, and cry out with the prophet, *O Domine,* etc.—"O Lord, how wonderful art thou in thy woorks."

. . . Now for the verifying of this report (which to soe wil seem absurd, although the sensibleness of the thing it self confirmeth it to be a trueth) as testimonies and witnesses of the force which rested in this straunge shaped thing, there are remaining in the stones of the church,

and likewise in the church dore which are mer-
velously reten and torne, ye marks as it were of
his clawes or talans. Beside, that all the wires,
the wheeles, and other things belonging to the
clock, were wrung in sunder, and broken in
peces.

And (which I should haue tolde you in the
beginning of this report, if I had regarded the
observing of order) at the time that this tempest
lasted, and while these storms endured, ye whole
church was so darkened, yea with such a palp-
able darknesse, that one persone could not per-
ceive another, neither yet might discern any light
at all though it were lesser then the least, but
onely when ye great flashing of fire and lightning appeared . . .

On the self-same day, in like manner, into the
parish church of another towne called Blibery,
not above seve miles distant from Bongay above
said, the like thing Entred, in the same shape
and similitude, where placing himself uppon a
maine balke or beam, whereon some ye Rood
did stand, sodainely he gave a swinge downe
through ye church, and there also, as before,
slew two men and a lad, and burned the hand
of another person that was there among the rest
of the company, of whom divers were blasted.

This mischief thus wrought, he flew with wonderful force to no little feare of the assembly,
out of the church in a hideous and hellish
likenes.

A straunge and terrible Wunder wrought very
late in the parish Church of Bongay, a Town of
no great distance from the citie of Norwich,
namely the fourth of this August in ye yccrc of
our Lord 1577, in a great tempest of violent
raine, lightning, and thunder, the like whereof
hath been seldome seene. With the appearance
of an horrible shaped thing, sensibly perceiued
of the people then and there assembled. Drawen

into a plain method, according to the written copye by *Abraham Fleming*.

Black dogs are not solely a British phenomenon. Stories of their appearances can be found in American folklore texts. Often these incidents are reported not as popular yarns, but as actual experiences of the informants. Theodore Ebert of Pottsville, Pennsylvania, gave this fairly typical account to George Korson, who printed it in his *Black Rock: Mining Folklore of the Pennsylvania Dutch:*

One night when I was a boy walking with friends along Seven Stars Road, a big black dog appeared from nowhere and came between me and one of my pals. And I went to pet the dog but it disappeared right from under me. I couldn't see where it got to. Just like the snap of a finger it disappeared. Well, I'll tell you, I had about two miles to go to get home, and I made it in nothing flat. I never seen anything like that and I never hope to see anything like it again. This happened later to others. No one in the locality had a dog of that type and it was seen by others with practically the same experience. No one could ever explain why or where it came from.

The following story, which Sidney Benton of Horncastle, Lincolnshire, related to British Fortean Nigel Watson, is of particular interest to us, for reasons which will become clear very shortly:

It was during the winter months of 1922 and 1923, when I was employed at a small local dairy, my job was to fetch up the cows from the fields, help to milk them and then deliver it to local people.

Part of my deliveries took me to one of the

oldest parts of town. I usually took a short cut by going past an old Iron Foundry, over a small bridge with a water-wheel near it, then by the back of the Vicarage and past the old church-yard. On this particular evening I had made my deliveries and had just climbed over the small wooden palings on my way back to the dairy, when all at once, right in the center of the path, appeared two great bright shining eyes.

I called out thinking the dog from the dairy had followed me, but got no answer. I climbed back over the fence and stood there almost petri-fied with fear. I don't know how long I stood there but suddenly the eyes were just blotted out. I must have been braver then than I am now, for I took my courage in both hands and got back over the fence and walked back over to the spot where the eyes had been.

My employer and his wife and niece, noting that I looked white and frightened, asked the reason. They informed me that the dog had not left the dairy. After this experience, I was always sent on this particular part of my deliveries in daylight. On mentioning my experience to an old lady neighbor, she said that the spot was reputed to be haunted, as some people had been drowned when the ice gave way on the moat of what used to be an old castle there. A workmate friend tells me that he had seen the same thing years earlier.

It was such a long time ago, but all I can remember of that night are the eyes appearing quite suddenly, only a few yards in front of me, at about two or three feet from the ground. I do remember that everything was still and quiet and that after what seemed quite a few minutes the eyes were just blotted out. I have always been convinced that this was something very strange and the attitude of my employers at the time strengthened my belief. They did not wish to talk about it, and would never let me go that way at night afterwards; and also someone would accompany me when I had to take the pony to the field at nights.

At almost the same time, between 1921 and 1923, D. R. Clark, the father of Jerome Clark, had a remarkably similar experience. It left such a vivid impression on him that when he recalled the incident in May 1976, he said, "I can still see it clearly as I talk now. It was the strangest experience I've ever had."

It began one evening as he was walking home with his parents, Mr. and Mrs. A. L. Clark, from a church function on the north side of LaCrosse, Wisconsin. He was five or six years old at the time. About a block from their house he noticed "something that looked with shining eyes, with the face of a dog." The eyes were yellowish-gold in color, with no detail in the center. The teeth were also luminous but not so bright as the eyes. Behind the eyes and mouth young Clark had the impression of a "dark black body" about the size of a rat terrier.

Frightened, he called his parents' attention to it, but they could not see it. They assured him it was only his imagination at work and they went on their way.

One evening a week or two later, as the three of them passed the same spot, once more returning from church, Clark saw the apparition again. As before, it was on the boulevard side of the sidewalk, halfway through the block where the light from the streetlights was dimmest. Again the child was terrified. Again his parents couldn't see it.

Not long afterwards, the thing appeared for the third and final time, as usual when the family were coming home from church at night. Young Clark was walking on the outside, closest to the creature, and this time when he saw it, he overcame his fear sufficiently to kick at it, only to discover, just as if the thing were anticipating just such an action, his foot landed inside its mouth and it bit down on his shoe. The startled boy could feel its teeth. When he screamed, the black dog vanished and he never saw it again.

The following incident took place during World War II and was reported in a letter to writer Janet Bord:

The cottage where we lived is still in existence, in Bredon, Worcestershire. My encounter took place one late afternoon in summer, when I had been sent to bed, but was far from sleepy. I was sitting at the end of the big brass bedstead, playing with the ornamental knobs [the witness was a young girl], and looking out of the window, when I was aware of a scratching noise, and an enormous black dog had walked from the direction of the fireplace to my left. It passed round the end of the bed, between me and the window, round the other corner of the bed, towards the door. As the dog passed between me and the window, it swung its head round to stare at me—it had very large, very red eyes, which glowed from inside as if lit up, and as it looked at me I was quite terrified, and very much aware of the creature's breath, which was warm and strong as a gust of wind. The animal must have been very tall, as I was sitting on the old-fashioned bedstead, which was quite high, and our eyes were level. Funnily enough, by the time it reached the door, it had vanished. I assure you that I was wide awake at the time, and sat for quite some long while wondering about what I had seen, and to be truthful, too scared to get into bed, under the covers, and go to sleep. I clearly remember my mother and our host, sitting in the garden in the late sun, talking, and hearing the ringing of the bell on the weekly fried-fish van from Birmingham, as it went through the village! I am sure I was not dreaming, and have never forgotten the experience, remembering to the last detail how I felt, what the dog looked like, etc.

The years following World War II bring UFOs into the black dog picture. In the first chapter we looked at a Savannah, Georgia, report of ten black dogs running from a landed UFO.

There is also a 1963 story from South Africa. Two men driving at night on the Potchefstroom/Vereeniging road were startled to see a strange, large doglike animal cross the road in front of them. Curious, they stopped, only to have a UFO buzz their car several times, frightening them severely and driving all thoughts of the peculiar animal out of their heads.

The following fascinating account comes to us via letter from Betty Hill, herself a percipient in a famous and much-publicized UFO case:

In the spring of 1966, Eliot, Maine, was the scene of unusual UFO activity. They came up the river in early evening in groups, night after night. Since this river runs by the flight line at Pease AF Base, they had numerous planes flying, as well as helicopters, and private planes. So it was a spectacular sight—with the sky full of UFOs and flying craft. People came for miles —traffic was bumper to bumper. Police called in police from other areas to direct traffic. People had telescopes, cameras, binoculars. Someone had set up a huge searchlight in a field. Pushcarts sold hot dogs, hamburgers, snacks, cold and hot drinks. In the two to three months that this activity covered, many strange things happened.

One night a group of prominent people from Portsmouth [New Hampshire] decided to go to Eliot to watch the UFOs. After driving around in a caravan of three or four cars, in all the traffic, they decided to pull over in a gravel pit and watch the skies. They all got out when they saw a huge dark "dog" run through the pit. This dog was larger than any they knew so they decided to try to follow it. They ran through the pit, but unfortunately for the last one in the line, he was stopped by a strange odor. He tried to identify it, and as he was standing there, suddenly a form glided towards him. The form was giving off this odor and he had the feeling he was to follow this gliding form. He broke away and ran back to the car, and told a person who remained behind what had happened. She got out of the car and called for the others to return to the car.

Fortunately they did, for at this moment, the first man jumped out of the car, saying that he had to go back, and started for the woods. The others grabbed him and held him until he quieted down, and then they all left the area, promising not to reveal what had happened. This was told to me in confidence by two who were there, but I do not know the identity of the others involved, although there must have been a large number—possibly 20 or more.

In the previous chapter we have discussed the paranormal manimals which have haunted western Pennsylvania in recent years. Stan Gordon, the leading investigator of the occurrences, has written (MU-FON 1974 UFO Symposium Proceedings):

Besides the reports of large hairy bipeds being observed . . . there were sightings of animals

159

about as large as a German Shepherd dog. These animals baffled the witnesses because they couldn't figure out just what kind of animal they were looking at. The creature looked like a cross between a monkey and a dog. It had a tail with rings around it and large red eyes. These creatures at times came up on people's porches and were scared away by the occupants of the house. The witnesses normally were attracted to the creature by the sound of a crying baby, which they speculated that someone had dropped off. When they went to the porch, they found the creature making the sound.

9.

On July 8, 1970, the *Topeka Daily Capital* editorialized about some peculiar events in Kansas:

> Even in this practical era when people take scientific marvels for granted, many quickly turn to the supernatural if they can't explain something that has happened.
>
> Nearly everyone has a mysterious episode to relate which apparently defies rational interpretation.
>
> Whole communities can become involved, as witness reaction to several incidents which have taken place near Humboldt Hill, south of Iola [Kansas]. As background, it is explained that the area is reputed to be the location of an Indian burial ground.
>
> Twice recently, motor vehicles traveling nearby have experienced strange losses of power in their electrical systems and conked out.
>
> Add to this a report that cattle stampeded in fright from a pasture at the top of the hill and

there is grist for the superstitious to grind in their mills.

Some even report having seen strange lights and sighting large cat tracks. How the latter ties in with the former isn't explained either.

But people do love mysteries—as shown by the rash of flying saucers reported sighted some time ago.

Then there was the Perry Panther and other such manifestations . . .

Mike Busby's experience suggests that there may well be a connection between MAs of the phantom cat variety and auto stoppages, which are usually associated with UFO sightings. Ufologists, who believe that UFOs are the products of a superior extraterrestrial technology, theorize that such stoppages are caused by the objects' propulsion system. An interesting idea, but it is by no means clear how it applies to such incidents as one that took place in 1969, along the Choccolocco-Iron, Alabama, road, where all that spring residents had been reporting creatures they called "boogers" and "varmints."

A man is said to have shot at one of the things, causing it to run back into the hills uttering "an almost humanlike cry." "It's darn scary when you hear it," one witness said. "Like something from another world."

Late in May of that year a man driving down the road between Choccolocco and Iron saw a "varmint," described as faintly resembling a humpback combination of bear and panther, appear out of nowhere and force him off the road.

The following night Johnny Ray Teague and three companions were on the same road when their car abruptly stalled. While they were out looking at the motor, they heard something crashing through the leaves and branches. Before they knew what was happening, the "booger" was upon them—so close, in fact, that they could hear it breathing. They jumped back into the car, rolled the windows up, locked the doors and sat petrified with fear as the creature circled the car several times.

It was, they would claim later, "awful looking," the size of a cow, gray to black in color, humped similarly to a camel, with a large head and prominent teeth. It did not try to attack the witnesses.

Soon after the creature had disappeared back into the woods, the car miraculously started right up and the occupants sped away. Half a mile down the road they saw "three or four" more of the creatures, larger than the first.

A Surrey puma story directly links UFOs and a phantom cat. The story was told by Edward Blanks, who farmed near Godalming and who claimed that over a two-year period between 1962 and 1964 the puma had regularly crossed his land and unnerved him with its "yowling" cries. When Charles Bowen, editor of *Flying Saucer Review,* came to the farm to investigate, he discovered the following:

Part of Mr. Blanks' routine is to make the rounds of his farm before retiring for the night. On two occasions he suddenly became aware of a mysterious light on the roofs of the farm buildings. The light moved from roof to roof, yet he could not see the beam which produced the light. It was certainly *not* produced by car headlights from the Odiham Road: the local topography precluded that possibility. Mr. Blanks could not trace the source of the light, and he was puzzled and worried by the phenomenon, because on each occasion the mystery puma arrived on the scene shortly afterwards!

We are reminded of A. V. Hamm's Pana, Illinois, experience when we read this item from an article by Eileen Buckle in *FSR Case Histories* #6:

Recently a young man related . . . a remarkable low-level sighting he had at the age of 15 when traveling by car with his family. An apparently solid object kept pace with the car for 20 minutes. All the family saw it clearly, except the father. Strangely, he was unable to see it at all.

10.

There seems little doubt that our mystery felines are not conventional animals but paranormal phenomena of some kind. We base that conclusion upon these considerations:

1.) *Their appearance.* Black pumas are extremely rare and far too many of them show up in the reports we have examined. African lions, for another thing, do not live in the wild in midwestern America. Neither do cats have "glowing" eyes, nor do they leave tracks with claw marks in them.

2.) *Their geographical distribution.* Our MAs appear in areas where conventional large cats either have long been extinct or have never existed.

3.) *Their behavior.* They are extremely hostile to human beings, unlike normal cats. They stand, and even walk, on their hind legs. They are seen frequently, whereas "real" felines, which are very shy, are seldom observed. They sometimes appear in "waves" during which other unknown animals are observed.

4.) *Their elusiveness.* There is no conclusive physical evidence of their existence. No bodies have ever been found and none has ever been killed. Bullets seem not even to affect them particularly. They have managed to elude innumerable large posses over the years.

5.) *Their tie, direct and indirect, with other MA, UFO and psi phenomena.* Car engines may stop in their presence. They may make sounds similar to those heard in other "monster" and poltergeist manifestations. They may materialize suddenly and be selective as to whom they appear. There may also be a certain ambiguity in the descriptions when they are compared to one another.

Before we begin to make sense of all of this, we must go down to south Texas and follow the path of other, even more bizarre Mystery Animals.

CHAPTER FIVE

Things With Wings

1.

By the time we had come to the Rio Grande Valley, in early March 1976, Big Bird was already old hat. When we'd ask about it, people would almost invariably laugh and say, "That was a long time ago," when actually it had been only a couple of months before.

But memories are short there, because life is fast and busy, as fast and busy as the big cars that barrel down Highway 77 on what the promoters proudly call the "longest Main Street in the world," which moves south from Raymondville through a couple of small towns, and down to Harlingen less than twenty miles away. Harlingen fades into San Benito, which soon becomes Olmito, which fades into Brownsville. What little distance separates the cities and towns is bridged by an unending string of farms, barbeque (or, as the signs always have it, "BBQ") stands, Mexican-food joints and roadside bars. "The

Lower Valley towns are so closely linked with rural districts," the tourist guide says, "that the whole area is largely urban. It is the most cosmopolitan district in Texas."

The Rio Grande Valley is not, in short, a wild and primitive place. In fact, the wild and primitive areas in the depressingly overpopulated region are few. One, in eastern Willacy County near Port Mansfield, is on private property owned by the famous King family. It houses an assortment of unlikely animals, including the nilgai, 900-pound antelopes imported from India, and the javelina, piglike mammals which are often dangerous. The birds there include ducks, Canadian geese, storks, cranes, herons and even African cattle egrets, blown over to Texas which keep ticks off grazing cattle. A fairly exotic collection, to be sure, but there is nothing there that is anything like the Big Bird—even though many people insisted, often with a certain unmistakable note of desperation (or at least exasperation) in their tones, that there was, and that it had to be one of the above.

But it wasn't. Not *the* Big Bird anyway.

If you were gullible or indifferent enough, you could believe birdwatcher Gladys Donohue of Mission, who asserted it was nothing more than a large barn owl. Of course, she conceded, barn owls don't look at all like what witnesses were reporting, but then she had an explanation for that, too: "People don't always see what they think they see."

Television stations and private individuals contributed to the nonsense by offering rewards for the Bird's capture, then hastily withdrawing them when zoologists "identified" it as the great blue heron, an endangered species protected by some of the harshest conservation laws in the books. That, however, did not stop gun-toting teenagers from taking to the back roads in search of the thing. And the Bird's presence, real or imagined, gave at least one drunk a story to tell his wife when he staggered home late at night from a barroom brawl—the Bird, he said, had attacked him. And a young Brownsville farmer roared down a country road late one night, terrified that the Big Bird was about to get him, while behind him a pelican sailed in hot pursuit.

There was, it seemed, no end to the silliness. But there was also the Big Bird, and that was quite something else.

2.

Armando Grimaldo says he "wasn't drunk and wasn't smoking marijuana or anything like that" when it happened. What he was doing, he insists, was sitting quietly in his mother-in-law's back yard on the north side of Raymondville and smoking a cigarette. His estranged wife Christina, whom Grimaldo had come to visit, lay sleeping inside. It was 10:30 p.m., January 14, 1976.

"Then all of a sudden," he claims, "I heard a sound like the flapping of batlike wings, and a funny kind of whistling. The dogs in the neighborhood started barking. I looked around but I couldn't see nothing. I don't know why I never looked up. I guess I should have, but as I was turning to go look over on the other side of the house, I felt something grab me, something with big claws. I looked back and saw it and started running. I've never been scared of nothing before but this time I really was. That was the most scared I've ever been in my whole life."

Grimaldo saw it just long enough to determine that it was as big as he was (5'8"), with a wingspan of from ten to twelve feet. Its face was bat- or monkeylike, its eyes two or three inches round and

167

bright red. It did not have a beak and its "blackish-brown" skin looked leathery and was featherless.

Grimaldo could manage no more than a scream at that point—and a face-first sprawl into the dirt when he attempted to propel himself to safety. As he struggled back to his feet, he felt his pants, coat, and shirt being ripped open, his flesh remaining curiously untouched—a feature of the story which would generate as much skepticism as wonderment in the days and weeks to follow. Finally he dashed under a tree and his attacker, now breathing heavily, elected to pursue the matter no further and lumbered off into the night and back into the nether regions.

Christina Grimaldo, who had been awakened by her husband's shouting, came downstairs just as he stumbled through the back door and gasped that something had attacked him from out of the sky. Christina immediately phoned the police, who rushed to the scene and found Grimaldo "in some kind of shock," muttering *"pajaro"* (Spanish for bird) over and over again, still incapable of speaking coherently. He was taken to the Willacy County Hospital and released after half an hour when doctors found there were no physical injuries. Nonetheless, the distraught Grimaldo spent the next two days in bed.

A month and a half later, when we made the rounds in Raymondville inquiring about the supposed incident, the story had become something of an embarrassment to the community, even to Grimaldo's family, who responded to questions about it with either giggles or scowls.

Sheriff Oscar Correa discounted the story entirely. "Oh," he said, "I think he was sincere in what he said. But I firmly think it didn't happen as reported. If this was real, there would have been one or two scratches on his flesh. A bird's going to land on the head if it's going to attack, not on the feet or back. If there were such a thing as this bird, the people we have out on the roads would have spotted it by now."

And in any case, two days after Grimaldo's alleged encounter, Conovia Tijerina had called the sheriff's office to report a huge gray bird with a long beak sitting immobile in the middle of a field three and a half miles northeast of Raymondville. It proved to be a dead pelican. So the mystery of Grimaldo's sighting was "solved"—and never mind that the bird he said he saw was dark brown, not gray, and possessed neither beak nor feathers.

Unfortunately it was still not clear who or what killed Joe Suarez's goat during the early morning hours of December 26. Suarez, a Raymondville resident, had left the animal tied up in a corral behind his barn the night before. The next morning he found it ripped to pieces. Mauled from the right side, the goat lay in a pool of blood, the heart and lungs missing, the snout cut or bitten away. The blood was still wet and warm when police officers examined the carcass. There were no footprints around the body.

Armando Grimaldo was not, by any means, the first Texan to claim an encounter with "Big Bird," as someone dubbed it after the Sesame Street television character. There was, for example, this story which James Rowe, a retired Corpus Christi newsman, recalled hearing many years ago from a man who ran a grocery store along Corpus Christi Beach:

"It was on the Nueces River back before they built the Wesley Seale Dam [in 1958]," Rowe said. "He was fishing up at Swinney Switch with a rod and reel and something grabbed his hook and took off downstream. The thing almost took all of his line before he got it turned around. Then it headed upstream just about as far.

"He fought it and fought it. Then finally the thing just climbed out of the water on a sandbar across the

169

river from where he was standing. It was this creature with fur and feathers and it just took the hook out of its mouth. Then it climbed up a tree.

"The fellow had a pistol in his tackle box, so he took it out and started to shoot at the animal. Then as he took aim, the thing just flew away."

If that sounds suspiciously like a Texas tall tale, the rumors that began in Rio Grande City in November 1975 perhaps deserve more serious consideration, though they are difficult to substantiate. The rumors, which were in circulation before the Big Bird story hit the papers, had it that various citizens, including children, Mexican-Americans and "winter" Texans (northerners who reside in the Valley during the cold months), had observed a "man-bird" skulking about in the darkness. The creature, supposed to be about four feet tall, had a bird's body and a man's head. It was spotted—during nonbusiness hours, we're assured—on the roof of a tavern north of town. Another story had the thing above the Starr County Courthouse, a story which Sheriff Ray Alvarez, who presumably should know if anyone does, discounts as nonsense. Certainly the witnesses seemed as reluctant to step forward and identify themselves as other townsfolk seemed eager to spread wild and unsubstantiated tales.

The first report—that is, an account with which names, places and dates can be connected—is curiously unimpressive, despite the massive media attention and the quality of the witnesses. The witnesses, Patrolmen Arturo Padilla and Homero Galvan, watched a white "stork or pelican type of bird" sailing over San Benito, 75 miles east of Rio Grande City, at 5:15 a.m. on December 28. The two officers, who were in separate squad cars, described the bird as having a foot-long neck "that sort of bent as it glided."

It seems virtually certain that this particular sighting was in fact of a white pelican, a larger than ordinary white pelican, possibly, but still a white pelican. Actually, that is what Padilla and Galvan now believe it to have been, we were told. The bird's estimated wingspan, twelve to fifteen feet, is only slightly larger than the ten-foot span of many pelicans, and it is always possible that the early morning darkness and mist may have caused the bird to appear larger than it really was. Moreover, pelicans retract their necks when they fly.

The San Benito report probably would have received little attention if it had not been for a weird incident that occurred just four days later in neighboring Harlingen. The witnesses were Tracey Lawson, 11, and her cousin Jackie Davies, 14.

The sighting, unlike most of the others, took place in the daylight hours. On January 1, while the children's parents slept off the excesses of New Year's Eve, Tracey and Jackie were playing in the Lawsons' back yard, which faces a plowed field five miles south of Harlingen along Ed Carey Road. Suddenly Tracey noticed something standing a hundred yards away. Dashing inside, she picked up a pair of binoculars and returned to focus on a "horrible-looking" huge black bird. It was over five feet tall and had big, dark red eyes, with wings bunched up at its shoulders, which were three feet wide. Its face was "gorillalike" and gray, and its sharp, thick beak was at least six inches long. The head was bald. On one occasion during their sighting the thing made a loud, shrill *eeeee* sound.

Tracey and Jackie were stunned and frightened. The next thing they knew, the creature, which had been standing near a borrow pit which borders an irrigation canal, had disappeared—apparently, the parents inferred later, running or flying low through the pit—only to reappear on the northeast corner of the property, its head poking above a small clump of trees. That was all Tracey and Jackie cared to see. They went inside the house and stayed there.

When the parents finally awoke, the children told them what they had seen. Perhaps understandably the adults did not take the story seriously.

The next day, however, Jackie's stepfather, Tom Waldon, went out to look for tracks, still skeptical of the tale but concerned at his stepson's insistence that it was true.

The tracks were there. Waldon did a double take before kneeling down to examine them carefully. The first three were close to the fence behind the house. The fourth print was twenty yards out into the field and the fifth twenty yards beyond that. The tracks were three-toed, eight inches across, square at the head, and were pressed an inch and a half into the hard ground.

Waldon called Mrs. Lawson, who was at work. She phoned the Cameron County Sheriff's office and then her husband, who raced home to find that an officer had already beaten him there.

Stan Lawson, who weighs 170 pounds, pressed his own foot down alongside the bird print and found it made practically no impression. "That thing must have been pretty heavy," he said later.

He noticed something strange about his dog's behavior, too. All day it cowered inside the doghouse, leaving it only once, at suppertime, when Lawson went to feed it and it bolted through the door into the main house. It had to be dragged back outside. And that night, around 10:00, Lawson heard something like large wings scraping across his bedroom window screen, but he saw nothing. In the morning he discovered that there was a tear in the screen. He was not sure if it had been there before or not.

Among those who came to talk with the Lawsons after the incident had been publicized on the local television station was Sgt. Sam Esparza of the San Benito police force. Esparza, who lives in the same general area as the Lawsons, told them—and confirmed to us later—that the night of January 1 he had left his house at 10:00 and returned at 11:00. Looking into his back yard, he was startled to see blood on some of the clothing that had been hanging on the line. Two of the four stained items had large, dark stains, rather, he thought, like liver that something had chewed on and disgorged. His wife, who had been inside all the while, had heard nothing. The dog hadn't even barked. As a matter of fact, the Doberman, an animal not known for its timidity, seemed oddly frightened. Apparently, unlikely as it seemed, it had been *too scared* to bark.

Esparza uneasily recalled that the night before something had whammed into his trailerhome. Of course this had happened during a windstorm, but afterwards he hadn't been able to find the cause. He was by no means certain that there was a connection; on the other hand, he was by no means certain that there *wasn't* a connection, either.

On January 7, at 8:30 p.m., Alverico Guajardo of Brownsville heard something hit *his* trailer. Unlike Esparza, Guajardo dashed outside immediately to see what had happened. "It was a little like somebody was shoving something against the trailer, maybe a sack of cement," he recalled.

Guajardo, who did not own a flashlight, got into his station wagon, drove it slowly around the south side of the trailer and shone his headlights on "something from another planet." As the lights hit it, the thing, which had been lying on the ground, suddenly rose up and stared at Guajardo with blazing red eyes the size of silver dollars. For the next two or three minutes it stood gazing at the man, who sat immobilized with fear.

The creature was four feet tall, with black feathers

173

and a beak whose length Guajardo estimated at between two and four feet. It was making a "horrible-sounding noise" from its throat, which he could see pulsating. Its long, batlike wings were folded around its shoulders.

While Guajardo watched it, the thing backed carefully toward a dirt road three feet away. By the time Guajardo had gathered enough courage to bolt out of the vehicle toward a neighbor's house, it was just vanishing into the darkness.

The next morning, at 9:30, reporter George Cox of the *Brownsville Herald* interviewed Guajardo, who was plainly still terrified. "You could see this was no jive," Cox told us later. "This guy did see something. He's the most convincing Big Bird witness I've met so far. If any of these stories are legitimate, this is the one."

3

By this time Big Bird had become a Valley sensation, but it was being played strictly for laughs, and for ratings. Harlingen's KGBT-TV, which had been first on the scene when the Lawsons reported the Bird and the tracks, led the way with assorted contests to draw or explain the Bird, though privately news director Ray Norton discounted the story. "People have been seeing something, no doubt about it," he said. "They may be seeing a common bird and imagining the rest of it."

Jack Grimm, an Abilene, Texas, geologist who put up a $5000 reward for the Bird's capture, narrowed down the possibilities to three *un*common birds. The first was an Abyssinian ground hornbill, which stands four feet high and sports a four-foot wingspread. Grimm does not explain, however, how the bird made its way from sub-Saharan Africa, its usual abode, to Texas, nor does he tell us why not one witness remarked on its bright red, decidedly unmonkeylike face.

Grimm, an energetic and imaginative man whose enthusiasms include the Loch Ness Monster and the search for Noah's Ark, suggests the jabiru stork as another possible explanation, though the jabiru's dark eyes, red and black neck, white wings, and long black legs again do not match witnesses' descriptions. The marabou stork, Grimm's final candidate, sounds more promising, if only because of its enormous size (four and a half feet) and wingspan (ten feet). Unfortunately, marabous reside in central India and Borneo. In addition, their backs, wings, and tail are slate gray with green iridescence. The wings, moreover, have white edges on the outside and are completely white on the underside.

David Thompson and Don Farst, resident zoologists at the Gladys Porter Zoo in Brownsville, dismissed as "extremely improbable" a theory held, for example, by the Lawson parents, who had not seen the thing themselves, that the Bird was actually a California or Andean condor, neither of which is native to south Texas, nor matches observers' descriptions.

That left those resolutely determined to find a conventional explanation with two alternatives: a pelican and a great blue heron.

The pelican was almost certainly the cause of some reports, as we have seen. The great blue heron undoubtedly generated at least one report (and probably others). This one report led at least one newspaper to bury the mystery a bit prematurely, proclaiming in a headline, "Legend of Bird Is Dead."

In reality, what had happened was that one day in early February farm workers south of Alamo had panicked at the sight of a large bird roosting in a fruit orchard. They quickly spread the word and within the hour a crowd of fifty had gathered, among them a television reporter who shot footage of the fowl as it stood, looking slightly bored, in the orchard's plowed turf. When the film was shown, bird watchers and zoologists had no trouble identifying the subject as a great blue heron.

The great blue heron, an endangered species protected by federal law, is native to south Texas but still not a particularly common sight. The excitement its appearance at Alamo caused says more about the hysteria the Big Bird scare generated than it does about the Big Bird itself, which looked not at all like the heron, a silvery-blue and white creature with a long, winding neck.

Another Big Bird sighting, this one near Laredo, was most likely of a great blue heron. On January 14 Arturo Rodriguez, nineteen, and his nine-year-old nephew were fishing on the banks of the Rio Grande when they heard a rustle of leaves, looked up and saw a large gray bird gliding over the river at a height of approximately fifty feet. They did not stick around to study the sight, choosing instead to scurry home. Two hours later Roberto Gonzalez saw the bird over U.S. Highway 83, which runs parallel to the river.

The bird's appearance and habits—herons forage along river banks and stand silently in or near the water while watching for fish—suggest that this was a big bird (the heron) but not *the* Big Bird.

But apparently the ill-tempered beast which an Eagle Pass man reported was neither.

At 12:45 a.m. on January 21, so the story went, the man had just arrived home and had stepped into his back yard when he spotted a large something stooped over near a clothesline post. Before he knew what was happening, the thing made a hissing sound, jumped him, ripped into his shoulders, and then hopped off. He described it initially, according to the police report, as having "a brown or almost black body, bright red eyes and the wings of a bat . . . short, stubby legs and two arms, each about two and a half feet long. It had pointed ears, the face of a pig, but didn't have a snout." Investigators found mysterious feathers and hair at the scene.

At first these investigators took the story seriously —a UPI account noted, for example, that this was "the first such attack being given credence by officials"—especially after an Eagle Pass physician testified that the wounds, clawlike marks three and a half inches long and half an inch deep, had almost certainly been caused by a large bird or animal. The witness, furthermore, agreed to take a lie detector test, once a Spanish-speaking operator could be found. The man spoke no English.

But unfortunately for those who were trying to find some firm evidence for Big Bird's existence, the story proceeded to collapse in the days that followed, a fact about which the press was oddly silent. Nonetheless an Engle Pass police officer who participated in the investigation, and who has asked not to be identified, passed on the following information to us:

1). Because of the man's past history, local officers regarded the man as unreliable.

2.) The police had interviewed him four times. There were major conflicts between the first account and the second one, and further, less dramatic conflicts in the subsequent versions. The first day, for instance, he said the thing had feathers, the next day that the skin was featherless, leathery and batlike.

3.) The feathers proved to be from a member of the redbird family, while some of the hair was linked to a domestic cat and the rest to a javelina.

4.) The doctor whose testimony had seemed to substantiate the man's report was a close personal friend of the alleged witness. No other physician agreed that a bird or animal had caused the wounds.

The wounds, they said, looked as if they might have been inflicted with cut glass.

5.) None of the man's neighbors had heard anything unusual at the supposed time of the attack. Neither, evidently, did the neighborhood dogs, which did not bark. Across a street a huge mastiff had not made a sound.

6.) Though the Eagle Pass police did locate a Spanish-speaking polygraph operator, the man repeatedly begged off taking the test, giving increasingly unconvincing excuses each time.

Still, the officer hedges his bet slightly by conceding, "There's a possibility it could be true." But not a very great one, apparently.

The report three San Antonio elementary school teachers made on February 24 was something else entirely. Patricia Bryant, Marsha Dahlberg, and David Rendon, driving to work down an isolated road southwest of the city, were startled to see something with a wingspan of "15 or 20 feet, if not more." The enormous bird swooped low over the cars, casting a shadow that covered the entire road.

"I could see the skeleton of this bird through the skin or feathers or whatever," Mrs. Bryant said, "and it stood out black against the background of the gray feathers."

Rendon added, "It just glided. It didn't fly. It was no higher than the telephone line. It had a huge breast. It had different legs and it had huge wings, but the wings were very peculiar like. It had a bony structure, you know, like when you hold a bat by the wing tips, like it has bones at the top and in-between."

Oddly, the same time they were watching the mysterious bird, they saw another unusually large flying object. This one was off in the distance circling like a buzzard over a herd of cattle. It resembled, the teachers thought, an "oversized sea gull."

The first bird, though, was unlike anything they had ever seen. But when they got to school, they rummaged through a set of encyclopedias until at last they found what they had seen: a pteranodon. The only trouble with that was that the pteranodon, a kind of flying dinosaur, has been extinct for about 150 million years.

The teachers were not the first to call the Bird a pteranodon. That achievement went to two sisters, Libby and Deany Ford, who in mid-January spotted a "big black bird" near a pond several miles northeast of Brownsville. "It was as big as me," Libby said, "and it had a face like a bat." Later, paging through a book on paleontology, they came upon a drawing of a pteranodon and concluded that was what they had seen.

Jesse Garcia and Vanacio Rodriguez may have seen the same thing on January 11. Checking out a stock tank on a ranch just north of Poteet, the two sighted a five-foot bird standing in the water. "He started flying," Garcia said, "but I never saw him flap his wings. He made no noise at all." Paleontologists believe that pteranodons and their cousins, the pterodactyls, did not actually fly but used their enormous wings to glide through the air.

The San Antonio sighting was the last Big Bird sighting to make the papers. In fact, it came a month after skeptics, whose numbers included virtually everybody but the witnesses themselves (plus a few reporters who had actually bothered to talk with the witnesses), had declared the Bird a dead issue and press attention had drifted back toward more conventional media pursuits. We did not arrive on the scene until after the scare had run its course. Almost everyone we met was either perplexed, amused, or annoyed when we told them of our interest in gathering material on Big Bird.

But as we probed into the incidents, it became

179

clear that something, or *somethings,* called Big Bird did exist, that it was not a conventional bird, and that it was more than a delusion born out of the folk imagination. Nearly everyone subscribed to some version of this theory and newspapers gave prominent play to old Mexican folk tales about flying monsters, strongly implying a connection, while failing to note that some of the witnesses were northern-born Anglos.

Furthermore, the armchair theorists did not bother to ascertain whether or not there is a *living* folklore about giant supernatural birds, and whether those who claimed to have seen the Big Bird related the thing to this folklore.

4.

And so it was that we ended up in San Benito hearing stories about the mysterious bird that had haunted the La Palma section of the city for at least thirty years.

We came upon the story purely by accident. We had driven to the San Benito police station in hopes of interviewing Officers Padilla and Galvan, who had seen the pelican the press had transformed into Big Bird, and found ourselves desperately trying to convince a hostile desk officer that we should not be thrown out into the street. Discouraged, we had begun packing up our notebook and tape recorder when Lt. Ernest Flores, who had been listening to the exchange, beckoned us into his office.

"You might be interested in this," he said, searching into a file cabinet. He retrieved several jars of some kind of fecal material and handed them to us. "We've been getting them from a young guy who lives around here. He thinks they're from Big Bird."

The droppings were dried, whitish lumps about one inch thick and two to three inches long.

"We don't have the facilities to analyze this stuff," Flores went on, "and we really don't know where to take it. But I'm sure there's something to it. The guy who brought it to us is honest and intelligent and we know him well. He's telling the truth about it. We've studied this material informally and we've found things like Johnson grass, grain, fragments of hair and even a whole cockroach. In one dropping there's even an inch-long bone, something from a skull, it looks like.

"We've even had some possums in here and had them eliminate. This doesn't look like possum waste. It's not from an owl either. An owl spits out its droppings in pellet form.

"Whatever this thing is, it appears to have a very primitive digestive system."

Flores' informant and supplier proved to be nineteen-year-old Guadalupe Cantu III, a thoughtful, intense young man who had lived in San Benito all his life. Cantu told us that after graduating from the local high school he had worked until recently as a carry-out in a supermarket. Now unemployed, he planned to enter vocational school in the near future. In the meantime he was obsessed with finding out what had caused the droppings.

His father had discovered them on the roof of the house in May 1975. "That was before the sightings of Big Bird, you know," Cantu remarked, "so there was no fuss about it. That was the first droppings but that was what got me interested in climbing up the roof to see if I could find others.

"I live on the city limits near the City Power and Light plant. I first heard it—the Bird—when I was eight years old. I was living in the same house I live in now. I was inside and suddenly I heard a cat sound from up on the roof. The dogs were barking at it. It was real heavy and we heard it for over an hour. Then I heard it fly away and there was no more cat sound.

"Everybody's heard it, my grandparents, uncles, aunts. It makes a cat sound and two other sounds. I've heard just the 'meow' sound and the other, a very rough sound like an eagle or a horse would make, only once. The other sound is a clacking sound, like teeth. Well, of course, I've heard the wings flapping. You can tell the Bird must be pretty big but I've never seen it."

We glanced a bit incredulously at Lt. Flores and another officer, who were sitting by impassively during the interview. Obviously they had heard the story before.

We drove with Cantu down to nearby Brownsville with two jars of feces, which we showed to Curator David Thompson of the Gladys Porter Zoo. Since zoo spokesmen had made it clear some time earlier that they did not care to involve themselves in the Bird controversy, we carefully refrained from using the offending word in Thompson's presence. It did not stop him from asking us, after we'd inquired about "what kind of bird" he thought might have dropped the feces, "You think they might be from Big Bird, right?"

Fortunately he took it all in good humor, explaining that the zoo had no facilities for analyzing feces. "Besides," he said, "it's very difficult to determine what kind of animal made the dropping just from the dropping alone. You can tell what it ate, and that's about all." Thompson theorized that the droppings were from a possum.

At this writing the droppings are being analyzed by scientists connected with the Society for the Investigation of the Unexplained, a New Jersey-based group founded by the late Ivan Sanderson.

As we headed back to San Benito, we asked

Cantu if he would introduce us to some of the other witnesses he had mentioned. "Oh," he said, "they won't talk. They're too shy. They don't want their names in the papers. They know that people will make fun of them."

We said we could understand that. "But how do we know you're not making all of this up out of your head?"

Cantu was silent for a while, then said he would see if he could persuade some of the people to talk with us. When we met the next day in front of the San Benito police station, he had one of the supposed witnesses with him, a man who asked to be identified only by his first name, Chris.

Chris, twenty-six, a bus driver and part-time carpenter, is a life-long resident of San Benito. Shyly, occasionally laughing in embarrassment, he told us, "Yes, I've heard the Bird. I've even been close to it but I've never seen it.

"When I was thirteen or fourteen—about the time I dropped out of school—I used to go out and come back home about 1:00 or 2:00 in the morning. That's when I would hear it. It would make a sound like *tch-tch-tch,* with a whistle, very loud. I told my mother about it. She'd heard those sounds before and she warned me not to be out when it's around because it's a bad bird. She said a lady around here was beaten by the Bird. Another lady, she's dead now, saw it often through her window. Another woman said it has a cat face and no beak. The face is a foot in diameter and it has a thick, foot-long neck. It has big eyes.

"In 1964 or 1965, during the summer, my cousin and I had gone to the drive-in and I came home late through the alley. I could hear the Bird following me. I ran. I was very frightened. I told my mother, 'The Bird's after me!' My mother, dad, and sisters went out. We couldn't see nothing because we didn't have a flashlight. My father hit the tree where the Bird was with a broom until finally it flew to another tree in our neighbor's lot. Three dogs were barking, with their teeth showing. We never did see the Bird. We could just hear it moving among the leaves on the trees.

"Then about three weeks ago [mid-February] something heavy fell on the roof of our house. The TV antenna began shaking. I had a rifle but I didn't want to go out, but not because I'm afraid. I've been living with this for a long time. When I was young, it kind of followed me, you know. That hasn't happened lately, though.

"I used to pick cotton when I was young. Around Santa Rosa. There was a very old lady who would talk about it. That's when I first heard about it. She was scared. She talked about it like it was an evil bird."

"My uncle saw it in 1945," Cantu interjected. "It was an extremely large bird. My father saw it, too, also another uncle. It was a very, very big bird. My father saw it twenty years ago, flying at tree-top level. It had a white breast.

"I could get you twenty people, like that," he added, snapping his fingers. "But they're afraid, too, shy. The descriptions are all the same. They say it has a cat face."

First in the company of Cantu and Chris, and later alone, we drove down the streets of the La-Palma Colony, the name given the Mexican-American neighborhood on San Benito's northwest side where the sightings supposedly occurred. The first person we talked with was Chris' mother, Leonor, a small, wrinkled 62-year-old woman who does not speak English. As our two companions did the talking and translating, we watched her as she vividly reenacted the Bird's cries and motions.

She said, according to the translation, that it was

true about the Bird. She had first heard it when Chris was about twelve, one day when she was out feeding the rabbits. It was in a tree, which she pointed to, and making a whistling, clicking sound, which she imitated. She had seen it around 10:00 one evening last year as she was coming from church. It was a big white bird and it flew across the street.

Over ten years ago a lady named Ignacia—she did not know her last name—had been walking to the outhouse when the Bird attacked her from behind. She had heard it flying and was just turning around when it ripped into her with "long, long" claws and tore off some of her clothing. (As Leonor spoke, she enacted the clawing with her own thin, almost bird-like arms.) It had an ugly, catlike face, enormous wings, black feathers, and no bill. The woman, who had been ill long before the attack, was dead now and had left no relatives.

Later, we stopped a young woman on the street and asked her if she knew anything about a strange bird in the neighborhood. Frowning, clearly reluctant to speak, she finally said, "Yes, it is true. We've heard it. It makes a lot of noise and sometimes we can hear it walking on top of the shack back of our house. There was a lady who lived down the street and the Bird attacked her. But she's dead now. That happened a long time ago, over ten years."

She pointed to a house where she said the woman lived. We went over and knocked on the door, but no one was home. Maybe just as well. The young woman had told us that the people living there now were not relatives. The woman had left no relatives, so far as she knew.

A forty-year-old car mechanic related his experience with the Bird three decades earlier, when he was eleven. He and a friend had been lying on top of a trailer filled with cotton, parked between a truck with a small trailer attached and a barn. Suddenly they heard a flapping sound from behind the barn. Soon an enormous bird glided over the barn and passed by about twenty feet above the ground. Its wingspan surpassed the combined length of the truck (twelve feet) and the attached trailer (seven feet), putting the size at well over twenty feet. He did not see its face but saw that it had no feathers.

Tony, twenty-seven, said he and his wife-to-be had seen something very strange in August 1966. "It was about 1:00 a.m.," he recalled. "Maria and I were sitting in the car over by my mother's house and we saw this thing standing on a telephone pole. It was dark so we couldn't see well but I could see enough of it to know I'd never seen anything like it. It was a weird big bird, bigger than a man, a yard wide, with wings folded around it. It was black. We could see it staring at us. We ran over to my mother's house. I haven't seen or heard it since.

"One time in 1967 my mother was sleeping in the living room and she heard something flapping against the house. She was too scared to go outside.

"Once a bird hurt a woman. A little boy was scratched, too. Everybody knew about it."

Maybe everybody did know about it, but we were never able to get direct confirmation of the supposed incident. Nonetheless the story fits so well into the pattern that we are willing to accept it as something other than pure folklore.

There seems little real question that something very weird indeed has been taking place in San Benito for at least the past thirty years, and it is irrelevant to point to old superstitions as the stimulus for the alleged sightings. The hoary legends the newspapers revived did not seem to be part of the living folklore of the LaPalma Colony. The people we talked with, even the old ones, either had never heard the old stories about *Lechuza* (a girl who, having been rejected by her suitor, turned into a bird and attacked evil-doers), or did not connect them with what they had seen. The Bird was not viewed as a supernatural omen. It was "bad" and "evil" for a very simple reason: it attacked people.

That is not to say that a certain folklore had not grown up around it. For example, one informant assured us the Bird was "known" to hide every night in a big tree on Virginia Street, near a certain man's residence. When we called on the fellow in question, our questions were greeted with blank incomprehension. Finally the man said that not only did he not harbor the Bird in his yard, he did not even believe in its existence.

The incidents in San Benito continue. On April 7, 1976, Cantu, whose honesty and common sense we, like the San Benito police, had come to respect, wrote, "My aunt heard it walk on the roof twice since the day you were gone. She said it sounded loud . . . The dogs were barking at it. I got on top of the roof and walked on it. I asked my aunt if she heard me . . . She said no. This kind of gives you the idea of how heavy or strong that bird really is." April 20: "Since the last time I wrote to you, Big Bird stopped on a tree at my aunt's home. The bird stopped at 5:00 a.m."

While Texas' Big Bird was the one that got all the attention, it was not the only one being seen anywhere. On January 1, 1976, Dr. Berthold Eric Schwarz, a Montclair, New Jersey, psychiatrist, author and parapsychologist whom we have already mentioned in another context, was driving down Highway 46 past the quarry near Great Notch when suddenly he spotted an enormous long-necked bird sailing by, hardly flapping its wings as it flew close to the ground.

"I wouldn't have thought anything of it," he said to us, "except that it was so huge and its wings didn't

187

seem to be flapping much at all. But what disturbed me the most was that it was so white, even as dark as it was. *How could it have been so white?* Unless— I know this sounds ridiculous—it was luminous."

But the weirdest one of all appeared on Easter Sunday, April 17, 1976, at Mawnan, Cornwall, England. The witnesses were two girls, June and Vicky Melling, who were there on a holiday outing from their Preston, Lancashire, home when they saw a grotesque-looking "big feathered bird-man" as it hovered over the church tower. The sight so upset them that the family cut their holiday short and returned to Preston three days early.

Fortean investigator Doc Shiels interviewed the girls' father, Don Melling, who gave him a sketch of the thing which June had drawn that same day. The sketch, reprinted in the June 1976 issue of Bob Rickard's *Fortean Times,* shows an unbelievable phenomenon which almost defies description. Firm believers in the old saw that one picture is worth any number of words, we reproduce the drawing here:

The same or a very similar creature was allegedly seen on July 3, 1976, by two fourteen-year-old girls who were camping among the trees near the Mawnan Church, where the first sighting took place. Around 10:00 p.m. they heard a peculiar "hissing" sound, which made them look up and observe a weird figure standing in the trees about twenty yards away.

"It was like a big owl with pointed ears, as big as a man," Sally Chapman told Shiels. "The eyes were red and glowing. At first, I thought it was someone dressed up, playing a joke, trying to scare us. I laughed at it, we both did, then it went up in the air and we both screamed. When it went up, you could see its feet were like pincers."

Barbara Perry added, "It's true. It was horrible, a nasty owl-face with big ears and big red eyes. It was covered in gray feathers. The claws on its feet were black. It just flew straight up and disappeared in the tree-tops."

The sighting lasted only a few seconds.

Shiels separated the two girls and had them draw sketches of what they had seen. The drawings were very similar, though Sally thought Barbara had "done the wings wrong." Sally depicted the wings as being more birdlike, whereas Barbara's illustration showed somewhat humanlike arms with feathers attached. Neither picture precisely matches the one above, but the differences can perhaps be explained as the product of faulty observation caused by poor lighting conditions, the brevity of the sightings, and the extreme fright they evoked in the witnesses.

The next day three women saw the "Owlman" in almost the same spot. This letter from Jane Greenwood of Southport appeared in the *Falmouth Packet* for July 9:

"I am on holiday in Cornwall with my sister and our mother. I too have seen a big bird-thing like that pictured . . . It was Sunday (4th) morning and the place was in the trees near Mawnan Church, above the rocky beach. It was in the trees standing like a full-grown man, but the legs bent backwards like a bird's. It saw us and quickly jumped up and rose straight up through the trees. My sister and I saw it very clearly before it rose up. It has red slanting eyes and a very large mouth. The feathers are silver gray and so are his body and legs. The feet are like big black crab's claws. We were frightened at the time. It was so strange, like something out of a horror film. After the thing went up there were crackling sounds in the tree-tops for ages. Our mother thinks we made it all up just because we read about these things, but that is not true. We really saw the birdman, though it could have been somebody playing a trick in very good costume and make-up. But how could it rise up like that? If we imagined it, then we both imagined the same thing at the same time."

Big Bird (or, at any rate, a big bird) returned to Texas for some final appearances in December 1976. This time, however, it was in east-central Texas, not the Rio Grande Valley. And this time someone shot it and got some physical evidence, which is being analyzed at we write this.

On the afternoon of December 8, John S. Carroll, Jr., a Montalba area hog rancher, was walking out of a shed in his back yard when he saw an enormous bird standing in the middle of a pond a hundred feet away. It was trying to fly but seemed to be having a difficult time getting airborne. Stunned, Carroll stared at it for a few moments, observing something about eight feet tall, bluish steel-gray in color, with a golden-hued breast and a twelve-inch bill.

"I was thinking that I didn't want a thing that

big hanging around my place, that I had no idea what it was or what it might do to my pigs," Carroll said later. He dashed to his pickup to retrieve his deer rifle. As he did so, the bird took flight, heading north several hundred feet, then circling briefly before rising above the ravine to the northwest. Finally it alighted in a hardwood tree and stood on a limb about 25 feet above the ground.

"When it settled on that limb," Carroll said, "the whole tree shook and vibrated violently. That bird must weigh 100 pounds."

By this time the rancher was ready to shoot, even though he knew the distance—about a thousand feet —was fairly large. Carroll sighted the target through the scope, squeezed off a single shot and was amazed to see the bird drop from the tree and out of his range of vision.

Neighbor Mike Ellis heard the shot and, thinking Carroll had fired on a deer, came over to help. The two of them raced to the scene but found nothing, at least at first. As they broadened the area of the search, they discovered a blood-stained feather 75 feet from the tree.

Carroll did not exactly hasten to the local newspaper office to tell his story. "I didn't call the newspaper for fear folks would think I was losing my marbles or was drunk," he explained. "What would you do if you saw something almost as big as a horse flying?"

But then he heard of a similar sighting made by a youth from nearby Palestine, Texas. Carroll called the witness, Donnie Simmons, and the two compared notes. Reporter Ernest Jones heard of the incident from a friend of Simmons' and soon after interviewed the reluctant Carroll.

On December 17 Carroll, one of the leading swine breeders in Texas, gave the feather to Palestine biologist Larry Lamely, who in turn sent it on to Steve

Wylie, curator of birds at the St. Louis, Missouri, Zoo. Carroll, who once lived near the Arkansas National Wildlife Refuge, home of the whooping cranes, said he was familiar with many varieties of large birds, but the thing he saw was none of them. Lamely showed Carroll several books which contained numerous pictures of birds, and still the rancher was unable to identify it.

The resulting newspaper publicity caused several other persons to admit they had seen the bird prior to its appearance on Carroll's land. After that, on December 17, a Bethel, Texas, woman named Dolois Moore saw the thing through a window of her home. She described it as "very large, like a big crane seen through a magnifying glass . . .

"The bird was about 150 yards away from me. Our big Brahman bull was trying to get close to the bird. Every time he did, the bird took wing and flew off a short distance, then resumed feeding in our oats and rye pasture."

Mrs. Moore said it appeared to have an injured wing. Her place is fifteen miles northwest of the Carroll farm.

A further sighting was made by a woman near Catfish Creek, three miles south of the Moore residence, on the morning of December 22.

5.

Winged weirdos are hardly new to the American landscape. The first Americans, the Indians, spoke of giant flying creatures they called "thunderbirds." Sightings, or alleged sightings, are made from time to time even today. In Anglo-American folklore the "Jersey Devil" is often described as a manlike bird with horns.

But if the legends are the stuff of fantasy, there

remain the testimonies of many living persons who attest to the existence of Unidentified Flapping Objects. Undoubtedly the weirdest of all was something called "Mothman," the subject of a 1975 book by John Keel *(The Mothman Prophecies)*.

Mothman, named after a character in the once-popular Batman television series, first showed up in the Ohio River Valley before anyone thought to give it a name—as long ago, apparently, as 1960 or 1961, when several unpublicized sightings were made. It was not until the fall of 1966 that the residents of the Valley realized they had a visitor, one which, though distinctly unwelcome, stayed fourteen months and introduced itself to over a hundred persons, none of whom were pleased to make the acquaintance.

Mothman was usually described as being between five and seven feet tall, gray in color, with large glowing red eyes set in or near the top of the shoulders. The wings, which had a spread of ten feet or so, did not flap in flight.

As usual, there were certain variations from the common description. A few witnesses said it looked like an enormous winged man. Two said they thought it might be a machine of some kind, because they had heard a mechanical humming sound as the thing passed overhead. Obviously Mothman, like most monsters, had something for everyone.

It certainly had something for the authors of this book.

In April 1976, after Jerome Clark had returned from his investigatory jaunt through the Rio Grande Valley, he was interviewed by telephone by Vic Wheatman, who hosts a Fortean radio show on Boston's WBUR-FM, and Loren Coleman. The interview, taped for later broadcast (it eventually aired on May 24), went without incident. It was only when Wheatman and Coleman played the tape back that they realized something extremely odd had occurred.

Midway through the conversation Coleman had asked Clark if he saw any similarity between the Big Bird reports and the "Mothman" reports ten years earlier.

"Very definite similarity," Clark replied. "Now, John Keel, of course, is the man who did the research on Mothman. Keel claimed that there is a connection between these sightings and UFOs. If there's any such connection with the Big Bird, I was unable to prove it. . . . All I know is that this thing doesn't have any business existing in the Rio Grande Valley or anywhere. This is really something out of the ordinary. I have no idea where it is coming from."

As he spoke these lines, Clark heard nothing out of the ordinary on his end. Neither did Wheatman and Coleman on theirs. Yet on the tape, immediately after the word "sightings" in the third sentence, there is a loud, unmistakable and very startling EEPPP! sound—precisely the sound Mothman is supposed to have made. ("It squeaked like a big mouse," one of the original Mothman witnesses had commented in 1966.)

When radio station personnel heard the sound, they could offer no explanation, unless it originated with Clark, which it didn't.

And now, our journey through wonderland completed, it is time to make sense of all this nonsense.

CHAPTER SIX

Phantasms

1.

Throughout this book we have had occasion to refer to UFOs, but their role in all of this has never been too clear. In some cases these creatures, especially the manimals, have appeared to be UFO occupants. In other instances UFOs have been sighted in areas where people were encountering creatures, and the link between them has only been implied. Most of the time UFOs have not entered the picture at all.

Whatever the case, we think this much is clear: *UFOs and creatures are generated by a single paranormal mechanism.* The parallels between the phenomena are undeniable:

1.) *Both are far more elusive than they have a right to be—if they are what they appear to be.*

Both have given us what Dr. J. Allen Hynek calls an "embarrassment of riches." We plainly have far too many of them. Extraterrestrial spaceships simply could not be touring the earth in the massive numbers UFO sightings suggest. The mathematical foundations for this statement are ably explained in Chapter 28 of Carl Sagan's *The Cosmic Connection,* to which we refer interested readers. Neither could massive numbers of large unknown animals be roaming countrysides and city streets without long ago having been officially recognized and catalogued (and probably driven into extinction as well).

Moreover, they could not have done all this in such numbers without providing us with more conclusive physical evidence than they have given us so far. The "physical evidence" is always just enough to suggest that the reported manifestation was not purely hallucinatory; it is never enough to prove that it was objectively real. And the "physical evidence," most often ground traces in the form of landing marks (as in UFO cases) or tracks (creature cases), less frequently physical parts in the form of metallic residue or hair, is frustratingly ambiguous and inconclusive. The ground traces differ from incident to incident, and at best some are only very generally similar. The investigator cannot use them to predict the kind of trace a particular kind of UFO or creature will make. The alleged physical parts are invariably agonizingly ambiguous. The most one can expect from them is the suggestion that their cause *could* have been an unknown craft or creature. More often, however, the alleged evidence proves to be something completely mundane.

2.) *They appear in a wide variety of shapes but tend toward certain very general types.*

As we have shown in *The Unidentified,* there are so many different kinds of UFO beings described in the reports that if they are extraterrestrial they must be coming from at least a thousand different planets. Nonetheless most of them do have one head, two arms, and two legs and most are small in size. Many of the dwarfs are said to wear what look like "diving suits."

Beyond that, though, the similarities end for the most part. (There is a small minority of incidents in which precisely similar beings have been observed in different areas.) The humanoids have big heads, little heads and medium-sized heads; bug eyes, slanted eyes, one eye, or no eye; long noses, short noses, or just two holes where a nose should be; a lipless slit for a mouth, a fishlike mouth, or a "normal" human one; any number of fingers or claws on the hand; just about any shade of skin color; and so on and on.

For reasons of space (and maybe sanity, too) we have confined ourselves to several basic creature types, but as we noted in the introduction, that does not mean a virtually endless number are not reported. For instance, a Montana woman recently discovered a huge glob of jellylike substance in her front lawn. An English policeman named Bishop encountered a "walking fir-cone" in a park in Ramsgate, Kent, on April 16, 1954. During the summer of 1969 a number of Texans reported seeing a "half-man, half-goat thing with fur and scales."

Godfrey H. Anderson claimed that while strolling down an Edinburgh, Scotland, street on November 23, 1904, he saw a "vague black shape about four feet long and two and a half feet high" rise out of the gutter. It was shaped, he said, "like an hourglass and moved like a huge caterpillar," and it sprang at the throat of a horse, which abruptly reared up in terror. While it was doing so, the thing vanished.

In 1951 a Calumet, Oklahoma, farm woman spotted a creature that "looked like a cross between a wolf and a deer." Something very similar appeared to two hunters near Canby, Minnesota, on March

27, 1971. That same year a quadrapedal "wolf-woman" terrorized the Delphos, Kansas, area. On July 4, 1974, a father and his two sons observed "a medium-sized dog with a monkey face" and a curved, monkeylike tail leap across a country road near Oakland, Nebraska.

Obviously, we could go on and on* but we hardly need belabor the point. Still, as with UFO occupants, certain creature types predominate, despite their considerable variety. The Texas Big Bird sightings provide the most graphic demonstration of this principle, as we have seen, but even among the relatively "stable" manimals we encounter such variations as:

a). Two-, three-, four-, five- and six-toed tracks, plus varying shapes even among tracks with the same number of toes.

b.) Eyes that glow red, green, orange or yellow, and eyes that do not glow at all.

c.) Long, ape-length arms and shorter, human-length ones.

d.) Machinelike behavior and animal-like behavior.

e.) Enormously huge, broad-shouldered specimens and others that are relatively slender.

f.) Ones that stink and ones that don't.

g.) Some that have large fangs jutting out of their mouths and some that have no visible teeth.

h.) Ones that resemble "apemen" and others that resemble "wolfmen."

3.) *People who see them may experience other types of paranormal phenomena as well.*

Witnesses may find themselves plagued with poltergeists or visited by men in black. They may

* Those who care to pursue the matter should consult *The Books of Charles Fort* and John A. Keel's *Strange Creatures from Time and Space.*

receive odd, sometimes threatening phone calls, or receive psychic "revelations" of an apocalyptic nature. They may find that car engines die mysteriously or electric lights fade when the manifestation is near.

These kinds of things happen to relatively few percipients, and usually only to those who have had some sort of prolonged exposure to a UFO or a creature. The considerable majority of sightings are of short duration and are free of either obvious paranormal content or subsequent paranormal fallout. John Keel has suggested that when a rash of manifestations break out in an area one person or one family is actually the target; it is he, she, or they who are subjected to the whole range of paranormal infestation. Other witnesses are just outsiders whose sightings are of no particular significance, since these people are seeing nothing more than the most obvious surface manifestations. We don't know at this point if that is really the case or not, but it is an extremely interesting idea that researchers should bear in mind during future investigations.

4.) *The phenomena encompass "opposite" qualities at the same time.*

UFOs are at once "technological" and "magical." They look like machines but they behave much like ghosts or fairy-ships. Many of their allegedly extraterrestrial occupants resemble angels (in several instances they have even identified themselves as such!), and so the manifestations are "scientific" and "religious" at the same time; the angels are androgynous beings, with features of both male and female; and so on. The supposed technical powers of the ufonauts (their abilities to vanish instantaneously, to paralyze witnesses, to stop vehicles, and so on) are identical with the supernatural powers long attributed to fairies and other mythical folk.

Creatures may resemble biological animals. Up to a point they may even behave like them, sleeping, eating, defecating, even showing some evidence of a sex drive. There may even be apparent "creature families." Yet at the same time a creature seen eating food on a sandy bank will fail to leave footprints—an apparition, it seems, with purely biological hunger. In other cases the creatures may give every appearance of being zoological while acting mechanical. In the UFO-related episodes, creatures from our evolutionary past manifest in the company of, or even inside, vehicles from our technological future. Werewolves and demon-dogs prowl the countryside while spaceships from other planets zoom overhead.

Most of all, though, UFOs and creatures seem both to exist and not to exist. Neither their existence nor their nonexistence can be proved. They are like fantasies that have come mysteriously, and briefly, to life. Trying to establish their reality is like trying to preserve a revelation one has had in a dream. One of the authors remembers a dream he had several years ago in which he was told how to levitate himself through the air. In the dream it seemed a simple enough matter, and as he felt himself starting to awaken, he thought frantically, "I've got to remember this!" But the instant his eyes opened, the secret was gone.

Likewise, percipients of strange phenomena struggle to prove the things they have encountered are "real." Like D. K. and innumerable others, they seek frantically to hold on to something—a body, a mechanical implement, a new truth—which will survive the encounter and will place it in "this" world. They never succeed. They grasp for the substance and touch only the shadow.

Man is trapped between his past and his future. On one hand he looks beyond the dust speck which has always been his home and gazes out into the unimaginable reaches of infinity, wondering what, and who, waits out there, knowing that one day, inevitably, his curiosity will overcome his qualms and he will go out there to find what he must find.

He is of two minds about it. That future, that prospect, fascinates and frightens. Will he find salvation there? Or beings so superior that all human endeavor seems a futile joke by comparison?

Even more immediately, as his burgeoning technology directs him inexorably toward some distant cosmic perspective, that technology begins to trouble him deeply. Looking about, seeing the terrifying uses to which totalitarian states have put technology, he wonders if it will ultimately enslave him—or already has. Will it also destroy the planet he lives on? He sees the development of weapons of hideous destructive power. He sees the forests disappearing, rivers turning into streams of sewage, whole species of animals disappearing daily, while human beings are packed tightly into little boxes from which they fear to emerge, lest savages who prowl the streets after dark knife them for pocket change.

It is not particularly surprising that the Age of Ecology should follow the Age of Space. It was not so much a rejection of the prospect of space travel as the fear of the technology that sired the Space Age, which caused human beings to think about their role in the terrestrial natural order. The understanding grew that in some way human physical and spiritual survival was tied to the preservation of the natural environment, that if we were surrounded by nothing but machines we might become such ourselves. Nature, once feared and hated, once seen as something from which one must escape, now seemed a more benevolent place, the true home of the soul.

Skeptics have often remarked on what a coincidence it is that, just when we began thinking seriously about space travel and space beings, "spaceships" started showing up in our atmosphere. The implication is that UFOs are nothing but delusions born of the cultural imagination. That is only half true. The skeptics have failed miserably in all their myriad efforts to prove that what are called UFOs are nothing but misinterpreted conventional phenomena and hoaxes. Yet believers in UFOs as spaceships have failed just as fully to make their case. All that we have been able to establish so far is that something unknown, something which has the *appearance* of being extraterrestrial, is being seen and reported with great frequency. Evidently, in some mysterious fashion, our own psychological obsessions created corresponding physical phantasms. As Fort remarked, "If our existence is an organism, in which all phenomena are continuous, dreams cannot be utterly different, in the view of continuity, from occurrences that are said to be real."

The UFO occupants, as we came to "know" them through repeated encounters and contacts, proved to be a curious lot. While they seemed to possess an advanced technology, they were forever warning contactees that technology is dangerously two-edged and that the uses we have made of it are all wrong. Some ufonauts, especially those of the androgynous "Venusian" variety, seemed as much priest/philosophers as scientists. "I would say that their religion and their science are all in one," one contactee observed. They constantly warned percipients that *homo sapiens* is "upsetting the balance of the universe" in its mad obsession with material values over spiritual ones.

No wonder the "scientific ufologists," trapped in a mechanistic view of the universe, despised the contactees.

Other UFO beings were not so benevolent. Though possessed like their kindlier brethren of what seemed to be a "superior technology," they still were the worst kind of savage primitives, grotesque, destructive, stupid. Others, neither friendly nor unfriendly, were machinelike in either appearance or behavior, soul-less and unfeeling, indifferent to the human beings with whom they dealt, betraying no sense but one of overwhelmingly superior authority.

On many levels a message began to emerge. The reports produced wonder and excitement. They also produced bewilderment and fear. On one side, mankind realized that a tremendous adventure—the confrontation with the cosmos—awaited it, and that such a confrontation was made possible by its development of an incredibly sophisticated technology. But it could just as easily lead to the establishment of a frightening order in which men could play out their most violent fantasies on a new and infinitely more dangerous scale. Or it could destroy their every human impulse and reduce them to machines whose sole function was to run other machines, automatons who had lost their capacity for communion with their fellows.

These concerns were not engendered solely by UFO reports, of course. The UFO reports reflected deep concerns of the human psyche, acting out these concerns in what essentially were metaphorical displays. One of the few intellectuals to understand the significance of the UFO phenomenon, the late psychoanalyst C. G. Jung, saw them as symbols of a great crisis in the psychic life of mankind and as portents of an impending profound change in consciousness.

UFOs represented the promise and the peril of

technology, the wonders and dangers of a cosmic consciousness to which technology would ultimately lead. As humanity's doubts about technology grew and as governments curtailed space programs, the back-to-the-earth movement started and societal consciousness shifted to a new awareness of mankind's immediate natural environment. While there were clear logical reasons for doing so (such as the realization that we could not go on polluting the planet indefinitely without serious consequences), there were also decidedly alogical impulses involved. At its core the Ecology Movement was a spiritual movement.

Accompanying the new ecological concern were less attractive manifestations, such as the revival of fundamentalist Christianity, Satanism, and any number of offbeat cults which eschewed the process of reason altogether. As William Irwin Thompson remarked, "The death of materialism will open man up to beasts and demons he has not feared since the Middle Ages." These cults trafficked in unreason and rank superstition.

Just as our obsession with technology and interplanetary visitors brought UFOs to everyone's attention, so did the new concern with nature and intuitive thought bring the creature phenomenon to the forefront. It was as if ghosts from another age in the planet's natural history had returned to haunt us.

Significantly enough, the most prominent were those most like us, or as we probably were in the early days of our evolutionary development: reclusive, hairy, apelike beings living in woods and caves. Actually, the archetype of the beast in the wilderness is an ancient one which has always expressed man's memory of his primordial past, but in recent times it has assumed a new role in what Jung termed "the constellation of psychic dominants." The manimal archetype symbolizes the animal in man, the elemental man freed of the demands of technological order, returned to the forests and caves to live in gentle harmony with nature. In the sense the manimal exists in counterpoint to the flying saucer.

But of course it is not quite that simple. What about those manimals seen in or near UFOs? Such reports are in a minority but that does not mean that we should ignore them or that they have no significance. In fact, we should expect them because, as we have noted several times, *Fortean manifestations tend toward their opposites*. "Everything," Fort wrote, "merges away into everything else." If such events have any meaning that can be expressed intellectually, they may be telling us that "natural man" and "technological man"—the intuitive man and the rational man—can live together in balance. If we can contain technology from being wholly dominated by our natural, arational impulses, with such inevitable consequences as violence, madness and superstition, we will not lose our souls but survive to achieve the cosmic perspective.

There are great dangers in all of this. To maintain what the ufonaut philosophers call "the balance of the universe," we must tread the thin line between conscious rational, technological impulses and unconscious intuitive, natural ones, favoring neither one nor the other, always seeing one as only half of the whole.

The danger we face, as in the current crisis in human affairs we contemplate a return to the wilderness, to the elemental mode, is implied particularly in the phantom cat, dog and bird stories, with their recurring motifs of violence and hostility. They remind us that nature is not quite the benevolent place modern-day sentimentalists would have us believe it is. Perhaps these visions reflect ancestral memories of a time in our dim prehistoric past when men lived in fear of animal adversaries.

Even more fundamentally we confront the prospect of psychic annihilation. Stephen Pulaski was turned into an animal because the archetypal implications of the situation (the appearance of two creatures) were so incredibly powerful that they literally "possessed" him. During his terrifying experience he had a vision which warned him, and all of us, that the stakes are very high indeed. The human race may well be destroyed if it allows itself to be overcome by the contents of the collective unconscious, if it wanders too far into the wilderness.

The man in black who appears in the vision is an archetypal representation of the "shadow" side of the unconscious mind, that part of the psyche in which we repress our darkest impulses. When men in black, in UFO and creature lore go about threatening percipients, they are in effect warning them of the dangers inherent in dealing with paranormal occurrences, whose dreamlike ambience may lure an individual into a shadowy realm of madness and terror from which he may never return. Such a warning is only implicit, of course; often the effect of the MIB visitation is to draw the victim even farther into this other realm. The individual percipient—and by extension the whole human race—stands in danger of losing his hold on the world of conscious reality. When that happens, the individual personality, and all of civilized society, cannot long survive.

3.

If Fortean phenomena do tend toward their opposites, then we can see, at least on one level, why they appear both to exist and not to exist. After all, what is more fundamental than the dichotomy between reality and fantasy? But what are they? Where do they come from? How are they generated? What will happen to us when they force us to alter our perception of the universe?

The answers to these questions await us some time in the unforseeable future. In the meantime, if we keep our bearings, we will learn much from the strange phenomena we have discussed in these pages. Once we understand them, or as much of them as we are capable of understanding—once we come to know that we should neither fear them nor revere them—we will see them for what they are: companions with whom we are walking, in balance, on our way to the next great human adventure.

EPILOGUE

1977—A Year Filled With Monsters

"I know I saw the creature!"
—Abby Brabham commenting on her sighting of the
Dover Demon

The mystery animals discussed in the preceding pages have continued to creep, crawl, fly, and run through the lives of humanity. As this opus quickly approaches publication, we felt it might be interesting to give a cross-section of a few noteworthy cases of 1977: cases which, in fact, further demonstrate the meanderings of the manifestations of the phenomena.

The year was a good one for sightings of the creatures of the outer edge. Bigfoot was allegedly photographed on Mount Baker in Washington State. The "skunk ape" was photographed in Florida, but the photographer and his pictures soon disappeared. The manimals were active in such widely separated locations as Easton, Pennsylvania, and Abilene, Texas. The so-called Bigfoot of Little Eagle, South Dakota, made the Halloween issue of *Newsweek*.

The manimals also returned to the Ohio County, Indiana, "window." As we noted elsewhere in this book (see pages 75 and 123), Rising Sun has been the focus of EM, UFO, and MA activity in the past. In 1977, Tom and Connie Courter saw their hairy, apelike, 12-foot-tall creature on the 12th and 13th of April, outside of Rising Sun. The first night, the couple left Mrs. Courter's parents' home around 11 p.m., and were getting ready to drive home. Tom was reaching into the back seat to get their baby's diaper bag when the creature crashed into the side of the car, denting it. They quickly called the police, but no trace of the thing was found. It was 11:45 p.m. the next night when they saw and heard it. "It was a real funny noise—like an ugh—and then we saw him sitting perched on the hill," Mrs. Courter said. Her husband had come prepared, armed with a sixteen shot .22 caliber rifle, and he emptied all 16 shots into it. Once again, the deputy sheriff found nothing. The creature had simply left.

As for phantom cat activity, we were able to personally check into the reports of a sheep killer in Ohio. Most of the publicity surrounding the Richland Township, Ohio, killings began after Sherwood Burkholder was interviewed by Dayton TV-7, and other local media. On the 25th of April, 1977, Burkholder lost forty sheep to some unknown animal killer. On the 26th, he lost another seventeen.

William Reeder, Dog Warden and Executive Director of the Allen County Humane Society, had been involved with the investigations of the killings for more than a month before Burkholder's sheep were attacked. Reeder was the person most often quoted in the press, and it was with him that Loren Coleman spent the better part of June 29, 1977, discussing the problem. Reeder told us the Burkholder sheep had been grabbed at the rear of their jaws, and then clawed forward. Eight claw marks were visible on the side of the sheep. Although most of the sheep were not dead when Reeder arrived on the scene, he had to destroy all of them. Later he went back and took plaster casts of what he believed were the killer's tracks.

The Burkholder sheep were kept in a large pen located near Tom Fett and Rockport Roads. The killer struck before dawn the first time, then early the next day, and finally on the afternoon of that same day. Carol Benson, who rents the trailer that sits on Burkholder's land (Sherwood Burkholder lives on a farm many miles north), told us she did not hear a thing, and even came home the second time it happened to find Reeder destroying the clawed-up sheep. A month later, Carol Benson, her son Bryan, and Burkholder saw a large black cat walking back and forth among the trees near the creek out back.

While the Burkholder story got most of the media coverage, the killings at the Elmer Nesbaum farm in March are more interesting from an investigative and human point of view. On March 22, 1977, something got into Elmer Nesbaum's sheep. Through interviews with William Reeder and Mr. and Mrs. Elmer Nesbaum, we were able to reconstruct the events as follows.

Elmer Nesbaum, 74, and his wife, a Reformed Mennonite couple, live on a 94-acre farm a couple miles northwest of Burkholder's land. The first time the mystery animal came, it was a windy, snowy March night. Elmer Nesbaum had penned his sheep because most of them were about ready to lamb. He liked sheep; they were easy to keep and these had become his friends; they would all crowd around him when he came out to see them. "When I came in the first morning," Nesbaum said, "only a few were standing. They were all red, and I wondered what happened with these sheep. Something terrible went on in there! It was a bad sight to see." What Nesbaum found was a "bloody mess" of deeply clawed and dying sheep at the end of the pen. He called a veterinarian, and had what sheep could be saved sewed up.

Then Elmer Nesbaum made preparations to protect the survivors. His sheep were housed in a pen at the back part of a U-shaped area, between his barn and his machine and lofting sheds. Nesbaum had heavy farm gates across the front of the pen, regular wire fencing up to the roof of the barn, and then chicken wire on the top. He put six steel muskrat traps in front of the pen.

When the creature came back on the 26th of March, it set off all six traps, and clawed the gate apart. It left chunks of wood strewn about, pockmarked with teeth marks, and apparent claw marks. When we inspected the pen and ground area, pieces of wood, one to two feet long, were still in the same position Nesbaum had found them on the 26th. He had not moved a thing. The wood slats of the fencing showed many signs of teeth and claw. Nesbaum gave us several of these wood chunks. Many semi-circular bites out of the wood and fang-like punctures are quite visible.

At the time, Nesbaum noticed clumps of black and blackish-brown hair sticking to the wood fencing. He did not keep it, not thinking it important at the time. "I didn't realize it was goin' to become such a mystery," Elmer explained.

As Bill Reeder described it, the animal had "literally clawed the Nesbaum sheep; it didn't eat the sheep; didn't hamstring the sheep; didn't gut the sheep. It just put eight perfect claw marks down the side—from the backbone to the stomach. One of the ewes had her udder completely torn off. Also," Reeder continued, "there was fang marks across the neck. Definitely punctures of four in nature, two on each side." That was after the first attack. The second time, Reeder noticed "only clawing, no biting. The only one with fang marks was a lamb which had been born between the first and second attacks. It had the four perfect fang marks. The vet tried to save it, but its ribcage was crushed."

Because the pen was on a concrete slab covered by straw, Reeder and the Nesbaums only found one track. In all, the Nesbaums had lost twenty sheep, most of them pregnant.

To Elmer Nesbaum and his wife, it was a personal tragedy. They had been looking forward to selling their sheep and new lambs, selling the farm, and retiring to a smaller place. Mrs. Nesbaum had been ill over the winter, and Elmer wanted to move closer to the city. The killings ended their hopes, and Nesbaum felt he was "out of the business, but you hate it to go out like that."

Elmer Nesbaum spoke to us of his affection for his sheep and was obviously deeply moved in his retelling of the "bloody mess" he discovered. Bill Reeder told us how the couple had stood there and cried. They finally had had to walk into their farmhouse, for they could not watch Reeder destroy their sheep. Mrs. Nesbaum was philosophical in trying to sum it up: "Well, it's a mystery. The thing'll never be solved."

After the Nesbaum and Burkholder sheep were killed, William Reeder found events occurring rapidly. He took plaster casts of what he felt were the killer's tracks on the 28th of April, at the Burkholders'. On the first of May, five sheep were killed at the

Richard Etter farm on Pandora Road, and two days later Herman Hilty of Lugabill Road lost some tame ducks. At the Hilty farm, Reeder found and took casts of what he was beginning to feel were cat tracks. (The Hilty casts exactly match the Burkholder ones.) Although catlike, the tracks had the by now familiar non-retractable claw marks well known in the historical annals of phantom panthers.

Bill Reeder began getting reports of other sheep kills from Phillips Road. The killer appeared to be moving south down that road towards the town of Lafayette. At about the same time actual sightings of a large cat began to occur. Bill Reeder pulled out a stack of reports for us and started reading through them.

28 April—Maria Henderson was the first person to see the cat. In her statement to the Bluffton Police, she said she was going to work by way of Bentley Road, near the County Line Road, when she saw what she thought was a dog in the road. When she got closer, she saw it was a cat. Finally, out of her car, she walked within four feet of it and definitely saw it was a cat ... a big cat, black and gray in color, and approximately one and a half feet tall. The Bluffton Police checked and found Henderson to be a "good, substantial, solid citizen".

29 April—Bob Cross, an employee at the Lima State Hospital and member of the local news media, watched a large cat, black and gray, with a long tail, for ten minutes.

1 May—Near Lafayette, at 2:30 a.m., the "glassy eyes of a cat" were spotted by a deputy with a spotlight. Reeder later found tracks like the other ones. At the Hardestys' place, this same date, casts of tracks were made by the residents.

6 May—Lou Abial of Napoleon Road went

out to his barn at about 6:45 p.m., and then, returning, found cat tracks in an area that a moment before had been undisturbed. Reeder said it appeared the cat had jumped from a hay loft. They tracked it to the end of Abial's property, but never saw it.

9 May—At 7:30 a.m., Barbara Price reported seeing a 140-pound, black and gray cat with a big head and long tail cross in front of her on Highway 81, near Swaney Road. Two off-duty deputies and Reeder searched the area for two hours. Many tracks were visible, but they failed to locate the cat. On this same day, Mr. Rutherford, 9890 Reservoir Road, found tracks on his property.

12 May—An Allen County veterinarian examined a dead German Shepherd. The dog had fang marks in its neck.

By mid-May, the sheep killer was getting a big play in the local newspapers. The thing was being held responsible for killing five peacocks, some tame ducks, a German Shepherd, and at least 140 head of sheep. William Reeder found a hot political potato had dropped into his lap. The Allen County Sheriff, Charles Harrod, called Reeder into his office and more or less told him they were taking over the investigations. The Sheriff believed the killings were being caused by a pack of dogs, and William Reeder's findings were making them feel a bit uncomfortable.

About the same time Bill Reeder was being confronted by the Sheriff's intrusion and dog-pack theories, the cat "woke up half of Lafayette" at 1:15 a.m. one morning in May. On May 17 two residents (Reeder gave the names to the Sheriff's office, and they never returned his file) of the Lafayette area reported a large dark-colored cat was drinking from their pond.

214

Despite the Sheriff's Department, Bill Reeder was becoming more and more convinced that what he had on his hands was a large black-and-gray feline. On May 20, Reeder held a news conference and announced his conclusions based upon the mounting body of evidence. Besides the sightings and footprints, Reeder had also found some droppings. He told us these had been found on the farm next to the Burkholder place, and he had given them to Dr. Wayne Kaufman and Dr. R. L. McMahn, veterinarians practicing in Lima, Ohio. The silver-dollar-sized stools had contained balls of hair and hookworms, characteristic of cat scat. ("What color was the hair?" we asked Reeder upon hearing about the hair balls. "I don't know. You're the first people to ask me that question," Bill Reeder responded.) After Dr. McMahn had examined the droppings and sheep kills, he candidly told Reeder: "Bill, this a panther-type animal."

William Reeder was told to not hold any more news conferences.

Then on May 27, the Mayor of Lafayette called Reeder and told him the cat was in Lafayette. Reeder and one other officer joined the Mayor and two Lafayette Police Officers, but failed to locate the animal. Bill Reeder went home and soon got another call. This time it was from the manager of a lake resort and camping area southeast of Lafayette. He said the cat was drinking from a swimming hole near the camping grounds, but asked Reeder not to go down there because it might panic the campers. Reeder "determined" that the cat was not bothering anyone, so he did not go after it.

Home again, the Allen County Dog Warden sat down to a cup of coffee and tried to settle down after the hectic events of the day. His phone rang again. It was the Lafayette Police, and they had the cat in their sights in a plowed field near Lafayette.

Bill Reeder flew out there and quickly located the stakeout. It was 2 a.m. by then and Reeder, an off-duty Sheriff's deputy, and two Lafayette Police Officers were using large flashlights and spotlights. The deputy circled around into the nearby woods. They all had a pretty good view of it in the light of their spotlamps. Reeder slowly began walking toward the cat. They all were within 35 yards of it. Then it began to calmly walk towards them, "like it was going to be a docile animal," Reeder said. It was now only about twenty yards away, and "within tranquilizer gun range." All of a sudden, it broke for the woods and ran "150 yards in two seconds flat." As it came into the woods, it was sighted by the deputy stationed there. And then it was gone.

Bill Reeder's description matched those of the other witnesses in the area. He said it was black, one and a half to two feet tall, and had "the pointed ears of a cat." Because of the animal's position in relationship to Reeder, the tail could not be seen. He strongly felt the "movement was that of a cat, not of a dog". The beam-type flashlights caught the glassy eyes, and they appeared to be gold or yellow. After the cat escaped into the woods, Reeder discovered tracks with claw marks exactly like the Hilty–Burkholder casts.

William Reeder was forbidden to give a news release on the sighting he and the officers had made, and no one in the local media knows about it. We are the first writers with whom he discussed the incidents of May 27. Reeder is a no-nonsense sort of fellow who has taken a good deal of flack because of his "big, black cat" theory, and he was initially cautious as we started examining and cross-examining the Richland Township events. Only after some basic trust was established did Bill Reeder detail his personal experience. He is not looking for publicity and appears to be happily and personally vindicated. Bill

Reeder was very much at peace with himself, finally, after some extremely trying months.

The black cat, the sheep killer, seems to have left Allen County, Ohio. During the first week of June, area newspapers carried articles telling of the sighting of a "large black cat" near the town of Ada which is ten miles due east of Lafayette, in Hardin County. Hancock County Game Protector Brad Lindsey and Hardin County Game Protector Gary Braun were out looking for the cat because of reports from Ada area residents. Braun was quoted as saying he got a good look at the animal and it was definitely a large black animal of the feline family. Braun watched the cat for twelve to twenty seconds through field glasses before it walked into the woods. No livestock has yet been killed in Hardin County.

So what are we to do? Here again, we find a large, black cat in an area where tawny pumas have been extinct for over a hundred years. It is easy to recognize the classic nature of this 1977 Ohio case: the cat's elusiveness, its clawed footprints, its savage attacks on livestock, and the overwhelming number of first-hand sightings. Allen County, Ohio, seems to have been visited by one of our old friends, the phantom panther.

1977 is shaping up as a sychronistically interesting year for the cats. 1877 saw mystery feline reports from Ohio and Indiana. During 1977, besides the Ohio events, there have been sightings in Bay Springs, Mississippi; Edwardsville, Illinois; and California, Kentucky. And as we continued our investigations into the matter of the "Dover Demon" of Dover, Massachusetts, word came of a maned lion's having attacked two dogs near Dover, Arkansas.

Dover, the wealthiest town in Massachusetts, is fifteen miles southwest of Boston. Although it is heavily wooded and its houses are spaced several hundred feet apart, it is hardly a place in which one would

217

expect to encounter a strange creature unknown to science, but that's exactly what four teenagers claim they saw over a 25½-hour period in April 1977.

The bizarre affair began at 10:30 on the evening of April 21 as three seventeen-year-olds, Bill Bartlett, Mike Mazzocca and Andy Brodie, were driving north on Dover's Farm Street.* Bartlett, who was behind the wheel, spotted something creeping along a low wall of loose stones on the left side of the road. At first he thought it was a dog or a cat until his headlights hit the thing directly and Bartlett realized it was nothing he had ever seen before.

The figure slowly turned its head and stared into the light, its two large, round, glassy, lidless eyes shining brightly "like two orange marbles." Its watermelon-shaped head, resting at the top of a thin neck, was fully the size of the rest of the body. Except for its oversized head, the creature was thin, with long spindly arms and legs, and large hands and feet. The skin was hairless and peach-colored and appeared

---

* Sometime after the end of the Dover Demon flap, we happened to stumble across this passage in Frank Smith's 1914 book, *Dover Farms:*

Farm Street extends from the Medfield line on the south to Springfield park, on the north, and is the second oldest road in town. This street as present laid out, forms only a part of the original layout, which followed Indian trails. . . . In the early time (i.e. 1600s) this road went around by the picturesque Polka rock which was called for a man by that name, of whom it is remembered, that amid the superstitions of the age he thought he saw his Satanic Majesty as he was riding on horseback by this secluded spot. The location has long been looked upon as one in which treasures are hid, but why anyone should go so far inland to hide treasures has never been told; however, there has been at times unmistakable evidence of considerable digging in the immediate vicinity of the rock. (page 7)

Furthermore, Loren Coleman was able to talk to the Acheson family who saw a barn-sized UFO in this area in June of 1969 with red lights rotating on the bottom and a white triangle underneath. One could begin to wonder if we are dealing with a "window" area.

© 1978 by Loren Coleman

Dover Demon seen by
William Bartlett, 21 April 1977

to have a rough texture ("like wet sandpaper," Bill subsequently told Loren Coleman).

The figure, which stood no more than three and a half to four feet tall, was shaped like "a baby's body with long arms and legs." It had been making its way uncertainly along the wall, its long fingers curling around the rocks, when the car lights surprised it.

Unfortunately neither of Bill's companions saw the creature. Mike was watching his own side of the road, and Andy was sitting in back talking with him. The sighting lasted only a few seconds and before Bill could speak he had passed the scene. Mike and Andy told Coleman, however, that their friend was "pretty scared" and sounded "genuinely frightened." At first they were skeptical but Bill's obvious fear forced them to change their minds.

"I really flew after I saw it," Bill said. "I took that corner at 45, which is pretty fast. I said to my friends, 'Did you see that?' And they said, 'Nah, describe it.' I did and they said, 'Go back. Go back!' And I said, 'No way. No way.' When you see something like that, you don't want to stand around and see what it's going to do.

"They finally got me to go back and Mike was leaning out of the window yelling, 'Come on, creature!' And I was saying, 'Will you cut that out?' Andy was yelling, 'I want to see you!' "

But the creature was gone. Bill dropped his friends off and went home. He was visibly upset as he walked through the door and his father asked him what was wrong. Young Bartlett related the story, then withdrew to sketch what he had seen.

In the meantime another teenager was about to see the creature. Around midnight John Baxter, fifteen, left his girlfriend Cathy Cronin's house at the south end of Millers High Road in Dover and started walking up the street on his way home. Half an hour later, after he had walked about a mile, he observed someone approaching him. Because the figure was quite short, John assumed it was an acquaintance of his, M. G. Bouchard, who lived on the street. John called out, "M. G., is that you?"

There was no response. But John and the figure continued to approach each other until finally the latter stopped. John then halted as well and asked, "Who is that?" The sky was dark and overcast and he could see only a shadowy form.

Trying to get a better look he took one step forward and the figure scurried off to the left, running down a shallow wooded gully and up the opposite bank. As it ran John could hear its footfalls on the dry leaves.

He followed the thing down the slope, then stopped and looked across the gulley. The creature —for now John could see that was what it was— stood in silhouette about thirty feet away, its feet "molded" around the top of a rock several feet from a tree. It was leaning toward the tree and had the long fingers of both hands entwined around the trunk, which was eight inches in diameter, as if for support.

The creature's body reminded John of a monkey's, except for its dark "figure-eight"-shaped head. Its eyes, two lighter spots in the middle of the head, were looking straight at John, who after a few minutes began to feel decidedly uneasy. Realizing that he had never seen or heard of such a creature before and fearing what it might do next, he backed carefully up the slope, his heart pounding, and "walked very fast" down the road to the intersection at Farm Street. There a couple passing in a car picked him up and drove him home.

The next day Bill Bartlett told his close friend Will Taintor, eighteen, of his sighting. And that night —around midnight—Taintor himself would catch a fleeting glimpse of the creature.

He was driving Abby Brabham, fifteen, home when the encounter took place. As they passed along Springdale Avenue, Abby spotted something in the headlights on the left side of the road. The "something" was a creature crouched on all fours and facing the car. Its body was thin and monkeylike but its head was large and oblong, with no nose, ears or mouth. The thing was hairless and its skin was tan or beige in color. The facial area around the eyes was lighter and the eyes glowed *green*. Abby insisted this was the case, even after investigators told her that Bill Bartlett had said the eyes were orange.

Will saw the creature only momentarily and had the impression of something with a large head and tan body, with its front legs in the air. He didn't know what it was but he did know that it was not a dog.

Frightened, Abby urged him to speed up so that they could get away. Will claims that only after they left the scene did he recall Bill's sighting. His own had been so brief and unspectacular that he probably would have thought little of it if Abby had not been with him. He asked her to describe the figure, deliberately phrasing misleading questions about aspects of the creature's appearance he knew not to be true in order to check her story against Bartlett's, which he did not mention to her. But Abby stuck to her story.

On April 28, Loren Coleman, then living in nearby Needham, was visiting the Dover Country Store when a store employee, Melody Fryer, told him about Bill Bartlett's sighting and sketch. She promised to get him a copy and two days later provided him with two drawings. The next day Coleman interviewed Bartlett. On May 3 he questioned Baxter and Brabham and on the 5th talked with Taintor.

Two weeks later Coleman pulled in Walter Webb of the Aerial Phenomena Research Organization, Joseph Nyman of the Mutual UFO Network and Ed

Fogg of the New England UFO Study Group to join the investigation. Although none of the witnesses had reported seeing a UFO in connection with the Dover Demon, the ufologists were struck by the creature's apparent resemblance to humanoid beings sometimes associated with UFOs.*

The investigators interviewed the witnesses' parents, who said they believed the stories. The Bartletts said their son is "very honest and open" and not the kind of person who enjoys playing pranks. Mrs. Baxter remarked that her son "never made up stories"—meaning, apparently, that he never made up stories which he passed off as true; his father told a reporter that his son writes science fiction. But he still didn't question John's honesty. John confirmed that he is a science fiction enthusiast but insisted that had nothing to do with his report.

Will Taintor's father and mother both accepted his story. The father believed Will and Abby had mistaken a conventional animal for the creature; the mother, on the other hand, felt they had seen something genuinely unknown.

Alice Stewart, who owned the land closest to the spot where John Baxter allegedly saw the Demon, said she had not seen or heard anything unusual that night. Her dogs, which were inside at the time of the reported encounter, had not acted up.

Dover Police Chief Carl Sheridan spoke highly of young Bartlett and described him as "a reliable witness." High school principal Richard Wakely told Coleman, "I don't think these kids got together and invented it." They were not troublemakers—just "average students." A police officer said, "At first I was going to ask one of the witnesses to give me whatever it was he was smoking, but I know all four and I know that to all of us they're very reputable people."

* See Ted Bloecher's "Close Encounters of the Third Kind," FATE, January 1978.

223

On April 25, four days after the first sighting, Robert Linton, science instructor at Dover-Sherborn Regional High School, overheard Bill Bartlett discussing the encounter with classmates. Later Linton asked him about it and the youth provided a full account and drew a picture of the thing. (Bartlett is an accomplished artist and a member of Boston's Copley Art Society.) Linton, who said Bill had told him that the experience "scared the hell out of him," accepted the story because of the young man's good reputation.

The researchers were especially impressed with Bartlett and with Abby Brabham, who declared adamantly, "I know I saw the creature and don't care what happens!"

Is the Dover Demon a hoax? The investigators concluded that was possible, but doubted that this was the explanation. There was nothing in the witnesses' backgrounds to suggest they might be pranksters and much to suggest that they were honest, upright individuals.

As Webb observes, "None of the four was on drugs or drinking at the time of his or her sighting so far as we were able to determine. . . . None of the principals in this affair made any attempt to go to the newspapers or police to publicize their claims. Instead, the sightings gradually leaked out. Finally, the teenagers' own parents, the high school principal, the science instructor and other adults in Dover whose comments were solicited didn't believe the Dover Demon was a fabrication, implying the youths did indeed see 'something' . . .

"As for the idea the witnesses were victims of somebody else's stunt, this seems most unlikely, chiefly due to the virtual impossibility of creating an animated, lifelike 'demon' of the sort described."

But if the Demon is real, what is it? A UFO being? Perhaps—but then nothing precisely similar has ever been reported before, according to Ted Bloecher, who has collected over 1500 UFO-occupant accounts for the Center for UFO Studies.

On the other hand, maybe the Demon is a member of a curious race known to the Cree Indians of eastern Canada as the *Mannegishi*. The *Mannegishi*, Sigurd Olson says in his book *Listening Post,* are supposed to be "little people with round heads and no noses who live with only one purpose: to play jokes on travelers. The little creatures have long spidery legs, arms with six-fingered hands, and live between rocks in the rapids . . ."

Indeed, the creatures of 1977 seemed to be playing cosmic jokes on a number of people. The "Big Birds" were at it again during the year. One of these huge things with wings attacked a five-pound beagle puppy belonging to Mrs. Greg Schmitt of Rabbit Hash, Kentucky. The "large bird" snatched the dog from her farm and dropped it in a pond 600 yards away. While local wildlife officials argued over whether or not the dog was attacked by an American Bald Eagle, the dognapping appears to have been a dry run for something more sinister.

On July 25, 1977, a bizarre and dramatic event occurred unlike any in the Big Bird literature to date. At 8:10 p.m., ten-year-old Marlon Lowe was playing hide-and-seek outside his Lawndale, Illinois, home when he was picked up by a huge bird and carried over a distance of thirty feet.

On July 28, Loren Coleman's brother, Jerry Coleman of Decatur, Illinois, traveled to the Lawndale area. He talked with some of the people who were involved in the "big bird" sightings and sent us some notes on his investigations. The following passages are his observations:

Spoke with Ruth Lowe and Marlon Lowe. Mrs. Lowe is self employed, along with her husband, Jake. They own and operate a Standard Station in Lincoln, Ill. She is a grandmother of about 45 years of age. She, in my opinion, is a very honest woman, and stated if I didn't believe her she didn't even want to talk about it. People from all over the country have called her. The Logan County Game Warden allegedly sat at her table and called her a liar. All in all, she felt people were laughing at her for what she had seen.

Three officers of the State police went down to Kickapoo Creek, and walked around the open bank of the creek for less than fifteen minutes, and found nothing. There were no feathers or anything to be found in her yard. I also went across the street to an empty lot, and found nothing. This location was where the birds allegedly were starting up.

A Mr. Cox of Lawndale was the first to see the birds, coming out of the southwest. He saw them as they started their descent. That was all he saw.

Marlon states that as he was playing a game of hide-and-go-seek, he was running at the time the bird picked him up. The bird, along with another one, was flying at a height of eight feet from the ground. They were side by side, wingtip to wingtip. Distance of 35 feet. The weight of the boy is around sixty pounds; he is almost four feet tall, red hair. This happened at 8:10 p.m., Monday, July 25, 1977. It was comfortable, warm, with clear skies; sunset at 8:15 p.m.

Ruth Lowe describes the birds as having a white ring around a neck which was one and a half feet long. The rest of the body was all very black. The birds' bills were six inches long, and hooked at the end:

The claws on the feet were arranged with three front, one in back:

Each wing, less the body, was four feet at the very *least*. Although they did not land, the birds on the ground would have stood four and a half feet tall.

When Mrs. Lowe screamed, the boy was released and fell to the ground. At this point, she was within ten feet of the birds. All (there were six witnesses) watched the birds fly off to the northeast. One flap of the wings, and the birds went up. They leveled off at tree-top, and flew toward Kickapoo Creek, which is less than a mile from their house. When they last saw the birds, about nine blocks away, she said they still looked the size of ducks.

Lawndale is a very small town, less than 300 people. The biggest town nearby is Lincoln (17,000), about ten miles to the southwest. North and northwest of Lawndale is Kickapoo Creek—*very heavy* with underbrush and trees for miles. At the point where one might think the birds entered—less than 200 yards from the Lawndale site—Judy (Jerry's wife) and I were able to quickly encounter heavy woods.

By the way, in the front yard where Mrs. Lowe was standing when she screamed, was her Saint Bernard, about twenty feet away. The dog never barked. She said the dog barks at everything, all the time.

More big bird reports are still issuing from Illinois late in 1977. A film has been taken, and the experts have been trotted forth declaring the birds are only turkey vultures. Hmm, must be a big turkey vulture to pick up a sixty-pound boy, but we Forteans are used to such attempts to bury the incredible as quickly as possible.

For us, the circle remains broken

BIBLIOGRAPHY

CHAPTER ONE: Mystery Animals

Bloomington [Illinois] *Pantagraph,* August 11 and 12, 1970.

Champaign-Urbana [Illinois] *News-Gazette,* August 9, 1970.

Clark, Jerome and Coleman, Loren, *The Unidentified,* Warner Books, New York, New York, 1975.

Fodor, Nandor, *The Unaccountable,* Award Books, New York, New York, 1968.

Rimmer, John A., "The UFO Is Alive and Living in Fairyland," in *Merseyside UFO Bulletin,* December 1970.

Stringfield, Leonard H., "The 'Atitseld' Incident," Cincinnati, Ohio, 1973. Privately distributed document.

Swift, Mark, "The Strange Experiences of a Salem

Family," in *Gray Barker's Newsletter*, February 1976.

Webb, David with Hynek, Mimi (ed.), *1973—Year of the Humanoids: An Analysis of the Fall 1973 UFO/Humanoid Wave*, Center for UFO Studies, Evanston, Illinois, 1976.

CHAPTER TWO: The Bigfeet

Beck, Fred and R. A., *"I Fought the Apemen of Mt. St. Helens," Washington, 1967*.

Bowers, Mrs. Wallace, private communication, 1971.

Byrne, Peter, *The Search for Big Foot*, Acropolis, Washington, D. C., 1975.

Centralia-Chehalis [Washington] *Chronicle*, December 16, 1970.

Clark, Jerome, "Saucer Central U.S.A.," in *UFO Report*, April 1976.

Coon, Ken, "Sasquatch Footprint Variations," January 20, 1974. Privately distributed document.

Green, John, *Bigfoot: On the Track of the Sasquatch*, Ballantine Books, New York, New York, 1973.

Green, John, and Sanderson, Sabina W., "Alas, Poor Jacko," in *Pursuit*, January 1975.

Keel, John A., *Strange Creatures from Time and Space*, Fawcett/Gold Medal, Greenwich, Connecticut, 1970.

McClarin, Jim, private files.

Napier, John, *Bigfoot: The Yeti and Sasquatch in Myth and Reality*, E. P. Dutton, New York, New York, 1972, 1973.

Phenomena Research Report, November 1975.

Redding [California] *Record Searchlight*, January 21, 1972.

Slate, B. Ann, "Gods from Inner Space," in *UFO Report*, April 1976.

Albuquerque [New Mexico] *Journal,* October 15, 16, 17, 19, 20, 23 and 26, 1966.

Alexander, Hartley Burr, *North American Mythology* (vol. X of *Mythology of All Races*), L. H. Gray (ed.), Cooper Square Publishers, New York, New York, 1964.

Arkansas Gazette, June 27, 1971.

Bloomington [Illinois] *Pantagraph,* July 12, 17 and 25, 1970.

Brandon, Hembree, letter to Loren Coleman, August 25, 1968.

Cairo [Illinois] *Evening Citizen,* July 26, 1972.

Carbondale [Illinois] *Southern Illinoisan,* June 26 and 27, 1973.

Carmi [Illinois] *Times,* May 9, 1973.

Champaign-Urbana [Illinois] *Courier,* May 8 and 9; October 17, 1973.

Champaign-Urbana [Illinois] *News-Gazette,* August 9, 1970.

Clark, Jerome, "Indian Prophecy and the Prescott UFOs," in *Fate,* April 1971.

——"On the Track of Unidentified Furry Objects," in *Fate,* August 1973.

——"Oklahoma Monsters Come in Pairs," in *Fate,* December 1976.

Clark, Jerome and Coleman, Loren, "Anthropoids, Monsters and UFOs," in *Flying Saucer Review,* January/February 1973.

——"The Jersey Devil," in *Beyond Reality,* May 1973.

——"Swamp Slobs Invade Illinois," in *Fate,* July 1974.

——*The Unidentified,* Warner Books, New York, New York, 1975.

Coffeyville [Kansas] *Journal,* September 2, 1975.

Coleman, Sister Bernard, "The Religion of the Ojibwa of Northern Minnesota," in *Primitive Man* 10 (1937).

Coleman, Loren, "Mystery Animals in Illinois," in *Fate,* March 1971.

Coleman, Loren and Hall, Mark, "Some Bigfoot Traditions of the North American Indians," in *INFO Journal,* Fall/Winter 1970.

Colvin, Terry W., letter to Loren Coleman.

Cooper, John M., "The Cree Witiko Psychosis," in *Primitive Man* 6 (1933).

Crawfordsville [Indiana] *Journal and Review,* September 21, 1972.

Dallas [Texas] *Morning News,* September 6, 1975.

Days, Richard A., letter to Loren Coleman.

El Reno [Oklahoma] *Daily Tribune,* March 9, 1971.

Evansville [Indiana] *Press,* August 22, 1955, and August 15, 1970.

Eyewitness, Vol. 1, No. 7.

France, Richard G., letter to Loren Coleman.

Gordon, Stan, "UFOs, in Relation to Creature Sightings in Pennsylvania," in *MUFON 1974 UFO Symposium Proceedings,* Mutual UFO Network, Seguin, Texas, 1974.

Guinard, Joseph E., "Witiko Among the Tête-de-Boule," in *Primitive Man* 3 (1930).

Gurdon, Lady Eveline Camilla (ed.), *County Folk-Lore: Suffolk,* D. Nutt, Ipswich, England, 1893.

Hall, Rick, letters to Loren Coleman.

Harpole, Marsh, letter to Loren Coleman.

Harris, Jesse, "Strange Beast Stories," in *Hoosier Folklore* 5 (1946).

Heath, Roger, letter to Loren Coleman.

Holtz, Jay, letter to Ted Bloecher.

Idabel [Oklahoma] *McCurtain Gazette,* August 20 and September 5, 1975.

Keel, John A., *Strange Creatures from Time and Space,* Fawcett/Gold Medal, Greenwich, Connecticut, 1970.

Lawton [Oklahoma] *Morning Press,* March 2 and 3, 1971.

Levy, Jerrold E., letter to Loren Coleman.

Lincoln [Illinois] *Courier,* August 20, 1970.

Lorenzen, Coral and Jim, *Flying Saucer Occupants,* Signet, New York, New York, 1967.

Lumberton [North Carolina] *Robesonian,* September 30, 1973.

MacDougall, Curtis D., *Hoaxes,* Dover, New York, New York, 1968.

Middletown [Ohio] *Journal,* October 30, 1972.

Mietus, Kenneth J., letter to Loren Coleman.

Morgan, William, "Human-Wolves Among the Navaho," in *Yale Publications in Anthropology* XI (1936).

Noe, Allen V., "ABSMal Affairs in Pennsylvania and Elsewhere," in *Pursuit,* October 1973.

——"And Still the Reports Roll in," in *Pursuit,* January 1974.

Oklahoma City Daily Oklahoman, February 26, 1971.

Oklahoma City Oklahoma Journal, February 28, 1971.

Parsons, Elsie Clews, "Tales of the Micmac," in *Journal of American Folklore* 38 (1925).

Pekin [Illinois] *Daily Times,* July 26 and 27, 1972.

Peoria [Illinois] *Journal-Star,* July 26, 1972.

Personal interviews with witnesses, authorities, reporters and investigators in British Columbia, Illinois, Indiana and Oklahoma.

Petersburg [Indiana] *Press-Dispatch,* August 13, 1970.

Robinson [Illinois] *Daily News,* May 12 and 15, 1973.

Sanderson, Ivan T., *Abominable Snowmen: Legend Come to Life,* Chilton, New York, New York, 1961.

Schroat, Beulah, letter to *Decatur* [Illinois] *Review,* August 2, 1972.

Schwarz, Berthold Eric, "Berserk: A UFO-Creature Encounter," in *Flying Saucer Review,* Vol. 20, No. 1 (1974).

Slate, B. Ann, "Gods from Inner Space," in *UFO Report,* April 1976.

Slate, B. Ann and Berry, Alan, *Bigfoot,* Bantam, New York, New York, 1976.

Speck, Frank G., *Myths and Folklore of the Timiskaming Alongquin and Timagami Ojibwa,* Anthropological Series, Canada Department of Mines, Geological Survey, No. 9, 1915.

Steiger, Brad, *Mysteries of Time and Space,* Prentice-Hall, Englewood Cliffs, New Jersey, 1974.

Tabor City [North Carolina] *Tribune,* September 26, 1973.

Toledo [Ohio] *Blade,* August 2, 9 and 10, 1972.

Warth, Robert C., "A UFO-ABSM Link?", in *Pursuit,* April 1975.

Whetstone, Deward, letter to Thomas R. Adams.

White Hill [North Carolina] *News-Reporter,* September 27, 1973.

Worley, Don, personal interviews and investigations.

——"The UFO-Related Anthropoids," in *Proceedings of the 1976 CUFOS Conference,* Center for UFO Studies, Evanston, Illinois, 1976.

Young, Robert W., letter to Loren Coleman.

CHAPTER FOUR: Phantom Cats and Dogs

Anniston [Alabama] *Star,* May 30 and June 8, 1969.

Belleville [Illinois] *News-Democrat,* April 16, 1970.

Birmingham [Alabama] *News,* June 5, 1969.

Bord, Janet, "Some Fortean Ramblings," in *The News,* November 1974.

Boston New England Farmer, August 3, 1823.

Bowen, Charles, "Mystery Animals," in *Flying Saucer Review,* November/December 1964.

Bue, Gerald T. and Stenlund, Milton H., "Are There Mountain Lions in Minnesota?", in *The Conservation Volunteer,* September 1952.

Burton, Maurice, "Is This the Surrey Puma?", in *Animals,* December 1966.

Cairo [Illinois] *Evening Citizen,* April 20, 1966, and April 20, 1970.

Chester [Illinois] *Herald-Tribune,* April 16, 1970.

Clark, Jerome and Coleman, Loren, "On the Trail of Pumas, Panthers and ULAs," in *Fate,* June and July 1972.

——*The Unidentified,* Warner Books, New York, New York, 1975.

Coleman, Loren, "Mystery Animals in Illinois," in *Fate,* March 1971.

Decatur [Illinois] *Herald,* July 14, 16 to 20, and 30; August 1, 1917.

Decatur [Illinois] *Review,* September 15, October 27 and November 1, 1955; March 12, 1970.

Detroit News, November 23, 1972.

Fort, Charles, *The Books of Charles Fort,* Henry Holt, New York, New York, 1941.

Gordon, Stan, "UFOs, in Relation to Creature Sightings in Pennsylvania," in *MUFON 1974 UFO Symposium Proceedings,* Mutual UFO Network, Seguin, Texas, 1974.

Gurdon, Lady Eveline Camilla (ed.), *County Folk-Lore: Suffolk,* D. Nutt, Ipswich, England, 1893.

Hill, Betty, letter to Jerome Clark.

Huntington [Indiana] *Herald-Press,* June 27 to 29, 1962.

Jerseyville [Illinois] *Democrat News,* March 12, 1970.

Joliet [Illinois] *Herald-News,* April 24, 1963.

Joliet [Illinois] *Spectator,* August 20, 1964.

Korson, George, *Black Rock: Mining Folklore of the Pennsylvania Dutch,* Johns Hopkins, Baltimore, Maryland, 1960.

London Daily Express, October 14, 1925.

London Evening News, July 19, 1963, and April 27, 1972.

Marshall, Robert E., *The Onza,* Exposition Press, New York, New York, 1961.

Newton [Illinois] *Press,* February 19, 1970.

The New York Times, December 28, 1877, and June 27, 1931.

Paris [Texas] *News,* July 26, 1964.

Personal interviews with witnesses, authorities and reporters in Illinois and Minnesota.

Randolph, Vance, *We Always Lie to Strangers: Tall Tales from the Ozarks,* Columbia University Press, New York, New York, 1952.

Richmond [Indiana] *Palladium-Item,* July 28 and 30; August 3, 5, 6, 8 to 13, 15, 17, 22, 24, 29 to 31; September 1, 5 and 15, 1948; January 8, 1951.

Rickard, R. J. M., "If You Go Down to the Woods Today," in *INFO Journal,* May 1974.

——"The 'Surrey Puma' and Friends: More Mystery Animals," in *The News,* January 1976.

Robb, Dunbar, "Cougar in Missouri," in *Missouri Conservationist,* July 1955.

Rockford [Illinois] *Morning Star/Register-Republic,* May 30, June 2 and August 25, 1970.

St. Louis Post-Dispatch, July 26, 1964.

Sanderson, Ivan T., *Living Mammals of the World,* Doubleday, Garden City, New York, 1955.

Topeka [Kansas] *Daily Capital,* July 8, 1970.

Washington [D.C.] *Daily News,* February 8, 1971.

Watson, Nigel, "Notes on Lincolnshire Ghost Phenomena," in *The News,* September 1974.

Wright, Bruce S., *The Ghost of North America,* Vantage Press, New York, New York, 1959.

CHAPTER FIVE: Things with Wings

Brownsville [Texas] *Herald,* January 18, 1976.

Cantu, Lupe, letter to Jerome Clark.

Clark, Jerome, "Unidentified Flapping Objects," in *Oui,* October 1976.

Corpus Christi [Texas] *Caller,* January 16 and February 8, 1976.

Harlingen [Texas] *Valley Morning Star,* January 13, 1976.

Keel, John A., *The Mothman Prophecies,* Saturday Review/Dutton, New York, New York, 1975.

Palestine [Texas] *Herald-Press,* December 16, 19 and 22, 1976.

Personal interviews with witnesses, authorities and reporters in Texas and New Jersey.

Pretoria [South Africa] *News,* January 15, 1976.

Rickard, R. J. M., "Unidentifieds," in *Fortean Times,* June 1976.

——"Birdmen of the Apocalypse!", in *Fortean Times,* August 1976.

Rio Grande [Texas] *Herald,* January 8, 1976.

San Angelo [Texas] *Standard,* February 17, 1976.

San Antonio [Texas] *Evening News,* January 14, 15, 23 and 29; February 12, 1976.

San Antonio [Texas] *Light,* January 15, 22, 23 and 29; February 26, 1976.

CHAPTER SIX: Phantasms

Bowen, Charles (ed.), *The Humanoids,* Henry Regnery, Chicago, Illinois, 1970.

Clark, Jerome, " 'Manimals' Make Tracks in Oklahoma," in *Fate,* September 1971.

——"Are 'Manimals' Space Beings?", in *UFO Report,* Summer 1975.

———"A Message from Magonia," in *The News,* February 1975.

Clark, Jerome and Coleman, Loren, *The Unidentified,* Warner Books, New York, New York, 1975.

Fort, Charles, *The Books of Charles Fort,* Henry Holt, New York, New York, 1941.

Hynek, J. Allen, *The UFO Experience,* Henry Regnery, Chicago, Illinois, 1972.

Jung, C. G., *Flying Saucers: A Modern Myth of Things Seen in the Skies,* Harcourt, Brace and Company, New York, New York, 1959.

Keel, John A., *Strange Creatures from Time and Space,* Fawcett/Gold Medal, Greenwich, Connecticut, 1970.

———*UFOs: Operation Trojan Horse,* G. P. Putnam's, New York, New York, 1970.

Padrick, Sid, "The Padrick 'Space Contact,'" in *Little Listening Post,* Fall 1965.

Personal interviews with witnesses and authorities in Minnesota, Montana, Nebraska and Oklahoma.

"Psychic Records," in *Occult Review,* October 1905.

Sagan, Carl, *The Cosmic Connection,* Doubleday Anchor, Garden City, New York, 1973.

Thompson, William Irwin, *At the Edge of History,* Harper and Row, New York, New York, 1971.

FURTHER READING

Those interested in the kinds of phenomena with which this book has dealt should consult the following Fortean publications:

Anomaly Research Bulletin, 7098 Edinburgh St., Lambertville, Michigan 48144.

APRO Bulletin, Aerial Phenomena Research Organization, 3910 East Kleindale Road, Tucson, Arizona 85712.

The Bigfoot News, P. O. Box 777, Hood River, Oregon 97031.

Bigfoot/Sasquatch Information Service, P. O. Box 442, Sedro Woolley, Washington 98284.

Fate, 500 Hyacinth Place, Highland Park, Illinois 60035.

Flying Saucer Review, FSR Publications Ltd., West Malling, Maidstone, Kent, England.

Fortean Times, P. O. Box 152, London N10 1EP, England.

Gray Barker's Newsletter, Saucerian Press, Box 2228, Clarksburg, West Virginia 26301.

The INFO Journal, International Fortean Organization, 7317 Baltimore Avenue, College Park, Maryland 20740.

International UFO Reporter, Center for UFO Studies, 924 Chicago Avenue, Evanston, Illinois 60202.

MUFOB, John Rimmer, 11 Beverley Road, New Malden, Surrey KT3 4AW, England.

MUFON UFO Journal, Mutual UFO Network, 103 Oldtowne Road, Seguin, Texas 78155.

Pursuit, Society for the Investigation of the Unexplained, R.D. #5, Gales Ferry, Connecticut 06335.

Res Bureaux, Box 1598 Kingston, Ontario, K7L 5C8 Canada.

UFO Newsclipping Service, Route 1, Box 220, Plumerville, Arkansas 72127.

UFO Report, 333 Johnson Avenue, Brooklyn, New York 11206.

Vestica Newsletter, P. O. Box 1183, Perth Amboy, New Jersey 08861.

THE BEST OF THE BESTSELLERS
FROM WARNER BOOKS!